COMIC SANS FOR THE EX

Thistlewood Star Mysteries Book Five

C. RYSA WALKER

☆ Chapter One ☆

WREN and I pushed forward into the crosswalk with the other pedestrians, ignoring the sharp blast of a car horn just inches away. Yes, the light had long since turned green, but anyone driving in downtown Nashville on a Saturday night has to know that green doesn't automatically mean *go*.

I reached out and grabbed Wren's arm purely on instinct as the car swerved to the left of us. My grip didn't relax until our feet were firmly planted on the sidewalk.

The music coming from the open doorways of the clubs that line the main thoroughfare was so loud that I read the words on Wren's lips more than I heard them. "Why don't they just ban cars on this stretch of Broadway? This is total chaos!"

She was right. The scene felt surreal, with the noise and the constant motion of the crowd morphing into a blur of neon light. It was a bit like being on a carnival ride and, combined with the smell of auto exhaust, it left me almost queasy.

I used to work these streets as a reporter. How odd that it had only taken a little over a year in Thistlewood to erase three decades of city life. I'd become acclimated to the small town's silence, its unabashed stillness in the winter, and the way darkness seemed to pull at the sidewalks as soon as dusk fell and the shops along Main Street began closing down for the night.

This was my first trip back to Nashville since I piled my things into the Wrangler when my job and my marriage, both of which had just passed the quarter-century mark, ended abruptly. At first, I'd purposefully avoided Nashville, worried that the familiar sights and sounds would trigger a wave of homesickness. More recently, I'd been too busy and too happy in Thistlewood to bother with the four-hour drive. But Wren and my daughter, Cassie, had been itching for a shopping trip and I was tired of the two of them nagging me about the bleak state of my wardrobe. I'd have been happy to simply order new jeans and sweaters online, but Cassie rolled her eyes at the suggestion.

"Oh, come *on*, Mom!" she'd told me. "We've been working our butts off for the past six months. We need a girls' getaway. A little shopping and a trip to the spa. Maybe go to the Wildhorse for some line dancing? Or karaoke. It will be fun!"

And so I'd relented. We'd driven over the day before,

grabbing lunch at a little roadside joint on the way. We'd spent the evening and this morning shopping, much to the dismay of my credit card and my sanity, and then we relaxed for a few hours at the hotel spa. Cassie excused herself around two, just after the mani-pedi session, so that she could visit her friends at the metaphysical book-store where she once worked and then have dinner with her dad. I could tell she had mixed feelings about the latter, and I think she seriously considered sneaking into Nashville without letting him know she was here. They haven't been on particularly good terms since Cassie moved to Thistlewood last year. But Cassie said he sounded a bit lonely the last time she spoke to him, and she hadn't seen him in about six months, so her kind heart and sense of duty won out. She promised to meet us after dinner, once we decided whether we were in more of a singing mood or a dancing mood. I was inclined toward the latter. I love Ed dearly, but his hip injury rules out anything beyond a slow dance of the hug-and-sway variety.

The noise level dropped to something more manage-able when we turned onto Third Avenue. We stepped closer to the brick building on our right, and Wren smoothed her pale blue blouse back down into place, not that it needed it. She could be thoroughly flustered and still look calm and collected. "Tell me again why I insisted on staying downtown?" she asked with a wry grin.

"I believe your exact words were *that's where the*

action is. And I'm thinking you wanted to recapture our glory days. Which is fine with me. Maybe we should head down to that WannaB's place we saw for karaoke after dinner."

"I don't know, Ruth. You know how much I love karaoke but singing here without Tanya might stir up *too* many memories." Wren smiled softly. "She was the star. We were just her backup. This is the first time I've been down here since that trip."

That hadn't even occurred to me. Wren had visited numerous times over the years, and we'd gone out to eat a few times when she was here. But she never mentioned heading down to Broadway, and I never suggested going. It wasn't a conscious thing. The connection between downtown and Tanya had eventually faded for me. The *Nashville News-Journal*'s office is only a few blocks from here, and I'd worked downtown for years. I'd been on Broadway hundreds of times, but it was as if Wren and I'd had an unspoken agreement that it would be too painful to be here together without Tanya, our third Musketeer.

The last time we'd visited Broadway together was in 1987, a few weeks before graduation. Tanya had signed up to perform in a talent contest at Tootsie's Orchid Lounge. We had indeed sung backup, and not especially well. Even so, Tanya came in second, and we'd spent half the prize money on *way* too many drinks at a joint over on Demonbreun that didn't look twice at our fake IDs. Then the three of us had staggered back to a hotel much cheaper than the Westin, which didn't have a spa, but did have an outdoor pool that we'd jumped into after stripping down to our undies. It was, hands down, our wildest weekend, and we had thought it was the first of many to come.

It was our *last* wild weekend, as it turned out. A few months later, Tanya vanished without a trace and for thirty years, her disappearance had eaten at us, because it just didn't make sense. Tanya and I were planning to room together here in Nashville after high school. Wren was going to join us when she finished her tour in the military. We'd had it all planned and nothing could convince either of us that she'd simply packed up and run off on her own.

Being here together without her still felt strange, but it didn't *hurt* now because we finally knew what happened. At the beginning of last summer, the police had dragged Tanya's car from the river that is Thistlewood's main attraction. Walking along Broadway with Wren that night, trying to pinpoint which of the clubs was the one where we'd sang, felt like an homage to Tanya's memory.

We hadn't been sure what we wanted to eat when we left the hotel earlier, but on the way over, I remembered this little Italian restaurant where I'd eaten a few times, most recently just before taking Cassie and a friend to a Taylor Swift concert at nearby Bridgestone Arena when they were about fifteen. The place looked packed, but we weren't in any real hurry. Wren, who had been hunting for a bathroom for the past ten minutes, offered to squeeze through the crowd at the door and see how long we'd have to wait for a table.

I stood beneath the green awning, absorbing the sounds of the night. The late April air was warm, and I felt myself beginning to relax. Off to my right, a man leaned back against the wall, playing guitar, and singing softly. He had a nice voice and a few couples stopped to watch, one guy stepping forward to drop a crumpled dollar bill into the open guitar case. Just minutes before, I'd been thinking how nice it would be to get back to the calm and quiet of Thistlewood, but now that we were away from the worst of the noise, it was easier to remember the things I'd liked about living in the city.

Would this trip have the same effect on Cassie? She seemed happy in Thistlewood, especially now that she was dating Dean Jacobs, and she loved running The Buzz with him. But she'd been happy here in Nashville, too, before her father's mid-life crisis, in which he decided that he was no longer in love with me and that we didn't really have that much in common aside from a grown daughter. And while Joe definitely loved Cassie and vice versa, the simple truth was that he didn't have much in common with *her* either. The man I'd fallen in love with in college had enjoyed nature walks, movies, and music. When Cassie was small, he'd loved taking her to the park and reading her bedtime stories. But at some point along the way, he'd morphed into someone who was more interested in his growing business, Riverfront Realty, than in his growing daughter.

It was around eight fifteen, which meant Cassie would be in the middle of her dinner with Joe, but I decided to send her a text and see if she could meet us at Wildhorse when she finished. Looking down at my phone, I was surprised to see a missed call banner super-imposed on the lock screen photo of Cronkite, my Maine coon cat, snoozing in the sun on my deck. Poor Cronk was used to me being home when I wasn't at the office of my newspaper, the *Thistlewood Star*. He was going to be very annoyed at me for abandoning him for two whole nights, even with Ed and Dean both promising to stop in and keep him company.

I squinted down at the number. A 615 area code, which meant it was local to Nashville, but definitely not the number of anyone I knew. Or...at least not a number that I remembered. When I had finally updated my phone the previous spring, I'd kept many of the 615 contact numbers that were related to my previous job at the *News-Journal*, but I purged the vast majority of personal contacts. Most of them were more casual acquaintances than friends, neighbors whose kids played with Cassie when they were growing up, and so forth. They were part of my past. My present and future were in Thistlewood.

The only person I'd tipped off that Cassie and I were coming to town was our neighbor just across the street, Walter Petrie. He and his wife Madge had been one of the first families to move into the neighborhood. They were much older than me and Joe, closer to our parents' ages, and Cassie had more or less adopted them as spare grandparents, since Joe's folks were both gone by the time she was in elementary school and the Petries' grandchildren were all the way out in California. Walter and Madge always invited us over when they pulled out the ice-cream freezer on a hot summer day, and Santa had always seemed to leave a little something under the Petries' tree for Cassie. In turn, we'd always made sure to bring back a few extra pecan logs from Lida's Candy Kitchen when we visited my family in Thistlewood. Madge had died about a year before I moved, and I knew Walter had been toying with the idea of moving closer to his daughter and her kids. But he enjoyed his job teaching computer programming at a local community college and wasn't sure he'd be able to find a position in California. To the best of my knowledge, he hadn't moved yet, but he also hadn't answered the email I sent asking if he wanted to meet me and Cassie for lunch. While I was fairly certain the number on my screen wasn't his home number, he might have been calling from his cell phone. I'd still have thought caller ID would pop up, though.

That meant the call was *probably* a wrong number or spam. Even so, I felt a tiny tingle of worry, given that Cassie was off on her own for the evening. But just as I was about to dial back, Wren appeared, eyes gleaming.

"Only a ten-minute wait. And I'm pretty sure I saw Keith Urban in there."

"That's great." I flashed her a brief smile, but my mind was still on the missed call. What if it was the police station or hospital? What if something had happened to Cassie?

"Please tell me you know who Keith Urban is..." Wren was clearly revving up to tease me about my general disinterest in country music, something that is close to a mortal sin in Tennessee. But as soon as she saw my expression, she trailed off. "What's wrong?"

I tapped the middle of my screen, bringing it back to life. "Just a missed call."

"From whom?"

"No clue. Came in about fifteen minutes ago. I didn't feel it vibrate, and I certainly wouldn't have heard it ringing with all that craziness on Broadway. It's a Nashville number but not one in my contacts. It might be Walter Petrie, but it also has me a little worried--"

"About Cassie," Wren said. "Do we still want the table?"

"Oh, sure. I was just going to call the number back. Then maybe I'll call Cass. Just to be on the safe side."

Wren's own cell gave a loud chirp. "That's our table," she said, glancing down at the screen. "Quicker than they thought."

I told her to go on in and I'd follow as soon as I returned the call. She gave my arm a little squeeze and headed inside.

When I tapped the mystery number on my screen it connected, rang once, and went to a voicemail that hadn't been set up. Either someone was ignoring my call, or the phone was turned off. I breathed a small sigh of relief. That pretty much ruled out my mom-fears about it being a hospital or the police. In my experience, they do not send you straight to voicemail. And, come to think of it, they usually have numbers that show up on caller ID.

It probably wasn't Walter, either. Given his line of work, he was a far cry from the stereotypical older man who needed help setting up his phone or computer system. In fact, he'd helped us set up our router when Joe and I made our first forays into the computer age.

Next, I called Cassie and breathed an even deeper sigh of relief when she answered on the second ring. "Mom?" Her voice sounded a bit uncertain. I could hear glasses clinking and other restaurant noise in the background.

"Hi, sweetie. I just wanted to tell you we decided on Wildhorse, so you can meet us there when you're done with dinner."

"I was actually about to call you," she said. " Dad hasn't shown up. And I know it's a long shot, but I was wondering if maybe you'd heard from him?"

"No. He hasn't called." In fact, the last time I'd heard Joe's voice was when he'd phoned me out of the blue on Christmas Eve.

"Yeah, well...he's not answering my calls or texts. We were supposed to meet almost thirty minutes ago."

I frowned. This wasn't really in character. Joe had plenty of faults, but he prided himself on his punctuality.

"Maybe he got held up?"

"Without his phone? Not likely."

"Well...he could be out of range. Nashville is a whole lot better in that regard than Thistlewood, but there are still a few dead zones. And if he's working with a buyer, he might have had to drive them out into the boonies."

The last part is a reach. Joe almost never works with buyers, except on the occasional commercial deal. He usually hands off the buyers to Nathan Simpson, the junior agent he took into the brokerage about ten years ago.

"Maybe." Cassie's tone told me she wasn't convinced. "Or maybe he's still ticked off about..."

"Did you two have an argument? You never mentioned that to me."

"Sort of. And no, I didn't say anything because I didn't want to stir things up between the two of you. Or for you to feel like you were somehow responsible for any tension in our relationship, which you know you would have, even though I'm a big girl. All grown up now, remember?"

I ignored the snark, partly because I knew that she had a point. "So...what are you going to do?"

"Guess I'll wait a few minutes longer. Then I'll drop

by the house if I don't hear anything. I'm guessing he just forgot and is passed out in front of the TV or something."

A few years ago, I'd have said that definitely wasn't the case. But Joe's voice had been slurred when he called to wish me merry Christmas, and I'd thought then that he might be drinking too much.

"All right, hon," I said after a long pause. "Wren and I are about to eat. Call if you need anything, okay?"

She sniffed. "Dad is the one who's going to need help if he doesn't show up soon."

☆ Chapter Two ☆

I STARTED to slide the phone back into my pocket as I entered the restaurant but decided to keep it out. If it rang again, I wanted to make sure I heard the call.

Wren, who was in a booth near one of the windows overlooking the street, looked up from the small pitcher of clear liquid she was staring at when I approached. "It wasn't Keith Urban." She lifted the little jug. "What the heck is this for?"

I smiled. "It's sugar water. You pour it into your tea."

She gave me a look of mock horror. "Did someone move the Mason-Dixon line? Patsy swears it's illegal to serve anything other than sweet tea in the South."

"That doesn't surprise me at all," I told her with a laugh. "Pretty sure she dissolves a five-pound bag of sugar in each gallon."

The waitress showed up to take our drink orders. I

opted for a glass of merlot. Wren, on the other hand, ordered tea, probably because she wanted to give the sugar water a shot.

"Did you figure out who was trying to call you?" Wren asked.

"No. But I did talk to Cassie. She's fine. Just very annoyed. Joe's late for dinner. And...he's not answering her calls or texts."

"Hmm..." Wren frowned and wrinkled her nose the way she always does when she's thinking. "Maybe he was held up at work?"

"That's what I suggested, but to be honest it was mostly so she wouldn't worry. Like most realtors, he's never without his phone. He even sleeps with the blasted thing, terrified he'll miss a potential customer."

"I'm sure he'll show up soon," Wren said. "But I hope for his sake he has a good reason for being late. I get the sense he's already on Cassie's bad side. Now...what do we want to eat?"

I flipped open the menu. "I'm starving. I'll take one of everything."

Wren wagged her finger. "Oh, no you don't. We just bought you a brand new wardrobe." Her eyes sparkled teasingly. "Although...I suppose we *could* just go shopping again tomorrow and buy everything a size larger."

"Absolutely not," I said. "No more shopping. I'll be good. We can even skip dessert."

"Well, now you're just being ridiculous."

We selected our entrees and decided to split an order

of bruschetta. After the waitress deposited our drinks and left with our order, Wren tilted the jug over her iced tea and then paused. "Is there a specific ratio?"

"Nope. You just keep pouring until the southern voice inside you says it's sweet enough. Or if you're feeling nostalgic for Patsy's brew, just tip the whole thing in there."

Wren poured a thin stream into the glass, and then said, "How's Ed's investigation going? Is Olivia driving him crazy yet?"

I chuckled. A quilt owned by Ed's neighbor, Olivia Byrne, went missing several days ago. It was being displayed at Shepherd's Flock, the community church next to Wren's funeral home, because it won first prize in the local women's club's quilting contest. Olivia is convinced that her cousin Lillian swiped it, so she asked Ed to investigate.

"He hasn't turned anything up yet," I said. "I offered to assist when he told me about it the other day, but he very politely told me he could handle it. To be honest, I think he's glad to put his mind to a case without a corpse, given the body count in the books he writes, although he's running behind on getting his copy edits finished, so he might be ready to let me help out. Olivia's pretty upset about the whole thing."

Wren shrugged. "Well, I can't really blame her. Something like that takes a lot of time to create. The real mystery is how the darn thing was just carried out of the church without anyone noticing. And that goes double if it was actually her cousin. I can't imagine how a ninety-year old woman could get the thing off the wall and out of the church without anyone spotting her. She can barely get herself around, even with a walker."

"Apparently, the two of them have been squabbling since they were in their teens. Olivia thinks Lillian put one of her sons up to swiping it because she was jealous that her own quilt didn't win the contest. She told Ed that Lillian's sons would probably sell it online for beer money."

"Well, I'm glad Ed is helping her look into it," Wren said. "Olivia can be a pain in the patoot, but I like her. And I doubt Blevins took the issue seriously, which is probably why Ed got stuck with it."

"Ed said she never even called it in. Olivia taught Steve Blevins in Sunday school back in the day and said that he was a snot-nosed brat then *and* now. She taught Ed, too, and she told him it didn't matter who wore the badge, he was still *her* sheriff."

"Better be careful," Wren said with a grin. "Sounds like she's after your man."

I laughed. "Now that you mention it, Olivia does bring him a loaf of banana bread every few weeks. Maybe I should keep an eye on her."

We continued chatting about the various goings on in Thistlewood while we ate. At nine twenty-two, when I'd just finished my last bite of seafood fettuccine, my phone rang again, and Cassie's face popped up on the screen.

"Hey," I said. "What's going on?"

"Dad never showed." I could hear traffic behind her, so she'd apparently left the restaurant.

A small kernel of dread settled into my stomach. "Still not answering calls or texts either?"

"Nope. I'm going over to the house. Figured I could drop off Walter's pecan logs, too. So I may be a little late meeting you and Wren at Wildhorse. Didn't want you to worry."

Too late for that. I glanced up at Wren, who noticed my expression and signaled the waitress for the check. We'd be skipping dessert after all.

"We're on our way," I told Cassie. "Give us thirty minutes. Maybe a little more." It was only about ten miles from here to Brentwood, but we had to get back to the hotel first to get Wren's car, and the hotel was nearly a mile from the restaurant. And with traffic on a Saturday night, I couldn't be sure how long the drive would take.

I knew Cassie was going to protest before she even opened her mouth. "Mom, no. I'm sure everything is okay. I shouldn't even bother checking. He's probably not there. Maybe he forgot we were coming and went out of town for the weekend. He's been seeing someone, so..."

She paused, as if she thought the words might sting, and I was a little surprised to discover that they didn't. Maybe that *shouldn't* have surprised me. After all, I was much happier with Ed than I'd been with Joe. The only thing I felt was a mild sympathy for whoever Joe was seeing. Did the new woman realize that he'd work every weekend, even though he could retire quite comfortably on his savings? That he would expect everything on his agenda to take priority in their relationship? The man was horrible at give and take.

"You're probably right," I told Cassie. "But on the off chance that there *is* something wrong, you'd never forgive yourself if you didn't check. And—again, on the off chance that something is wrong—I don't want you checking on your own. Don't go in that house without us, Cassie. I'm serious."

It was closer to forty minutes by the time we turned into my old neighborhood, and while hearing that Joe had been dating someone hadn't really affected me, seeing the street where we'd lived together, where Cassie grew up, was a different story. The house coming up on the right had been a huge part of my life and I felt a tug of nostalgia, most of it involving Cassie. She learned to ride a bike on this sidewalk. Fractured her arm falling out of that tree. Cried on the front porch swing when she broke up with her high school boyfriend.

Wren, who had clearly picked up on my thoughts, turned to me from the driver's side. "You good?"

"Yes. I'm okay. It just feels strange coming back after all this time. Nothing here seems to have changed at all, and yet, somehow, everything is different."

"You aren't the same Ruth Townsend who packed up her Jeep and headed for the hills. You're a new version," she said as she pulled the car up to the curb. "A stronger one. Ruth 2.0."

I laughed. "Maybe."

Wren shook her head, her earrings gleaming in the light of the streetlamp. "No maybe about it. Good Lord, Ruth, you've solved not one but *four* murders."

It was actually six, if you counted the cold cases I solved along the way. Seven if you counted the bear. But I didn't correct her. "I had a lot of help. Wouldn't have been able to do it without you, Cassie, and Ed."

Wren snorted. "Don't forget Steve Blevins while you're rolling the credits."

"Pfft. What has Blevins ever done aside from being a royal pain in my backside?"

"Well, if he was even a half-decent sheriff, you'd never have unearthed your inner Jessica Fletcher."

She had a point. I got out of the car and sniffed the night air. It was fragrant, with the scent of magnolias and the azalea bushes that line the drive, but there was an undertone of something else. I tilted my head and sniffed again. Smoke? Maybe someone had decided it was still chilly enough to start up their fireplace. There was no smoke coming from the only chimney I could see, the one across the street at Walter's place. No lights either. It was about spring break time, though, so maybe he'd flown out to visit his daughter.

I looked around the lawn, which was immaculate thanks to the gardening service Joe used. Like the neighborhood, there were no obvious changes to the house. It looked much the same as it had the day I backed my Jeep out of the drive and headed for the mountains. There was no sign of Joe's car, but he usually kept it in the garage.

Cassie had taken an Uber over. At first, I thought we might have beaten her to the house, since I didn't see her, although she'd been angry enough that there was also a decent chance she hadn't waited on us like I'd asked. But then she stepped out of the shadows on the front porch.

"I knocked," she said, her arms hugging her body. "No answer. And I've called so many times that my stupid phone is dead."

She didn't look angry now. Her expression was troubled, and I had a brief flashback to her face as she stood outside Audrey Shaw's camper a few months earlier, trying to pick up a message from the woman's ghost. I was tempted to ask what she was sensing. Maybe it was better just to get this over with, though.

Cassie pulled her keys out of her purse. Her hands were shaking as she tried to insert the key into the lock. I was just about to take it from her and do it myself when she finally managed to work it. The lock clicked open, but she made no move to turn the knob.

"Cassie?"

She looked back at me. Her eyes were wide. "I have a...bad feeling, Mom."

"It's going to be okay," I said, placing my hand over hers on the doorknob. "Whatever it is. Wren and I are both here."

We turned the doorknob together.

Again, it was odd to see how *little* had changed. Joe didn't seem to have rearranged the photos or knickknacks on the shelves, even to fill in the odd holes left by the ones I packed up to take to Thistlewood. The only new addition I spied was a pair of running shoes by the front door that looked like they were barely used.

"Dad?" Cassie called out softly, almost as if she didn't want to be heard. Which was kind of counterproductive, but I understood the feeling.

There was no note on the refrigerator door, although unless the relationship Cassie mentioned had moved to the next level and Joe no longer lived alone, why would he leave a note? A glass was tipped on its side on the carpet, but that wasn't necessarily a sign of struggle. Joe was a bit on the clumsy side, doubly so if he'd been drinking, and he wasn't exactly a neat freak. The glass could have been there for days. Several travel brochures were on the coffee table, which was new, since Joe stopped being a fan of vacations around the time he started his company. I'd coerced him into a week in Thistlewood two years after my parents died, when Cassie was in high school, and that was the last vacation he'd taken aside from weekend fishing trips.

There were no medications on the kitchen counter to suggest a health emergency, just an array of empty takeout containers and cardboard wrappers from Marie Callender, personal chef to bachelors everywhere. A bottle of bourbon on the kitchen table completed the tableau...the expensive sort that Joe only drank on special occasions. Or at least that had been true when we were married.

"No wonder he's gained weight," Cassie said as she picked up an empty package of Oreos and dropped it into the trashcan at the end of the kitchen island.

A few dishes were in the sink and there was definitely some citrus going bad in the fruit bowl. I thought I picked up another slight whiff of smoke, too, but I doubted it was from a cooking mishap, given the proliferation of take-out trash. Probably just the lingering scent of the fire I'd picked up when we were outside.

The master suite was on the ground floor across from the home office that Joe and I had shared at one point, back when we had just one computer and most of our work was done elsewhere. Over time, as we'd both had more telecommuting days and more computer equipment, I'd let him have that space and shifted my computer up to a spare bedroom on the second floor. When I looked down the corridor toward the bedroom Joe and I had shared for roughly half my life, I saw that the door was closed. We certainly hadn't slept with it open, and if Joe was sick or asleep, he might still close it out of habit, even now that he lived alone. So, there was nothing at all *unusual* about the door being closed. For some reason, however, it struck a chord of foreboding within me. Cassie was definitely sensing something, too, because she sucked in a breath as we approached the door.

I was about to grab the knob when it occurred to me that Joe might have a very different reason for being in the bedroom with the door closed. If he wasn't alone, they might have decided to simply stay up here and keep quiet, hoping we'd leave. But surely he'd have heard our footsteps? Surely he'd have locked the door?

Cassie reached past me and flung the door open.

The room was empty. A flood of relief washed over me. Had I been expecting to find Joe sprawled across the king-size bed? Yes. That was *exactly* what I'd thought I would find. If not his dead body, then his naked body, or his *drunk* body. Possibly both.

I stepped into the room and flicked on the bedside lamp. Cassie and Wren followed close behind. At first, everything seemed okay. Then my eyes landed on the dresser.

"Mom," Cassie said, "what's wrong?"

I pointed to an item on the dresser. "Your dad's Rolex. It belonged to his father," I told Wren. "Unless it's broken, he'd be wearing it. He slept with it half the time. Even wore it during ...um...exercise," I finished lamely, as my face began to flush. Both Wren and Cassie almost certainly knew what I'd been about to say, but luckily, this wasn't an appropriate moment for Wren to tease me and it was probably far more information than Cassie had wanted to know about her parents' sex life.

The watch was working, however. Joe's life had probably not changed as much as mine had since the divorce, given that he was in the same house, working the same job, seeing many of the same people. But there would have been changes. It was just a bit hard to imagine that they'd have been so drastic that he'd have left his father's watch on the dresser.

"We should check the closet," Wren said. "Maybe you can tell if some of his clothes are missing? Or his suitcase?"

I open my mouth to tell her no. Cassie beat me to it, but we were both too late.

Wren opened the door.

From inside the closet, two wide, lifeless eyes stared back at us.

☆ Chapter Three ☆

THE MAN'S body slumped sideways, fell over, and landed on the carpet at Wren's feet. She jumped back, clutching at the air, and very nearly lost her balance. The breath whooshed out of me when I saw that it wasn't Joe, followed by a sharp intake of breath when I realized that I knew the man. It was Nathan Simpson, Joe's junior partner.

A brown extension cord was wrapped around his neck.

For a long moment, the three of us just stood staring at the man. Then Wren crouched down to examine him. It was a technicality. Anyone looking at him could tell that he was past the point of resuscitation, and given Wren's line of work, I was quite sure she knew a dead body when she saw one.

"He hasn't been dead long," she said. "Maybe an hour or two."

"We should go," Cassie said. She'd known Nathan since she was in middle school. He'd been over to the house on several social occasions and dropped by regularly to bring papers that Joe needed to sign as the firm's broker. She liked Nathan. We both did. And while she'd been surprised when the body tumbled from the closet, I couldn't tell if she was surprised that it was *Nathan's* body.

"Are you picking up anything? Did he see..." I trailed off, not wanting to ask her if Nathan had seen his killer, mostly because I was terrified that she would say yes...and that it would be Joe. I was still angry at the way he'd ended the marriage, even though I had to admit — eighteen months down the pike—that I was thankful he'd done it. But I didn't think Joe had it in him to kill someone. And while he'd occasionally complain that Nathan needed to work harder, they weren't just co-workers. They golfed together. Occasionally went fishing on the weekends out at Percy Priest. Truthfully, my bigger worry was that if Nathan's body was in this closet, Joe's might be somewhere else in the house.

Dear God, Joe. What have you gotten yourself into?

Cassie shook her head at my question. "I'm not picking up anything. He's not here."

I was tempted to push further and ask Cassie if she was sensing any other dead people in the house, but she'd probably piece together that I meant Joe. And she was upset, but not nearly as upset as I think she'd have been if she was picking up vibes from her dead father.

"Let's go." My suggestion didn't appear to have been necessary, strictly speaking, given that Wren and Cassie were already halfway to the door by the time I got the words out. I paused for a moment when I reached the hall and looked back into the room. It gave me a shiver to see poor Nathan there, just a few feet away from the bed where I'd slept for so many years. His eyes continued their unseeing stare, watching me leave, and I had to fight the urge to close the door behind me.

When we reached the living room, I told Wren and Cassie that I needed to call the police. As soon as I pulled the phone from my pocket, however, it gave a sharp *ting* and began vibrating with an incoming text. The message preview was turned off, but I could still see the number—and it was the same mystery caller from earlier, with the Nashville area code.

I swiped right on the notification. The message was seven short words.

Get out of the house. Right now.

A chill swept over me. Lightning flashed outside and I waited for the inevitable crash of thunder. Heat lightning was my first thought...although I know there's really no such thing. It's just lightning off in the distance, too far away for the sound to carry.

And why was I thinking about storms and lightning

right now, while holding a phone with a text telling me to get out of a house with a dead man in the bedroom closet?

I needed to focus. To call the police. Although maybe we should listen to the advice of my anonymous texter and *get out*. Was something lurking in the corner of the darkened living room off to the left?

Get out of the house.

Did I hear movement in the kitchen?

Right now.

The feeling of being watched was palpable.

I *did* hear something...a police siren. It was still in the distance, but definitely coming this way. I frowned, yet another knot of uneasiness tightening in my stomach and causing it to churn. The sound should have been comforting. Why wasn't it?

Because I hadn't *called* the police. Not yet. There hadn't been time. Either someone else had called them or they were headed into the neighborhood for an entirely different reason.

"Who was it?" Wren asked.

"What?"

"The text," she said, nodding toward my phone. "Who was it from?"

"Oh. It was the same number that called me before dinner." I handed my phone over so that she and Cassie could read the message. "Do you think maybe it's Walter? Did you check to see if he was home while you were waiting on us?"

Cassie shook her head. "I realized after I got here that the pecan logs were in your purse, not mine. And unless Walter has changed his habits, he'd be in bed by now. But regardless of who sent the message, that *get out of the house* part sounds like an excellent plan. I need to find Dad." She reached into her pocket when she stepped onto the porch, and then her feet shuffled to a stop as she apparently remembered she hadn't driven here.

"I have to call the police first," I told her. "Then we can work on finding Joe."

Cassie's eyes shifted toward the back of the house, no doubt thinking about Nathan's lifeless eyes staring back at us. "They're going to think Dad...had something to do with it." She squeezed her eyes shut. "He didn't. I'm sure of that. But you're right. We have to call it in. Or rather, one of you has to call it in since my cell is out of juice. Do you have an iPhone cable in your car, Wren?"

Wren nodded. "I swear, you're almost as bad about forgetting to charge a phone as your mama. Come on."

While I phoned the police, Cassie and Wren headed over to the Buick so that Cassie could plug in her phone. Then the three of us continued down the sidewalk to find out where the smoke was coming from. There had been only a faint hint in the air when we entered Joe's place, but it was much stronger now. The street was hazy with it, and the sky above the bank of trees off to the right had taken on an orange glow. I could hear the whooping wail of a fire truck in the distance, joining the chorus of police sirens.

The police were much closer, however, and seconds later, a Metro Police cruiser zoomed past as we stood in the driveway, its strobing lights painting the smoke with slashes of red and blue. A second police car followed, and then both stopped abruptly just down the road.

"Looks like you could have just waited and told them in person," Wren said, nodding toward the cruisers.

Neighbors were gathering on the sidewalks and carefully manicured front lawns across the street. *The bad side of the street,* as Cassie had called it once when she was going through one of her odd spells a teenager, and I kind of agreed. The families on this side of the street were nicer.

I scanned the neighbor's faces. Most were familiar, but there were a few new additions, too. I stuck to the shadows, not eager to engage in conversation.

Cassie seemed to be thinking the same thing. I hadn't been *close* friends with anyone in the neighborhood aside from Walter, but there were a few others with whom I was friendly, and I hadn't stopped in to say goodbye to anyone when I left town. People gossiped less here than they did in Thistlewood, where everyone knew everyone else's business, but I was sure that there had been at least some chatter about why Cassie and I were no longer around.

The road curved just beyond our lot, terminating in a cul-de-sac. We tentatively made our way down the sidewalk as the fire trucks arrived and screeched to a halt in front of the large two-story home three doors down. Windows on both floors were roaring with flickering orange light. The roof had already caved in, and tall flames arced up into the sky along with black pillars of smoke. I coughed and took an involuntary step back toward the row of shrubs.

Feeling eyes on me, I reluctantly looked across the street to find one of the neighbors, Tammy Roscoe, staring at me from her front porch. She'd been the only other person from the neighborhood to call and check on me when I moved out, something that surprised me because we'd never really been friends...I generally classed her as one of those on the bad side of the street. I'd returned her call, but kept things brief and vague, since Tammy was an inveterate gossip. She had pushed for more details, noting that most of the neighbors seemed to think the breakup was my idea, and she seemed a wee bit too pleased when I admitted that it hadn't been. I'd suspected it was a touch of schaden-freude, given that her own husband of fifteen years had taken off with his secretary more than a decade ago. When she called again a few weeks later, I didn't call back.

I couldn't really avoid acknowledging her now, since we were staring directly at each other, so I gave her a little finger wave. Her response was to turn on her heel and go back inside. Fair enough, since I'd dissed her first, but she must have been more ticked off about it than I'd thought, to be willing to go inside and miss the drama of a burning house.

The firemen were yelling back and forth, but they made no move to enter. No surprise because it was instantly apparent that the house was a total loss. The only thing they could do was prevent the fire from jumping to other houses.

Wren appeared beside me. "Wow. Those flames came out of nowhere."

"Yeah," I said. "I caught a whiff of smoke as we went inside, but...that was it. God. I hope no one was in the house."

Cassie shook her head. "Pretty sure it was empty."

She nodded toward the house. I took a few steps closer to her so that I could see around the fire trucks. Firelight flickered against a familiar sign. I'd helped paint the post it was attached to years ago, and there had always been a half-dozen or so in our garage.

A smaller metal sign—*Price Reduction!*—was attached at the bottom, flapping back and forth in the hellish breeze. The words *Riverfront Realty* were printed at the top. And just below that was my ex-husband's smiling face.

Chapter Four

WREN, Cassie, and I were still outside Joe's house an hour later, huddled together in the driveway. All the lights in the house were on and I could see shadowy figures moving to and fro behind the thin curtains. The neighbors were getting a double feature tonight. First the fire, and then they got to watch as yellow police tape was strung up along the perimeter of Joe's yard.

One of the fire trucks rolled back toward the main road. There were no sirens this time, no flashing lights to announce their departure. The house was still smoldering, and one truck remained behind, making sure that the neighboring homes were safe.

Unlike poor Nathan. And maybe Joe, too.

"That text message has to be from Dad," Cassie said for the third time.

I thought she was probably right. The only two other

possibilities would be Tammy Roscoe and Walter, although I still didn't even know if he was home. I'd tried the home phone, but just got the answering machine.

"It makes all of this seem even worse," Cassie added, "although I'm not sure how it could possibly *get* worse."

I had to admit it didn't look good for Joe. But things can *always* get worse. Anyone who says otherwise is inviting trouble.

"Just wish they'd hurry. It's getting cold." Cassie shivered as if to prove her point, rubbing her hands up and down her arms. She was right. The chill was working its way through the weave of my sweater.

"No reason we have to wait out here," Wren said. "I can have the car warm in a jiffy."

As we were getting into the car, a man stepped onto the porch. He appeared to be in his early forties, at least six-foot-four, and a solid wall of muscle. "Where are you going?" he asked. "The deputy said he told you not to leave."

"We're not *going* anywhere," Wren said. "Just trying to keep warm while we wait for someone to take our statements."

"Well, that someone is me." He glanced down at the notebook in his hand. "Ms. Townsend, I'll start with you."

Giving Wren and Cassie a nervous smile, I followed the detective into the house. The knot of dread in my stomach reminded me of the rare occasions when I'd been called into the principal's office in school. That was silly, though. I hadn't done anything wrong.

Well, not *yet*. But I was definitely planning it. Wren, Cassie, and I had decided there was no need to mention the text message until we had a better sense of what was going on with Joe. I had no intention of *hiding* anything from the police, but I couldn't see the harm in a brief delay before telling them about the message, especially since I still didn't know if it was from him. It was perfectly plausible for me to say that I hadn't discovered it until we got back to the hotel. If Joe had anything to do with Nathan's death, I wouldn't cover for him. The same was true if he was the one who started that fire down the street. I had a hard time believing that the two events weren't connected. I've always been suspicious of coincidences. In my experience, when something seems like a coincidence, that's usually because you don't understand enough about the situation to connect the dots.

The officer extended his hand and gave me a quick once over. "Detective Mark Webb. MNPD Homicide." He motioned for me to be seated on the sofa I'd bought the year before Cassie finished high school. "You know the deceased. The deputy said you made a positive ID before they even pulled out his wallet. Were you friends?"

"Yes."

"But you also told them you hadn't spoken to Mr. Simpson in over a year."

"You know how it is with divorces. Friends have to

pick sides, and in this case, Joe is also his boss, so Nathan really didn't have much choice. The last time I saw him was about a week before the divorce. He was going out of town for a few days, and he dropped off a gift for my daughter."

"Was she by any chance...involved with Mr. Simpson?"

I wrinkled my nose. "No. It was a thank-you gift for housesitting the week before. Nathan has known Cassie since she was in middle school."

Webb gave me a look that suggested this didn't rule anything out. "Do you know if he was involved with anyone?"

"He wasn't the last time I saw him. But again, that was over a year ago." I debated adding that I was fairly sure Nathan was gay, but since Webb didn't press the matter further, I decided to let him do his own detective work on Nathan's romantic attachments.

Webb consulted his notebook. "You said earlier that he has a sister in Hendersonville. Would she be his next of kin?"

"I don't know, but she's probably his only family in the area. He mentioned parents, but I got the sense that they weren't local."

"Okay, then. Let's move on to your husband."

"*Ex*-husband," I clarified.

I was quite certain he already knew that. But I'd conducted enough interviews to know that often you're looking less for the actual answer the person gives than for how they give the answer. Tone and expression can tell you far more than the words sometimes.

He placed his phone on the coffee table and adjusted the angle. Smart move. If he recorded me, he didn't have to glance down at the little notebook as he wrote. He could watch me with those piercing green eyes, hunting for clues as to whether I was lying. Or hiding something.

"Do you have any idea where your ex might be, Ms. Townsend?"

"No," I said, even though my mind was on the text message. *Get out of the house. Right now.* "We're not exactly on friendly terms these days."

"Never hurts to ask," he said with a humorless chuckle. "I know you told the responding officer what happened, but could you please tell me again. From the beginning."

I took a deep breath, opened my mouth, and told the full story again. When I finished, Mark Webb sat looking at me intently. I thought I detected a hint of suspicion in his eyes. Surely he didn't think I had anything to do with Nathan's death?

Of course he doesn't. You're just being paranoid, Townsend.

"Can you think of any reason why Joe Tate would want Nathan Simpson dead?"

"No."

"Any recent disagreements or fights between Joe and Nathan?"

"Not that I know of."

"Any recent disagreements or fights between *you* and Joe?"

A touch of anger bubbled up from the pit of my stomach. "No. We're past that. I haven't even seen him in over a year."

"What about your daughter and Joe?"

"Um, no," I said, although that answer was a bit less certain. "At least, not to my knowledge."

"What brought you back to town now?"

A freaking makeover, I thought. "Just a getaway. Shopping and so forth. The kinds of things you sometimes miss living in a small town."

"Where did you shop?"

"Opry Mills, mostly," I told him, although I really didn't see what that had to do with anything.

"And you didn't see Mr. Tate at all?

"No. I've spoken to him only once since the divorce was final. Like I said, we're not exactly BFFs these days. Again, Cassie was supposed to meet him for dinner. He didn't show and she couldn't reach him. She was worried, so we drove over. When we didn't find him, we checked the bedroom to see if he was sick."

"Or...hiding in the closet?"

"What?"

"I guess I'm just wondering what made you think to check the closet."

"Wren thought we could see if his suitcase was gone. If he was out of town." I'd told the other officer this already, and my voice must have sounded impatient, because he gave me a slight smile.

"I'm sorry, Ms. Townsend. These questions may seem redundant, but I have to ask them, as you probably know. Weren't you a reporter?"

"Still am. I own the local newspaper in Thistlewood."

Webb nodded. "Great place to visit. Some good fishing down that way. So, just to sum things up, we have one man dead, another missing, and the house down the street just burned to the ground. A house, oddly enough, that's listed with Mr. Tate's realty company. Seems like an odd coincidence."

"Except that's probably true of most houses currently for sale in this neighborhood," I told him, even though I'd been thinking that it probably wasn't a coincidence just a few minutes before. "When you put your house on the market, you want someone who knows the area. Who better than one of your neighbors? I really *do* wish I could tell you more, Detective Webb. He's Cassie's father, for crying out loud. She's worried. We both are."

He stood up. "And on that note, why don't you send Cassie in? I just need to get your contact information."

I pulled one of my cards out of the zip compartment in my phone case and handed it to him, then did as I was ordered. Webb was watching from the porch, so I just gave Cassie's arm a sympathetic squeeze and nodded toward the house.

Wren was sitting behind the wheel, searching for

something on her phone, when I slid into the passenger seat.

"Looking up info on the house that burned down," she said before I could ask what she was up to. "Five hundred and seventy-five thousand. Four bedrooms, three baths. Built in 1993. Last sold two years ago. Seems kind of odd that they'd be selling so soon."

"Probably investors trying to flip it and make a profit," I said as I scanned the listing on her phone. Joe's picture was at the bottom of the screen, along with his contact information and a cheery invitation to *Schedule an Appointment Today!*

"How do we find out who the current owners are?" Wren asked.

"Property tax records are available online."

We spent the next ten minutes trying to pull up the record, but the website was hard to navigate on her phone. I finally tossed it back to her. "I'll just check when I'm back at my computer."

Cassie was on her way down the porch steps. She tapped Wren on the shoulder as she slid into the backseat. "Tag. You're it."

"Oh, joy." Wren stashed her phone in the console, sighed heavily, and headed into the house.

"Did it go okay?" I asked Cassie.

She shrugged. "Just your standard police interrogation. I've had several of those in the past year, thanks to Steve Blevins, so it's kind of routine now. He just made me repeat everything several times and then gave me a stern caution about not trying to protect Dad. If he contacts me, I should call immediately and let the department know. Yada, yada."

Her attitude was a bit flip, but that was often the case when she was upset, so I didn't comment. We waited quietly for a few minutes, and then she tried calling Joe again. When the call went unanswered, she left him a terse message.

"This isn't like him," she mumbled. "You know how Dad is. He checks his messages obsessively. Remember me telling you how crazy he was when he lost his phone last..." She trailed off and stared at her phone for a moment. "Whoa. I don't know why I didn't think of this before. I have Dad's iCloud info. I helped him set it up last winter, when he lost his stupid Blackberry and I convinced him to switch to an iPhone."

"What good is his iCloud info?"

"Find my iPhone," she said, grinning. "If it's still on, we can track him. Assuming he hasn't changed the password."

"Which he almost certainly hasn't. Is it $Mr.C1990$ or $GoCommodores1990$?"

She arched an eyebrow. "The first one. How did you know?"

"Because he never changes passwords. He's used one or the other of those two since he graduated from Vanderbilt."

A few minutes later, she let out a little victory whoop and handed me the phone through the gap in the seats.

The map showed a green dot next to a large, irregular blue blob that anyone who lives in Nashville can identify instantly—Percy Priest Reservoir.

It was definitely too late for a fishing trip. What on earth was Joe doing out at Percy Priest?

☆ Chapter Five ☆

WREN'S TIME in Detective Webb's hot seat was a bit shorter than mine and Cassie's, possibly because she could honestly say that she hadn't seen Joe in nearly five years. He hadn't come with me and Cassie on our last two vacations to Thistlewood prior to the divorce. And while she'd threatened, in true best friend fashion, to drive to Nashville and kick Joe's butt for the abrupt manner in which he'd ended our marriage, I'd talked her out of it.

Webb followed her out to the car and handed me his card through the window, along with a reminder that we should call him if we heard from Joe. I promised to do so, happy that I didn't have to lie. We hadn't *actually* heard from Joe. All we had was a ping from his phone.

Detective Webb headed off to his SUV, which was parked at the curb. Wren glanced at the clock and then began backing out of the driveway.

"Given the time," she said, "I take it we're skipping line dancing and heading straight to the hotel."

"Yes to the first," Cassie said. "But no to the second. Take a left onto Edmonson, and then a right onto Old Hickory. We're heading to the reservoir."

"Okay then."

We filled her in on what we'd found out as she drove. About halfway there, I remembered that I'd promised to call Ed. It was late, though, and Thistlewood was an hour ahead of us. I told myself he'd almost certainly be asleep. He probably just thought we'd gone out to a club and lost track of the time. All of that was true, but I was also hesitant to call him because I was fairly sure he'd tell me that we needed to tell Detective Webb about the ping from Joe's phone, rather than heading out to investigate on our own.

Old Hickory became Bell Road. It was four lanes at first, but as we drew closer to the reservoir, the road narrowed into two lanes that meandered through tall trees. Every now and then you could catch a glimpse of the lake.

"Turn right at the next intersection," Cassie said. "The road is Hamilton Creek Park...which will take us down to the marina."

"How close will this get us to the signal?" I asked Cassie.

"Depends. Usually within a few hundred feet."

Wren turned onto the road following Cassie's

instructions. A few hundred yards in, she glanced into the rearview mirror and frowned.

"What's wrong?"

"Thought I saw a flash of headlights."

I looked into the side mirror and saw nothing at first. But a few seconds later I spotted it, too. "You're right. This isn't a private road, though."

"True," Wren said. "But this isn't exactly peak time for driving to a lake."

"It is if you're out on a date," Cassie said. "There are several popular parking spots on this stretch of road. And it *is* Saturday night. Most kids avoid the actual marina if they don't want to be interrupted because cops tend to patrol pretty heavily down there."

I decided that I really didn't want details on how Cassie knew about all of these popular parking spots that police didn't patrol.

"It looks like a truck. Maybe it's..." There was a pause and then Cassie continued. "I was going to say maybe it's Dad following us, but that's silly. He doesn't know what car we're in."

I exchanged a glance with Wren and could tell she was thinking exactly what I was. As much as I didn't want to worry Cassie unnecessarily, the only way Joe's phone being stationary right next to a massive body of water wasn't ominous was if he'd forgotten about his dinner with Cassie and taken the new girlfriend to one of those secluded lovers' lanes. Or if he'd been out here

earlier and lost the thing, but surely he'd have remembered about the find-my-phone feature?

The location was a puzzle, though. If someone killed
both Joe and Nathan, why leave Nathan's body in our
closet and bring Joe's all the way out here?

"How much farther?" Wren asked.

Cassie looked down at the glowing screen in her
hand. "The road ends in three-tenths of a mile at the
Upper Boat Launch. Which means the truck back there
would have turned off already if they were just looking
for a private spot. So, yeah. We're probably being
followed."

"Definitely not much going on here," Wren said as
she turned into the mostly empty parking lot. I could tell
from her tone that she was having second thoughts about
the wisdom of driving out here after midnight. On the
plus side, the headlights seemed to have disappeared.
Maybe they'd turned around?

Percy Priest Lake was created back in the 1960s
when the government dammed the Stones River,
forming a twenty-two square mile reservoir. It stretched
out before us like a giant black beast, slumbering uneasily
beneath the crescent moon. I've never been afraid of the
water but in the middle of the night, the sight was
unnerving.

"Look!" Cassie leaned between the seats and pointed
at one of the two vehicles parked at the far end of the lot.
"It's Dad's Denali."

Reluctantly, I repeated the question I'd asked back at the house. "Are you picking up anything?"

She shook her head. The fact that nothing was pinging Cassie's paranormal radar was a good sign, but she's said before that it can be a bit sporadic.

Wren parked on the far side of Joe's truck. It didn't look like anyone was inside, but it was dark, and if anything had happened to him, it was unlikely that he'd be sitting up behind the wheel. "I'll be right back," I said as I opened my door, hoping Cassie would take the hint and stay inside.

But she didn't, of course. She *is* my daughter. Her door was open before my feet hit the ground, and Wren was right behind her.

"Make way for the Three Musketeers," I muttered softly.

When I reached Joe's truck, I leaned toward the window to look inside the cab. Cassie reached for the door handle at the same time. It was unlocked and the window connected with my nose when she opened it. The impact wasn't hard enough to hurt, but when I stepped back, I bumped into Wren and we both barely kept our balance.

"More like the Three Stooges," Cassie said, shaking her head. The dome light clicked on inside the cab. "Well, at least we won't have to search for his phone."

It was in the middle of the driver's seat, face down. The floorboard had its usual array of takeout containers, assorted papers, and Mountain Dew bottles. I still think

one reason Joe stopped working as a buyer's agent was
that he had to clean out his vehicle every time he took
clients out to look at properties. The fact that he still
might have to ferry clients around on occasion, however,
had given him justification for spending extra to get an
extended crew cab.

A flash of crystal blue water, the polar opposite of the
cold dark lake in front of us, stared out at me from
beneath an Arby's box on the floorboard. *Visit Belize.*
Looks like he might have narrowed down his vacation
options.

I started to reach for it, but my hand froze in place
when I spotted the sheet of paper on the dash. Picking it
up by one corner, I placed it on top of the forgotten
phone.

Definitely Joe's handwriting, which is barely legible
in most cases. This was only two words, however, so it
was easy enough to make them out. *I'm sorry.* I turned
slowly and stared out at the dark mass of water, lapping
gently at the edge of the pavement. It felt like the water
was looking back, watching me, and I shivered.

I'm sorry.

Headlights swept across the parking lot, illuminating
the twin warning signs at the edge of the landing. *No
Swimming Near Ramp. No Parking on Ramp.*

"Great," Wren said. "We've got company."

Cassie was still staring at the note, apparently oblivious to our new arrival. The SUV approaching us
seemed familiar. In fact, I was almost certain it had been

parked in front of Joe's house a few hours ago. I could be wrong, though. It could be the owner of the marina. Someone out for a midnight fishing trip. Or maybe the murderer who had left a body in my former closet and was hoping to level up to serial killer?

The driver gave the siren one quick blast, a single little whooping noise. Better than a serial killer, to be sure, but bad in an entirely different way.

"What was that for?" Wren asked, frowning.

I gave her a grim smile. "Pretty sure that translates as *stay right there and don't even think about climbing back into your car.*"

For several long seconds we waited in the blinding glare of his headlights. And while I didn't climb back into the car, I did take a few tiny steps closer to the Denali so that I could place my hand on the hood. It was cool. Almost cold, in fact. While I had no idea exactly how long it would take the engine heat to dissipate, it seemed like a safe bet that the truck had been here for at least an hour. Maybe longer.

Finally, the door opened, and Detective Webb stepped out. "Seeing a lot of y'all tonight."

It wasn't until he spoke that I realized I'd been expecting a snarky tone and some lame joke. My brain seemed to be automatically equating all police officers with Steve Blevins. Webb just sounded tired, like he'd much rather be home in bed than standing on the shore of Percy Priest at the cusp of the witching hour.

"Detective Webb," I said. "I'm guessing you

followed us?"

"Yep. And I'm guessing that's your ex-husband's truck."

"There's a note," I told the detective in a soft voice. "I only touched the corner when I took it off the dashboard. It's Joe's handwriting."

He nodded toward the door. "May I?"

Cassie didn't respond, so I took her elbow and gently steered her away from the door.

Webb stared at the note for much longer than it would take even the slowest reader to digest two simple words. I took the opportunity to check out the bed of the truck. It was usually empty, but tonight there was a thick, dark slab of finished wood about six feet by three feet. It was polished to the point that I could see the moon's reflection, but there was a single streak of dirt running down the middle. A tire track, maybe?

"So..." he said finally. "All three of you ladies just finished telling me that you had no idea whatsoever where Joe might be. You also said you were heading back downtown to the Westin...but then you turned the wrong way coming out of the neighborhood, so I decided to tag along. The fact that you drove straight to his vehicle suggests that you weren't being entirely truthful. Unless one of you had some sudden epiphany that led you all the way out to Percy Priest?"

"That would be me." Cassie's voice was steadier than I would've thought. "I remembered that I had his iCloud info...and I tracked the phone."

"And you just happened to remember this as you were pulling out of the driveway?" He didn't sound convinced.

"Correct," she said. "I thought there was a decent chance that he was out here with the woman he's been dating. They're a little old for making out in cars, but..."

"This would be the woman you mentioned, right?"

Cassie nodded. "Right. We were planning to phone your office if we located him. But...as you know, since you were following us, we literally just got here."

She sounded entirely too chipper for someone who had just read what seemed to be a suicide note. I could tell from the tilt of Webb's head that her demeanor confused him, too. But then he gave her a sympathetic smile, probably thinking she was in denial.

And that was certainly a possibility. But given Cassie's odd quirk with spirits, I knew that it was far from the only possibility.

"Okay," Webb said, glancing out at the water. "I'm going to have someone come out and check your father's truck. When were you planning to return to Thistlewood?"

"Tomorrow," Wren said. "I have an appointment back in Thistlewood. So we were going to do a bit of shopping early in the day and then head out mid-afternoon. Will that be a problem?"

"I don't think so. But...don't leave until I contact you, okay?"

Wren nods and we head to our respective cars.

As I opened the door, Cassie grabbed my arm. Tears were in her eyes, but she was smiling. "He's not dead."

"Cassie..." I began, but she stopped me.

"No, Mom. He isn't. There's nothing here." She motioned around the dark parking lot and toward the still, darker water. "No *one* here. You don't kill yourself unless you're troubled, and troubled souls are the ones who stick around."

Wren and I exchanged a look, which Cassie caught from the backseat. "I know I didn't pick up anything from Nathan. But that was different. Nathan spirit had been in the house. I could tell that much. That's why I said I had a bad feeling. He was just gone by the time we got there. I'm not sensing Dad at all. He's *not* here."

I wasn't questioning her ability. I'd seen far too much in the past year to dismiss her instincts in that regard. But Wren was in a much better position than Cassie to understand why I might suspect that Cassie's certainty about her dad was wishful thinking. I'd confided in Wren years ago, back when she was still in the military, that Joe's father committed suicide when I was about six months pregnant with Cassie. Joe's mom had burned the note and told everyone that her husband had accidentally overdosed on a sleeping medication. She hadn't even told Joe's younger brother, who was away at college at the time, although he eventually found out. She probably wouldn't have told Joe, but he'd been the one who found the note on his dad's desk. Joe had a tough time dealing with it. At first, he'd been angry at his dad, wondering how he could do something like that with no explanation beyond a vague, terse note. Later, he'd felt as though he let his dad down by not picking up on the fact that he was so miserable.

No one ever questioned the story. Henry Tate had seemed a happy and cheerful man to the outside world, but he'd apparently held himself to impossibly high standards and suffered from periodic mood swings. And while he'd never consciously put that on his two sons, Joe had definitely inherited some aspects of his father's personality. No matter how well Joe's business did, how much it improved from year to year, his focus tended to be on the clients he'd lost, the deals he *didn't* make.

All Cassie knew was that her grandfather died a few months before she was born. Joe hadn't wanted to tell her that it was suicide. He said she might feel that he hadn't cared enough to stick around to meet her, when we both knew that he had been tickled pink to learn he had a grandchild on the way. It had made sense to keep it from her when she was younger, so I'd deferred to Joe's wishes. Henry was his dad, after all, and I'd been reluctant to reopen wounds that ran so deep.

And I certainly couldn't tell Cassie now. That would be beyond cruel, when she had just finished reading a note in her father's handwriting with the very same two words.

I'm sorry.

Chapter Six

WREN HANDED me her keys after pulling into a space at Green Hills Mall. "You're sure? We can go with you, Ruth. The girls definitely need a new support system or two," she said, snapping her bra strap, "but I can always order online."

I shook my head. "Go. Cassie still needs to find the shoes she promised to pick up for Dean. I'm just going to stop in and see if anyone I worked with is in the office today. I could call, but we might get more traction if I talk to them in person. If I give them what I know about the story, maybe they'll be willing to keep us updated on the investigation. I should be back by two, and we can grab a late lunch."

More than anything else, I wanted something to keep Cassie's mind occupied. We'd both tossed and turned all night, a problem that was amplified by the fact that we had to share a bed. For the most part, Cassie was still maintaining her positive attitude from the night before, insisting that Joe was okay. But I know my daughter. She's gotten much better over the past few years, but she's still really, really good at avoiding things she doesn't want to face. For years, she refused to go near graveyards and wouldn't even visit Wren's house because it's located above the funeral home.

And she was clearly distracted. Wren already had her door open, but Cassie was still in the backseat staring at her phone.

I reached back and gave her leg a pat. "Everything okay?"

"Yeah," she said. "Just trying to reset my phone. I didn't have a current backup so everything since March is pretty much gone."

I blinked. "What happened to your phone?"

"It was my own fault. I reset it so that I could log in with Dad's information. That way, we'd have had all of his messages, pictures, things like that. It might have helped to find him."

"I'm going to guess from your expression that it didn't work," Wren said.

She gave us a rueful smile. "You guessed right. It sent a code to his phone. It's a security thing to let you know if someone else is trying to log in as you."

"Webb is probably trying to figure out what's going on," I said. "Let's hope he logged the phone into the evidence locker and didn't have it sitting next to him when the alert went off."

The two of them gathered their things and headed
into the mall, and I backtracked into Nashville. This was
the first time I'd been back at the offices of the *Nashville
News-Journal* since they offered me early retirement as
part of yet another wave of downsizing. I very nearly
pulled into the employee parking lot out of habit.
Instead, I found a spot along the curb about a half block
down and dropped two quarters into the meter. Fifty
cents would only give me twenty minutes, however, so I
dug around in my purse for two more, just in case I
encountered any chatty former colleagues.

As it turned out, I could have stuck with two quarters. The receptionist remembered me, and let me go
back into the newsroom, but while I recognized a couple
of faces, they were only casual acquaintances. I spotted a
few familiar names on desk and door plates, but there
were quite a few empty slots, leading me to suspect that
there had been more layoffs and gentle nudgings into
retirement. Being in the room gave me the same odd,
slightly panicky sensation I'd felt at Joe's house last night.
It was strange to be in a place where I'd spent such a
huge portion of my life and feel like a fish out of water.

I made a mental note of two people that I could call
later, thanked the receptionist for her help and hurried
back to Wren's car. I'd promised to meet them at two.
That gave me right at ninety minutes to kill. I could join
them, of course, but yesterday's bout of shopping would
do me quite nicely for the next year. Maybe even two. I
contemplated heading to the little coffee shop just down

the block. They had tables outside and it was a nice morning. I could grab my laptop out of the trunk and do a bit of research.

But I could do that sort of digging when I got back to Thistlewood. Even though I ran the risk of arousing suspicion and possibly annoying Detective Webb, I needed to make the most of the few hours I had in Nashville. It couldn't hurt to drop by Joe's office. It would be closed, but I still had the key. Maybe I could poke around in the old neighborhood a bit. I could even drive by Nathan's house, too if there was time. Assuming, of course, that he still lived in the same place. He'd done his share of house-flipping when Joe first hired him, buying bargain fixer-uppers when prices were low, moving in, making the repairs in his spare time, and then selling them at a nice profit later. But about four years ago he found an older house near Nolensville with a little bit of land and fixed it up so nicely that he decided to keep it, at least for the time being. He'd seemed happy enough there that I thought there was a decent chance he hadn't sold it.

And so I pointed Wren's Buick toward Brentwood. I considered calling Ed, but decided to wait a few minutes until noon, when Owen, the husky he adopted a few months back, usually demanded a walk. I'd been supposed to call Ed last night, but it had been way after midnight when we got back to the hotel, and then we'd had to hustle to pack and check out of the hotel after we woke up. I hadn't been too keen on talking to him in front of Cassie anyway, since I didn't want to have to sugarcoat the events of the previous night.

Ed beat me to it, however. At eleven fifty-eight, my phone began playing "Paperback Writer," which is his ringtone. It's not entirely accurate, since his publisher had actually printed a limited run of hardbacks for his most recent book, but it was a close enough fit.

"Sorry for not calling last night," I said, happy to hear his voice. "Things got crazy."

"Thought that might be the case." The screen door closed behind him and I heard the jingle of Owen's leash as Ed continued. "Did you decide on karaoke or line dancing? Or were you having so much fun shopping that you stayed at the mall until they tossed you out at closing time?" His tone was amused on the last bit because he knows that I would generally prefer a trip to the dentist to a shopping spree.

"None of the above. It was an entirely different sort of crazy, and I think there's an off-chance we might have to stay in town another night if the police still have questions."

He laughed. "Dear Lord, woman. What have you gotten yourself into this time?"

"We found a body in Joe's closet." There was a sharp intake of breath on the other end, and I quickly added. "It wasn't Joe. But...then we found something that reads a lot like a suicide note in his truck."

I spent the next few minutes giving him an overview of the previous evening.

"You don't think Joe killed the guy, do you?" he asked when I reached the end.

"No. Nathan wasn't just Joe's employee. He was a friend."

There was a moment of silence, and I suspected Ed was thinking the same thing I was. The majority of murder victims are killed by friends or family.

"Anyway," I added, "Joe's not a murderer."

"So, what do you think the note meant? Do you believe it was a suicide note?"

This was one reason I had waited to call Ed when Cassie wasn't around. I wanted his unvarnished feedback, and we'd both have been reluctant to dig into this subject while she was within earshot.

"I'm not sure," I admit. "I would have sworn that Joe Tate would never commit suicide. That he would never do that to Cassie. He went through it with his own father, and it took him a long time to get past the anger. But you never really know, do you? And the note...it was the exact note his dad left. Just the two words...*I'm sorry*. The key issue here, though, is that Cassie doesn't believe he's dead. She swears she didn't pick up anything, and she's convinced that she would have if Joe was dead."

Ed was silent for a moment. "But her ability in that regard isn't foolproof, is it? And in this case, I would imagine there might be more than a little wishful thinking involved."

"I know. Either way, though, the note worries me.

Joe's either dead or in deep, deep trouble. Detective Webb seems competent enough, but..."

"Did you say *Webb*?" he asked. "Mark Webb?"

"Yeah. Do you know him?"

"Not well," Ed said. "He contacted me for information on a missing persons case about a year before I resigned. Seemed like a nice enough guy."

"I don't have any complaints," I said. "He could have given us a far rougher time since we didn't call him before heading out to the marina. Lord knows Blevins would have in that situation. But even a nice, competent detective will probably have a very real temptation to view that sheet of paper in Joe's truck not simply as a suicide note, but also as a confession. Especially if it turns out that Joe *did* kill himself, since that would offer up a very handy resolution to Nathan's murder."

After a pause, Ed said, "So that's why you're not at the mall. You're hunting for clues to clear his name."

"Yes. For Cassie's sake."

"For yours, too," he said. "I get it. Even after a divorce, you wouldn't want to think you were married for all those years to someone capable of killing a friend and stuffing him in the closet. Where are you heading now?"

"Back to Joe's place. I thought I might check in with a few of the neighbors and see what I can find out about the house that burned down. It was on the market with Joe's agency. Again. I'm almost positive that was a house that either he or Nathan sold a few months before we split up. I may drive past Nathan's place, too, if there's time. Just to make sure it's all locked up tight until his family arrives."

"Uh-huh," Ed said. "And if it's *not* locked up tight?"

"Why, I'll lock it, of course," I said in an angelic voice.

"Yeah. Right. Just be careful, okay? I'd prefer not to have to drive all the way to Nashville to bail you out."

I smiled. "Wren can bail me out."

"Except, if you end up in trouble, I suspect Wren will need bailing out, too. And probably Cassie, as well."

"How's your case going?" I asked, mostly to steer the subject away from my current activities. "Any leads?"

Ed groaned. "I've barely had time to work on it. I'm up to my eyeballs in copyedits, plus I have that panel at the writer's conference in Knoxville next week and I'm trying to think up something to say that won't bore the audience to tears. But Olivia's going to cut off my banana bread supply if I don't come up with some leads. And...you only asked me that to change the subject."

"That's not true," I lied. "I like her banana bread, too. But yes, I'm being careful. And I'll call you on the way home to discuss dinner plans."

"Good," he said. "Owen misses you."

The husky gave his usual response when Ed said his name, which is an utterance midway between a howl, a bark, and some semblance of human speech.

"So it's just *Owen* who misses me?"

"Well, maybe his owner, too. Just a bit."

About ten minutes later, I turned into my old subdivision, passing by Joe's house, where yellow police tape was stretched across the door. My first stop was Walt's place. It was still a bit risky, since I thought there was a decent chance that Detective Webb and his men would be stopping in to ask questions, and Walter might mention it. The last thing I wanted was for him to have to hide anything I said to him about getting a strange text message if the text hadn't actually been from him.

As much as I'd have liked to see him, I was a little relieved when he didn't answer. And also a little worried, even though I knew Walt had one of those medical trackers that alerts emergency services if he has a health crisis.

I got back into the car and drove down the block to the burned house, 115 Magnolia Way. Seeing Joe's face on the sign gave me far more of a twinge this time. I hoped that Cassie was right. Part of me was still a teensy bit angry at Joe, less for breaking up our marriage than for the manner in which he did it. But even in the darkest hours during the divorce, I'd never wished him ill. Okay, maybe a teensy bit of ill. A bad cold. Stubbing his toe on the coffee table. A permanent need for the little blue pill. But not dead. And the possibility that he might be some- where at the bottom of Percy Priest made my heart ache for Cassie, and doubly so if it he'd committed not just suicide, but also murder. I still couldn't believe the latter, but when you find a dead man in a house and then find a probable suicide note from the owner of that house, it's hard not to see the events as connected.

I was fairly certain that this blackened husk of a house was connected too, even if I wasn't sure how. Poking around inside a burned-out home seemed ill-advised, though. If not for the snarling expression Tammy Roscoe had been wearing the night before, I'd have tapped on her door to see if she had any gossip she was willing to share. I could play reporter and ask some of the other neighbors a few questions, but most of them would remember my face. The one exception I could think of off-hand was the house between Tammy's and this one. It had been on the market when I left town, one of the few neighborhood houses that Joe hadn't sold because the previous owner's sister was with Coldwell Banker and they preferred to keep the business in the family.

Two small kids were playing in the driveway with sidewalk chalk while their mom pulled weeds in the garden. Cassie had been just about the age of the youngest when Joe and I bought our place, and for several years, there had been a cluster of children ten and under. The cul-de-sac had been full of kids learning to ride their bikes and skateboarding on weekend mornings like this one. And then those kids had grown up and headed off to college. It was nice to see little ones in the neighborhood again.

I dug through my wallet, pulled out one of my old business cards from the *News-Journal*, and headed up the driveway, stopping briefly to admire the chalk rainbow that the little girl was making. Her younger brother was smudging it with one tiny sneaker, and I decided I'd better hurry before the mom had to referee a sibling squabble.

The woman, who appeared to be in her early thirties, looked up from her weeding with a reluctant smile, probably worried that I was selling something. After I introduced myself and flashed the business card, I told her that I was investigating a rash of housefires in the area and asked if she'd seen the fire the night before. To the best of my knowledge, there hadn't been any uptick in the number of housefires in Nashville, but it was vague enough that hopefully she wouldn't question it.

"Oh, we definitely saw it. Couldn't miss it. The kids were already asleep when it broke out, so I didn't come outside. Me and Kenny just kept an eye on it from the upstairs window in case it started spreading and we needed to evacuate. And then the police were over at the place across the street, so it was a busy night."

"Did you see any unusual activity in the neighborhood earlier in the evening?"

She shook her head. "We were outside after dinner, until around dark. Nothing out of the ordinary."

"Do you by any chance know if the owner still lives in the area? I'm curious as to whether there's any sort of pattern."

"No clue. I've seen him a few times. Keith…Hanson? Something like that. He travels a lot. You might want to ask Tammy Roscoe." She nodded toward the house on her right. "Pretty sure he was friends with her. And with

Joe Tate, but..." Her voice dropped and she looked a little uncomfortable. "The police took a body out of his house last night. He lives alone, so I'm guessing it was him."

I didn't correct her assumption, just thanked her for her time and headed over to Tammy's house. Even though I probably wouldn't get any information from her, her neighbor had pointed me in that direction. It might seem odd if I didn't follow up. And maybe I'd been reading too much into Tammy's expression. If there was anyone in the neighborhood who would have the 411 about the situation, it was Tammy Roscoe.

Tammy, however, was not home. So I walked around the corner to check one last time at Walt Petrie's place. Maybe he'd been in the shower.

A flash of nostalgia hit me when I caught sight of the Petrie's back porch. We'd had dinner there on several occasions over the years, and Cassie had spent hours on the old tire swing in their yard. It was gone now, which kind of surprised me. Walt said he liked to watch it sway in the wind because it reminded him of when he and Madge first moved into the house, back when his now-grown children were still in elementary school.

I walked to the front door and again rang the bell. After a minute, I tried a second time and decided he must be out. After grabbing the pecan logs from my purse, I opened the storm door and dropped the little bag inside. Then I trekked back to Wren's car, annoyed that I'd wasted all this time and hadn't gotten any real information. But what had I really thought I'd find out here on the street? Going inside Joe's house was out of the question given the police tape. I doubted I'd find much more than we had the night before, but if there were any clues, they'd be inside...

Or at his office. Which might not be cordoned off with police tape. His receptionist worked weekdays only, but I still had a key. I'd nearly tossed it out on several occasions after the divorce, but it was in the middle of a bunch of other keys and I'd have had to pull all of them off and rethread the darn things, and it just didn't seem worth the effort. There was a security system that Joe installed a few years back, but I thought the odds were good that he hadn't changed the code.

At least, I hoped he hadn't. I needed to get to the bottom of this, and preferably without either Wren or Ed having to post bail.

☆ Chapter Seven ☆

TEN MINUTES LATER, I pulled Wren's car into the lot of the upscale strip mall that housed the offices of Riverfront Realty. Joe's office was at the end of the strip, next to the yoga studio. Further down was a nail salon, several trendy restaurants, a jewelry store, and a vitamin shop. A substation for the Metro Nashville Police Department was just across the road, something that Joe had considered a positive in terms of security when he chose the site a few years after we married.

I was a bit nervous as I opened the door, even though I'd gone into his office after hours on many, many occasions in the past. When he first started the business, after working for six years with Century 21, I'd even filled in for his receptionist from time to time and helped him with basic research tasks. Joe had never asked for the key back or told me the place was off-limits, Detective Webb hadn't forbidden me coming here and there was no police tape barring the door, so I wasn't doing anything even remotely illegal. The code was still 121947, which was his father's birthday, so I didn't even have to worry about dealing with the security company.

There were two separate offices, a small conference room, and a desk out front for whoever the receptionist was at the moment. Joe went through them fairly quickly because he was cheap. He tended to hire receptionists with little or no credentials, and as soon as they had six months or so of work experience on their resumes, they left in search of greener pastures.

I went straight to Joe's door and was about to go in when I realized that the other office was empty. Well, not entirely empty. There was still a computer, a desk, and a phone. But all of Nathan's personal effects were gone. Which meant that he'd either quit or Joe had fired him. This made the possibility that the two had quarreled, that things might have gotten out of hand, seem much more likely than I'd assumed the night before.

Joe's office, however, was the usual chaos, which is why he always kept the office door closed. He met clients in the conference room, so he didn't have to worry too much about keeping things neat. This definitely wasn't the desk of a man who was getting his affairs in order. No other farewell notes. A quick flip through the Word-a-Day calendar he kept on his desk revealed two appointments penciled in for today, one at eleven and one at four, and a closing on Monday.

Having appointments on the calendar didn't prove anything, of course. If Joe had killed Nathan in a fit of anger last night, that realization alone could have been what pushed him toward suicide.

In addition to a mountain of papers, there were two pictures on the desk. One was of Joe with a huge fish he caught from Freedom River on one of the last trips he took with me and Cassie to Thistlewood. The other was of Cassie, age twelve, with a closed-mouth smile to hide her braces.

I flipped on his computer and while I waited for it to boot, I checked the phone where the red message light was blinking. This was a bit odd. Joe usually gave clients his cell number, since he had that phone with him at all times. I pressed the button and the voice announced that there was one new message and one saved message. After a brief pause, a man's voice said, "Not sure where you've gotten off to, Tate, but we had a deal. You're not answering your cell, you're not at the office, and you didn't follow through last night. If this goes south, it's on you. *Call me.*" The guy didn't give his name, but I jotted down the number. Then I checked the saved message, which was just a robocall.

The splash screen for Riverfront Realty was now showing on Joe's computer with a password window. I typed in the shorter of his two standard passwords, and once I was in, I pulled up the data system and ran a search for 115 Magnolia Way, hoping to find the name of the owner. Instead, I found a business. Capella Holdings, LLC, had purchased the property nearly two years earlier. It was a cash sale, something that's not that unusual for less expensive properties like condos, but a bit odd for a four-bedroom house. The company had bought the house for well under market value since it needed extensive repairs. The buyer's agent had been Nathan, and Joe had represented the seller. That sort of dual agency was legal in Tennessee as long as the client was informed, although Joe generally steered clear, feeling that it was safer for each party to have their own agent.

I remembered that the sign outside the house read *Under Contract*, but I couldn't find information on the buyer. The listing claimed that there had been nearly two hundred thousand dollars of renovations, including a newly finished basement and bonus room in the attic.

Running another search, I found that this was far from the only transaction for Capella Holdings. There were a couple of smaller residential purchases starting about four years ago, and about a dozen commercial transactions. This was the only major residential purchase, however. Joe had represented the company in seventeen transactions, total, as a selling agent. In every case, Nathan had represented the buyer.

I clicked the button to email myself the files and then checked the time. In just a little over an hour I was supposed to meet Wren and Cassie. If I was going to drive by Nathan's house, I'd have to head out soon, and I needed to get one more bit of access before I could finish this research remotely. I clicked on the EZBooks icon to open Joe's online bookkeeping software and typed in the short password. Then I tried the second, longer option. Neither one worked. Either he'd gotten security conscious on this one issue or else it was a program that required periodic password changes.

I opened the top drawer to look for a pen to write down the web addresses and a cheat sheet with that last password and found myself staring down at a framed wedding photo. A photo of *our* wedding. It was one of the staged shots where the couple feeds each other cake. It hadn't been in his office prior to the divorce. In fact, I could remember the exact spot where it had been on the bookshelves in our living room.

Beneath the photo was the cheat sheet. No pen, however. Rather than hunt further, I pulled out my phone and took a picture of the screen to record the web address and another of the cheat sheet with what I was suspected was his EZBooks password. I typed it in just to be sure the password worked, then I shut down Joe's computer and headed back into the front office. No point in hanging around here. Now that I had the password and the web address, I could look through his books once I got home.

That photograph was bugging me, though. Joe had been the one who wanted the divorce. I hadn't taken any of our wedding photos with me when I left Nashville and I certainly didn't keep one in my office at the *Thistle-wood Star*. The drawer wasn't exactly neat. In fact, it was full of papers, bills, and assorted junk. If he'd stashed the photo in there after the divorce, it seemed unlikely that it would still be on top. And if he was just in the habit of using it to hide his password cheat sheet, you'd think he'd at least have put the thing face down.

I grabbed a sheet of paper from the reception desk and scrawled a quick note saying the business was closed until further notice. Then I taped the note to the door, reset the alarm, and locked up. I had just cranked the engine of Wren's Buick when a sleek blue BMW pulled in a few spaces down. A woman with long dark hair who looked to be in her thirties was in the passenger seat. As I pulled out of the parking space, a stocky middle-aged man got out of the car and walked quickly to the door of Joe's office. Despite the sign I'd posted, he yanked on the door handle. When he found it locked, he put one hand up to the plate glass window to look inside.

Driving slowly toward the strip mall exit, I continued to monitor him in the rearview mirror. After a few seconds staring through the glass, he smacked the door-frame with the side of his fist and stormed back to his car. Maybe that was the client Joe had been supposed to meet today at eleven? Usually he met his clients at their houses since he was the selling agent. But with Nathan no longer working for him, perhaps he was having to handle homebuyers, too?

I turned right, heading in the direction of Nolensville. When Nathan bought his house four or five years back, he'd been looking for something located between the office and his sister's place in Smyrna. His sister had been in a motorcycle accident earlier that year and had required major surgery in order to walk again. Her husband had been incarcerated at the time for a drug offense, and Nathan had wanted to be nearby so that he could help out with his niece.

There were no cars in the driveway and no police tape across the doors when I arrived. I closed my eyes for a minute and tried to imagine the scene as Nathan left yesterday morning, although that assumed that he had gone to work and never returned. Given the empty desk, that theory might not hold water. The first thing I noticed was how immaculate the front yard was, with lush, vibrant green grass that made the other lawns on the quiet street pale in comparison. Unlike Joe, who was happy to contract out lawn maintenance, Nathan had taken pride in doing it himself.

That thought made my heart hurt. Nathan would never pull into the driveway again. Never check the mail or mow the grass or sell another condo. And I thought there was a decent chance that the same thing was true of Joe, although I didn't want to believe it.

A quick glance through the window of the garage door revealed that Nathan's car was inside. That had me wondering how Nathan had gotten to Joe's place, something that should probably have occurred to me the night before. There hadn't been any other cars at the curb or parked in the driveway when Wren, Cassie, and I arrived.

I rang the doorbell, and yes, checked to see if the door was locked. It was, and the key that Nathan used to keep under a blue ceramic flowerpot on the front porch was no longer there. I peered through the window, but there wasn't much to see. A car drove past, reminding me that the porch was clearly visible from the road. I felt a bit odd peeking in the windows, so I headed around to check the back door...which was also locked. It was immediately clear when I glanced through the kitchen window that Nathan kept a very neat house, something that really didn't surprise me. What *did* surprise me was the dining table...or rather, what was left of it. At first, I hadn't even realized that it *was* a table. All that remained were two large pedestals, surrounded by dining room chairs. It was possible that he'd bought a new dining set just before he died and hadn't finished assembling it, but I thought it was the same table he'd had since he moved in. Or maybe he was refinishing it? Nathan was fairly adept at furniture restoration. He'd done a decent job refinishing a coffee table that Joe inherited from his aunt three summers back.

This got me to thinking about the out-building, which served as a second garage and Nathan's workshop for his various home improvement projects. I probably wouldn't have bothered to check there, but the mystery of the decapitated dining table was bothering me. So I crossed the backyard and tried the knob. It didn't turn, but as soon as I let go, the door swung open a few inches. Inspecting the door jamb, I could see that someone had yanked on the door and forced it open. It looked fairly recent, too, because the wood splinters weren't weathered at all.

I pulled the door all the way open and stepped inside. Well...as far inside as I could. What had once been a workshop was now more of a storage area for building materials. Not just lumber, but also a couple of chandeliers, a whirlpool bath, and some top-of-the-line appliances. No tabletop, however. The shed was so packed that I couldn't even see the floor except for the area right in front of the doorway, where there was an empty patch of concrete divided down the middle by a single tire track of dried mud.

That was a bit of a surprise. Nathan rode a motorcycle regularly when he first started working with Joe. He didn't drive it *while* he was working, of course. There were very few real estate clients who would be willing to crawl on the back of a motorbike to go out house-hunting. But he'd often gone out riding on the weekends with friends and with his sister. Until the accident. Given how close his sister came to dying, he'd said he kind of lost interest in riding. I'd thought he might even have sold the bike, but the dirt tire treads looked fresh.

When I stepped back, I saw that the tire marks weren't just on the shed floor. There was also a print in a patch of mud a few yards away. Apparently, Nathan had gotten past his fear of riding the bike. Had he driven the bike to Joe's house? It hadn't been in the driveway, but it was entirely possible that it was parked in the backyard.

Something about the whole thing seemed off, but I couldn't quite put my finger on it. The lousy night's sleep was beginning to catch up with me. And I didn't really have time to suss it out right then, given that I was due to meet Wren and Cassie in twenty minutes. I took my phone out of my jeans pocket and snapped some shots of the storage room, including the tire track on the floor. Maybe after I had some coffee to give my tired brain a jolt, I'd be able to connect the dots.

I was just about to pull the door shut and head back to the car when I heard a vehicle turning into the drive. Worried that it might be Detective Webb, I ducked into the shed and peered through the tiny crack in the door jamb created by whoever had kicked the door in. It wasn't Webb's SUV. In fact, I doubted it was the police at all, since it was a pale green sedan. A Prius, maybe? A blonde woman was behind the wheel, but I couldn't see the face well enough to tell if I knew her. I was fairly certain it wasn't Nathan's sister, however. Unless her finances had changed drastically, she couldn't afford that car.

The woman parked next to Wren's Buick and walked over to peer through the windows. When she tried the handle, I realized I'd forgotten to lock the door. She glanced around quickly, then stuck her head inside the car to snoop.

That pissed me off, so I stepped out of the shed. Whoever she was, I had as much right to be here as she did. Nathan was my friend, or at least he had been before the divorce. Cassie and I both had come out here to water his plants when he was on vacation and we'd visited at least once a year for a cookout. And she had absolutely no right to be poking around in Wren's car.

The key fob was in my pocket. I pulled it out and pressed the panic button. The woman jumped, smacking her head against the top of the car. As she turned toward me, I realized it was Tammy Roscoe. I didn't see how she could have followed me from the neighborhood, given the stop at Joe's office. And I was fairly certain that she didn't know Nathan, so I actually had more reason to be here than she did.

I stormed off toward her, calling out, "Get away from my car."

Okay, technically it was Wren's car, but explaining that would have distracted from the main point.

"I didn't know it was your car, Ruth Townsend."

"Well, you most certainly knew that it wasn't yours," I countered. "What are you doing here?"

"I could ask the same of you." Tammy's voice had a shaky quality, wavering in and out, as if she were trying a little too hard to sound confident. Her arms were crossed against her ample, and if memory served me, recently amplified bosom. "For that matter, what are you even doing in Nashville? Did you get tired of living in the middle of nowhere?"

"I'm here as Nathan's friend. I wanted to make certain that his property was locked down before I head back home." If she knew Nathan at all, she'd probably remember that he had family in the area who could do that. But it was the best excuse I could muster on short notice. "And, to the best of my knowledge, there are no laws forbidding people who move away from Nashville for coming back to visit now and then to do a little shopping. Maybe take in a show. So, again, what are *you* doing here?"

Tammy was, of course, under no obligation to answer me, but since I'd been forced to come up with a lame excuse, I was bound and determined to make her do the same.

She didn't even try, though. Instead, she went straight into a verbal attack, propping her hands on her hips and puffing out her chest. "You always act so high and mighty. Always so sure that you're smarter...*better*...than anyone else. That anything that happens to *you* matters more."

I stared at her, confused. We'd had maybe a dozen conversations that were more than a greeting or a comment about the weather since she moved into the neighborhood about eight years ago. To the best of my knowledge, the only thing that I'd ever done to tick her off was refusing to give her any grist for the gossip mill when she'd called to inquire about why I left town. What had I done to make her this angry?

"You aren't the only one who cared about him, you know." Tammy poked a finger toward my face, giving me a faint whiff of acrylic. Her eyes were brimming with tears as she backed toward her Prius. "We've been seeing each other for nearly three years now. And you have no idea how hard I tried to make him love me." She slammed the car door, cranked the engine, and then screeched out of the driveway, leaving me staring after her as the taillights disappeared around the curve.

☆ Chapter Eight ☆

WREN AND CASSIE were almost finished with an order of avocado egg rolls when I arrived at the Cheesecake Factory.

"You are nearly fifteen minutes late, young lady," Wren said. "I had to swat Cassie's hand twice to keep her from eating your share."

"I'm sorry," I said, instantly regretting the words because they pulled my mind right back to the note in Joe's truck. "Traffic was worse than I thought it would be."

Usually I'd have taken my time with the menu, debating between two or three of my favorites, but both of them had already decided on their entrees and the waitress was hovering, so I opted for the Thai chicken salad and iced tea.

"Actually," I said as the waitress was leaving, "could you make that a mojito?"

"Well, I guess you're driving, Wren," Cassie said with a dry chuckle. "So...it wasn't just traffic. What happened that has you day-drinking?"

"Just a confrontation with a very unpleasant woman. A *confusing* confrontation, to be honest. You knew Nathan as well as I did, Cass. He was gay, right? Did he ever date women?"

She pulled a face that made it clear that wasn't even in the realm of the possible. "Never. Not even when he was a teenager. Why?"

"Well, the unpleasant woman I mentioned was apparently in love with him."

Wren shrugged. "It wouldn't be the first time a straight woman was attracted to a gay man. That's the plot of at least a dozen movies."

"I know," I said. "But I can't imagine Nathan even being *friends* with her, let alone her thinking they were compatible. He was a nice guy. And then the age difference. Tammy is almost my age and Nathan was what? Thirty-two? Thirty-three?"

"Tammy Roscoe?" Cassie snorted. "Nathan was definitely not involved with her. Even if he'd been tempted, I doubt he'd have risked his job by going after the boss's girlfriend."

My jaw dropped. "That's who your dad was dating?"

She nodded. "And I knew that would be your reaction, which is why I didn't name names."

"Who is Tammy Roscoe?" Wren asked.

"You saw her last night," Cassie said. "She was on

her lawn watching the fire and you asked me why she was glaring at Mom."

"Oh. You mean the one with the..." Wren held her cupped hands out about a foot from her own breasts.

"Yup," Cassie said, and then confirmed my earlier suspicions. "Those were her Christmas gift to herself a few years ago."

"So she didn't mean Nathan at all. That explains several things, actually. I couldn't understand why she was so angry at me, but maybe she thinks I'm in town trying to get Joe back. She's probably kind of sensitive on that front, given that her husband took off with his secretary years ago." My eyes narrowed as I remembered the other thing she'd said...that she'd been dating him for over three years. I'd moved to Thistlewood about eighteen months ago, so Joe had apparently been cheating on me for over a year before he found the nerve to say he wanted out of the marriage. Guess Tammy had decided that she'd rather be the other woman than be left for one. I didn't see any point in sharing that last bit with Cassie, however, especially when Joe might be dead anyway. She'd been mad enough at him over the divorce.

"Why was she at Nathan's house?" Wren asked. "For that matter, why were *you* at Nathan's? I thought you were only going to the *News-Journal*."

"No one I knew was at the office, so I decided to drive over and see if Walt was home. He wasn't, but while there, I figured I'd ask a few questions of the neighbors. Because I'm not buying that the house burning down was a coincidence. Then it occurred to me that I could still get into Joe's office to get that information--"

"You went to Dad's office?" Cassie asked with a note of alarm. "Why?"

"Like I said, I don't think the house burning down is a coincidence."

"Well, fine," she said. "But is it a good idea to go poking around there when detectives are likely to be combing the place?"

I gave her an annoyed look. "Oh, sure. Because you've never snooped around to get evidence..."

Wren, who was clearly trying to stay out of this, couldn't help but chuckle at that comment. We'd both had to escape onto the rooftop of her neighbor's house to avoid getting caught trying to sneak back in a piece of evidence that Cassie had sneaked out.

"Anyway," I continued, "I decided to see if there was anything odd at Nathan's while I was out that way. Tammy must have followed me when I left the neighborhood, but if so, she was pretty stealthy."

"Or she might have seen you as you were leaving the office," Cassie said. "Tammy took the receptionist position when the last girl quit. She'd been doing it occasionally when he needed a temp anyway. Dad said she's working on getting her real estate license. He tried using temp workers for a few months--I even filled in a couple of Saturdays--but he finally decided he needed someone there full-time."

I considered that. True, I hadn't seen her inside the

office, but there were quite a few cars in the lot so I might not have noticed the Prius. Maybe she was getting lunch or…having her nails done? That seemed likely given the scent of acrylic when she jabbed her finger at my face.

"So…what did you find out during this snooping session at dad's office?" Cassie asked after the waitress dropped off my drink.

"I don't know, really. I'm still trying to process everything. At least I now have access to Joe's bookkeeping software, so maybe there will be some clues there. I found out that Nathan apparently *quit* before he was killed, which…" I give Cassie an apologetic look. "Which unfortunately isn't going to be in the plus column for your dad if the police figure that out. And maybe I'll be able to piece something together from the photos I took in Nathan's storage shed, although it was so packed that I'd just be scratching the surface."

"Packed with what?" Wren asked.

I pulled up the photos I'd taken and pushed my phone across the table so that they could see them. Cassie scanned through for a moment and then handed the phone to Wren.

"What's he doing with all of that?" Wren asked.

I shrugged. "Home improvements, maybe."

"Or more likely, for one of the properties he'd been fixing up and selling." Cassie said. "Last time I saw him, he joked that he was going to have to take up another hobby, because he finally had everything exactly the way he wanted it. And I housesat for him enough times to

know that garden tub wouldn't fit in either of his bath-
rooms. Plus, those chandeliers... He'd have to knock out
the master bedroom upstairs in order to have a living
room ceiling high enough to hang either of those
monstrosities. And does any of that stuff look like
Nathan's style to you?"

I had to admit that they didn't. Nathan was into
clean lines, with furniture that was more about function-
ality than flash.

"If he's using that stuff to renovate houses," Cassie
added, "he's upped his game considerably, because those
items look more like they belong in a ritzy house. And
that isn't in Nathan's budget. Or rather *wasn't* in his
budget. It's still hard to think of him as gone."

That was actually something that Joe and I had quarreled about six months or so before we divorced. Nathan
had just had his annual review, and he had tried to nego-
tiate a more equitable split than he'd gotten in their orig-
inal partnership agreement. Joe balked at the idea of
paying Nathan a higher percentage, however, saying that
he carried the financial risk for the firm and that
warranted the forty-five percent he took from Nathan's
commissions. I'd pointed out that Nathan did a hell of a
lot more work at the firm after nine years on the job, and
that it might be time to treat him like an actual partner
rather than a lackey. To my surprise, Joe had actually
agreed, although he said it would have to wait until
Nathan's next review since he'd already drawn up the
paperwork and didn't want to redo it. Still, I was skep-

tical that Joe had followed through, especially since I was no longer around to nudge his conscience.

"Anyway," I continued, "I felt bad leaving the place unlocked with Tammy prowling around. Whatever is in there almost certainly belongs to Nathan's sister now. Which reminds me that we need to find out when services are being held. I don't think either of us can really afford to take the time off to drive all the way back, but at least we can send flowers."

As I said the words, it occurred to me that Cassie and I might be personae non gratae, given that Nathan's body was found in Joe's house. And I thought there was a decent chance that we would be driving back to Nashville anyway, if Mark Webb called to inform us that they'd located Joe's body out at Percy Priest.

☆ Chapter Nine ☆

"THAT'S the great thing about home," I said as I spotted the *Welcome to Thistlewood* sign. "Even though it's nice to get away sometimes, it always feels good to be back." The statement was especially true this time around. I was exhausted, drained in a way that I hadn't felt in months. Cassie and Wren seemed to be feeling it, too. I'd asked Cassie a few questions about the friends she'd visited the day before, and she'd given me mostly mono-syllabic answers that made me feel like we'd time-traveled back to when she was fifteen and perpetually sulky. The three of us had finally lapsed into silence about an hour ago, each lost in our own thoughts for the final leg of the trip.

"Right," Wren said. "You're just ready to see Ed."

"Well, yes. But I missed Cronkite, too. And Owen. They're all kind of wrapped up in the definition of home."

"You guys are so cute together that you almost make me question my preference for long-distance relationships," Wren said. "But then I remember the few times I actually had a roommate and...nope."

"We do have separate houses," I said primly.

"For *now*," Cassie chimed in from the backseat.

Wren nodded. "I give it six months."

I turned to look back at Cassie, trying to gauge her comment. Was this new phase in my relationship awkward for her? Cassie adored Ed and vice versa, and she was at Dean's at least three nights a week, usually even more often. So far, Ed and I had taken maximum advantage of the nights she was away, and occasionally I stayed at his place. We both joked that it was like being teenagers again. *My folks are out of town, so you can stay over.* There had only been one occasion when Cassie had returned unexpectedly around two in the morning. While she'd definitely seen Ed's truck in the drive, he had been up and out before she was awake.

But...

"You know, if you ever feel awkward about Ed being around so much," I told her, "all you have to do is let me know. It's your home, too."

Cassie snorted. "Hey, Wren...could you glance in the rear-view mirror real quick and answer a question for me? Do I look like I'm seven years old?"

Wren obliged her request. "You do not."

"Good. Because my mom seems to think I'm a little kid who's icked out that she has a normal sex life."

When I started to protest, Wren held up her hand. "I need one of you to very subtly check the *side* view mirror and tell me if that's what I think it is."

I turned in my seat.

"Girl, that is the direct opposite of *subtle*."

The unmistakable outline of a patrol car was pulling up fast behind us. As soon as I looked back, the blue lights atop the vehicle flashed on.

"Dear God," I said. "Is he really pulling us over?"

"Looks like." Wren tapped her brakes and began edging the car onto the shoulder of the road.

Great. Steve Blevins was the *absolute* last person that I wanted to see this afternoon. Pretty much the last person I wanted to see any afternoon, truth be told.

"Maybe he's after the car that passed us a minute ago?" I began, and then sighed as he pulled up directly behind Wren. "But of course not. Were you speeding?"

"No! You know I only speed on the interstate. And I'm kind of regretting saving his life right now. You'd think he'd cut us some slack."

I suspected that Blevins thought he *had* cut us some slack, since not a single word had been said about Wren's reindeer adventure just before Christmas. That still left him a long way from having paid his debt in full, in my opinion, but he probably viewed the matter differently.

He took his own sweet time getting out. After a minute, I turned sideways and stared at the cruiser willing my heretofore nonexistent telekinetic powers to activate and blow his car to bits. No luck.

Blevins unfolded himself from the car a few minutes later, nearly knocking off his Stetson-style sheriff's hat. He was the vainest person in our high school back in the day, and he can't seem to handle the simple fact that the mane of hair he sported back then is long gone. I'd seen him exactly once without a hat since I returned to Thistlewood and that was only because I'd caught him off-guard at his house. He's never bareheaded in public— he'd even worn a fedora to the Thistlewood Star Christmas party. The middle-aged spread was also beginning to take its toll on the man's waistline, and I suspected it wouldn't be long before he had the stereo-typical Southern sheriff's belly hanging over his gun belt.

"Afternoon, ladies," Blevins said with his sarcastic smile, which always hits me like nails on a chalkboard.

Wren didn't even bother to return his fake smile. "What gives, Blevins? I wasn't speeding."

"Taillight might be a bit loose," he said. "Left side."

"*Might* be?" Wren asked.

He nodded. "Flickered a tiny bit when you hit that dip in the road back there. Maybe it got bumped by one of the packages from your big-city shopping spree." The smile widened into a grin. "Should probably check and see if the bulb is loose when you get back to the mortuary."

"You actually stopped us for that?" I said.

"Absolutely. Safety first is always my motto. But while I have you..." His smile morphed into something I could only assume was supposed to be sympathy, since I'd never seen that expression on his face before. "Just wanted to share my condolences about your husband, Ruth."

My head jerked back. How did he know?

"He's not dead," Cassie snapped. "Not sure where you're getting your information, but you might want to seek out better sources."

"I'm sorry," Blevins said. "Guess I'm a little ahead of the curve, at least until they drag the reservoir. It just has to have been hard to have it happen when you were right there in Nashville and then be the ones to find the note. Quite a coincidence."

His expression wavered for a moment and I got a look at the malicious intent brewing just underneath the surface.

"News travels fast," I said, regaining my composure. I wasn't about to let Steve Blevins get the best of me. The day had already been long enough.

He shrugged and scratched the stumble on his chin. "Internet age," Blevins explained. "My mom spends a lot of time on the Facebook."

Wren and I exchanged a glance. *The* Facebook. God help us.

"She saw it on WKRN's page," he continued. "Joe must've been quite the big shot. Surprised you let a fish like that get away in order to take up with a guy like Ed, whose royalty checks barely pay the mortgage on that tiny little house of his."

The comment was mean-spirited, as usual, but not
entirely unfair. Ed had only earned out his advance on
his first book a few months back, and he'd told me that
advance hadn't exactly been anything to crow about. But
his mysteries are good, and he was increasing his fan base
with each one. And Ed didn't start writing because he
thought it would ever make him rich, anyway.

I could also add that Ed has a decent retirement and
disability check from the state, due to the hit-and-run
accident that forced him to retire early from the sheriff's
department. Steve Blevins is dumb as a rock, but he's still
savvy enough to realize he wouldn't be sheriff if not for
that accident. My only question was whether he knew
his then-teenage son was almost certainly behind the
wheel of the car that hit Ed. Was Blevins the one who
convinced his father-in-law to provide an alibi, or had the
judge acted on his own initiative to save his daughter's
only child from finishing high school with a DUI and
leaving the scene of an accident on his record? I wasn't
sure if we'd ever know the answer to that, but I trusted
Derrick Blevins even less than Steve, if that was actually
possible.

And so I just stared at him silently. I don't trust my
mouth very much, either.

My daughter, however, is younger and far less
inclined to hold her tongue. "You're lying," she said.
"That's not where you got the information. I've combed
through every media story that mentions my father's
disappearance and none of them mentions a note."

"Well, aren't we just the little budding journalist?" Blevins said. "I'm an officer of the law, so I have a few connections. Even in the big, bad city. Maybe, just maybe, someone called around to check on you. And maybe, just maybe, I was duty-bound to inform them that bodies tend to pile up wherever you girls go. Just professional courtesy, you know? But I'm thinking the next time you ladies go on a road trip you might want to take the hearse."

I heard Cassie's seatbelt unlatch and turned back to look at her. "Stay put, Cassie."

Her face was red, and she already had a hand on the door. After a few seconds, she pulled it away.

Blevins chuckled and gave the roof of Wren's car a hearty slap. "Y'all drive safe, okay?"

"Sure thing," Wren said as he turned to walk away. "Be sure to tell your mama I said hello. Word around town was that she took a tumble. Hope she's feeling better and that she's settling in okay at your place. Has to be kind of crowded with both her and Derrick back home."

Blevins turned back, his eyes narrowed as he stared at Wren. I struggled to keep my face straight because I couldn't believe she'd actually gone there, especially the last bit about his mom settling in okay. There was absolutely nothing in her words that would be interpreted as snide by an external observer and Wren's tone had been pure sweetness and light. In order to accuse her of any ill-intent, he have to at least tacitly admit that he preferred his mother in Knoxville where she'd been living for the past few years, which he wouldn't do, even though everyone in town knew it was true. The return of Bobbi Blevins had been the primary source of chatter at Pat's Diner for the past two months. Jesse Yarnell, Patsy's boyfriend, was apparently friends with a guy over in Maryville whose wife had been Jenny Blevins's best friend since they were in high school, so Jesse had been strolling in with a new juicy tidbit every couple of days.

"My mama is settling in just fine," Blevins said warily. "I'll be sure to pass along your greeting. And don't forget to take a look at that taillight, you hear? I'd sure hate to have to write you up."

"He can't just say stuff like that," Cassie grumbled after Blevins returned to his car.

"Of course, he can," Wren replied calmly. "He's the sheriff. As the saying goes, elections have consequences."

"And so does poking the bear," I told her. "Are you sure asking about his mom was a smart move?"

"Probably not," Wren said. "But I'm truly tired of that man's attitude."

I couldn't argue with her on that point.

Blevins whipped the cruiser around us, gave three short *beeps* of his horn, and was gone.

"And that's the not-so-great thing about coming home," Wren said with a wry twist of her mouth. "It's also home to people who know from experience how to get on your very last nerve."

"True," I said. "I thought Derrick was living on-campus at UT."

"Nope," Cassie said. "I suspect he couldn't cut it. He stopped by The Buzz a few days ago for a coffee. Said he was taking a semester off to figure out what he wanted to do next. I gave him a few suggestions but none of them seemed to appeal to him."

Wren and I laughed, because we both had a solid idea what sort of suggestions Cassie might have given to Derrick Blevins. I was quite certain none of them were polite.

Three minutes later, Wren pulled into the drive of Memory Gardens. It was a bit unusual for a funeral home, with its robin's-egg blue exterior. That was one of the first things Wren changed when she took over the place, and it took a while for folks in town to get used to it. It had taken them some time to adjust to Wren herself, truth be told. Thistlewood isn't exactly a diverse town, and the idea of an African American woman running the funeral home had been a bridge too far for some folks, who'd opted to take their business to Maryville or Pigeon Forge. I'll admit I was a little skeptical when Wren told me about her plans to repaint the place, but in the end, I think she was right. The stolid, stone-gray building was more traditional, but a little color can be comforting when you're mourning. Wren handled the funeral for my parents, so I could speak with some authority on that point.

I sighed, wishing my thoughts hadn't traveled in that

direction. Partly because I still missed them, but also because I was worried that Cassie might soon be burying her own dad. And despite everything we'd been through in the past eighteen months, it hurt to think of Joe being so miserable that he'd take his own life.

My Jeep was parked out back. Cassie grabbed her computer bag and was out the door almost as soon as Wren cut the engine.

"I'm gonna head over to The Buzz," she said.

I'd expected that she'd go home first, but then it occurred to me that in a sense, she *was* going home. As much as I loved my cabin, it was just four walls. The time I felt most at home was snuggled up with Ed on the couch, reading, watching a movie, or just staring out the windows at the night sky. Cassie clearly felt the same about Dean. The past twenty-four hours had been rough on her. It was only natural that she'd want that comfort, too. And she spent most of her waking hours at The Buzz, anyway. Dean was the owner of the combination bookstore, cafe, and esports parlor, but he had a day job delivering the mail. So, in every sense of the word, Cassie ran the place.

"Sure, sweetie," I said as I got out of the car. "Tell Dean I said hi. And call me if you need a ride home later, okay?"

She nodded and gave me a quick hug. We both knew the odds of her actually coming home that night were slim, but as her mom, I had to at least suggest it as a possibility, right?

Wren laughed as I watched Cassie sprint off toward the bookstore. "You want to come in for a cup of coffee?"

I glanced up at Wren's apartment and then at my own Jeep, waiting silently for me. "No, thanks. I need to be getting home as well. I'm supposed to meet Ed at Patsy's for dinner, but I may have to take a rain check. What I really need is a shower. Or maybe a long bubble bath and a glass of wine."

"Girl, you read my mind."

She popped the trunk and I looked down at the bags hidden there. "Guess I'll be taking Cassie's, too." I laughed.

Wren helped me carry the suitcases and assorted shopping bags over to the Wrangler. We loaded them into the back and then I climbed inside. It felt like I was home already.

My conscience tugged at me briefly when I drove past the office. This week's edition of the *Thistlewood Star* was going to be a bit on the light side. Everything was mostly ready. The only things left to do was setting up a new ad that had been purchased the week before, checking to see if there were any additions to the classifieds, and getting the print formes in their final order. I could easily accomplish all of that the next day, which would leave Tuesday for any last-minute changes before I printed out and collated the hundred and forty copies that I ran each week.

The sun was setting in the west, dipping over the mountain and rejuvenated trees, painting the edges of the new leaves in vibrant colors. I rolled down the window, letting the cool mountain air wash over me, and felt the stress of the last two days begin to lift. Not completely, but enough so that I could finally breathe freely. It's never hard for me to remember why I love this place.

Chapter Ten

I PULLED into my driveway and parked in front of the house. The bags in the back could wait, I decided, realizing that I'd probably curse myself for my laziness later.

When I was halfway to the door, I detected smoke. Not the fireplace kind, or the burning building kind, thank God, but the kind that can only mean there's food on the grill. Good food, too.

I peeked around the corner of the house. Sure enough, Ed's truck was in the back. And then I picked up a faint whimper from the other side of the door, followed by a plaintive howl and a very annoyed yowl. The whimper and howl were clearly from Ed's husky, Owen, and the yowl was from Cronkite, who was almost certainly already pissed at me for leaving and would be twice as annoyed if he had to share me with Owen tonight.

"No fighting, boys," I said as I opened the door. "I have enough hugs for everyone."

"Sit, Owen!" Ed responded from the kitchen. "Be good. She was Cronkite's mama long before you showed up. And save some lovin' for me. I've got okra all over my hands."

Owen cheerfully ignored the command, and it didn't matter to Cronkite anyway. He was giving me his disdainful look, after one annoyed twitch of his tail. Most days when I came in the door, he greeted me instantly, running figure-eights around my legs. I'd learned early on to stop in my tracks unless I wanted to trip and land facedown on the carpet. But then I didn't usually leave for two whole nights. The only exception had been the short New Year's Eve getaway that Ed and I took up at Sleepy Pines, and Cassie and Dean had been here the entire time. Cronk is, technically, *my* cat. He has lived with me his whole life and there have been stretches where he didn't see Cassie for a month or more, but that doesn't change the fact that *she* is his person. I'm a distant second. Joe was never in the running at all.

Almost as if reading my mind, the cat hopped down from the back of the chair and stalked into the kitchen to rub his shaggy gray self against Ed's legs as he washed his hands in the sink. Cronk's message was clear. *You abandoned me, short human. Now I will abandon you. Tall human has taken your place.* There would be no such punishment for Cassie, however. I had tried telling myself it was a sign that the beast was completely secure in my affection, but finally just had to admit the truth...Cassie owns his heart.

Sticking my tongue out at him, I crouched down next to Owen, who proceeded to bathe my face in doggy kisses. "Two can play that game, Cronk." The dog kisses almost certainly meant I'd need to shower before Cronkite would curl up in my lap, but there's generally no stopping Owen and a shower was on my agenda anyway. The cat confirmed my suspicions on that front by promptly leaving the kitchen as soon as I entered.

"You didn't have to cook, Ed. I thought we were going to do Patsy's because you're up to your ears in copyedits?"

"We were and I am," he said. "But I stopped in to grab a coffee to-go when Owen and I were on our walk and...I didn't think you'd want to deal with the Thistle-wood gossips tonight. Blevins was apparently in earlier. Patsy was smart enough to simply ask me if you'd heard anything more about Joe, but you know Jesse."

I nodded because I do indeed know Jesse.

"Anyway," Ed told me, "I've had a hankering, as they say, for my grandma's tomato gravy and rice, and thought it would go well with some grilled fish."

I peeked into the skillet, where a dark brown paste that smelled like bacon was bubbling around chopped okra, and what looked like onion and celery. It smelled good, and I was totally onboard with this veggie dish, whatever it was, until he tossed in a can of tomatoes.

Ed laughed at my expression. "You like okra. We had it in gumbo, remember?"

"Of course, I remember. You make exceptionally good gumbo. I'm just confused. I thought those were for the tomato gravy. The kind with meatballs that you serve over spaghetti?"

"No, ma'am," he said. "The stuff Italian grand-mothers make is tomato *sauce*. How can you call something gravy when it doesn't even start with roux? This stuff is the real deal."

"Well, it smells incredible," I said. "Nothing better than coming home to find a sexy man in your kitchen cooking dinner."

Ed grinned as he wiped his hands on the dishtowel. "Play your cards right and you might even get dessert. Now come here and let me give you a proper hello." The timer went off before he could finish the last word, and he sighed. "Make that a quick hello and a rain check, or our fish will be a crispy critter."

I gave him a quick but thorough hello kiss and then followed him onto the deck with the platter. The fish needed a minute more, so he closed the grill and gave me a searching look.

"You doin' okay?"

I shrugged, and was about to say *yeah, sure, I'm fine,* which was what I'd been telling myself since we'd seen Nathan's body tumble out of Joe's closet the night before. But it wasn't really true, and Ed could usually see straight through me. "I'm...I think I'm still in denial."

He nodded. "And you've been keeping strong for Cassie, too. How's she holding up?"

"I'd have said *fine*, but she was out of the car almost before Wren cut the engine. Which makes me think maybe she was trying to be strong for me, too. Finding Nathan like that was tough on both of us. We've known him for years. There was a time when he was at our place at least once a week for dinner. He came to Cassie's high school soccer games...and he was just a really good guy. A decent, kind-hearted man and he didn't deserve to die like that. As for Joe, I don't know what to think. There's his family history, and the last time we spoke, he sounded like he was drinking pretty heavily. I could almost believe the suicide, but...I simply can't believe he killed Nathan."

We continued the discussion over dinner. Unpleasant topics like murder and suicide probably aren't good for our digestion, but it certainly wasn't the first time we'd sorted out clues between bites.

"Hopefully, I'll have more to go on once I comb through his financial information," I said as we divvied up the scraps between our beasts and stacked the plates in the dishwasher. "I want to find out more about this Capella Holdings. The house burning down at the same time we found Nathan just doesn't feel like a coincidence to me. And I need to try and track down the number that sent me the text."

He frowned. "What text?"

"Oh. I guess I skipped that part. When we were

inside the house, someone texted telling us to get out. We were heading for the door by that time anyway, so it was a pretty pointless warning. The same number had called me earlier but didn't leave a message."

We carried the bottle of wine into the living room, along with a plate of the tiny frozen cream puffs that I tell myself I'm not going to buy when I go to the grocery store, and which I always end up buying anyway because it's a fifty-calorie dessert...if you only eat one of them, which I never, ever do.

"So, who do you think it was?" Ed asked.

"The *most* likely person is Walter Petrie, across the street."

"The old guy Cassie bought the pecan logs for? I thought you weren't able to get up with him."

"We weren't. But he's the only person other than Tammy Roscoe and Joe who would have had my number. Given her attitude at Nathan's place, I really don't think Tammy would be inclined to give me any helpful warnings and Joe was almost certainly out at the reservoir by then. The hood of his Denali was cold when we got there. But Walter could have seen the fire from his place. Maybe he was just out running errands or something when I stopped by this morning..."

"Maybe," Ed replied, with a touch of skepticism.

It felt off to me, as well, but it was still the most logical possibility. So, I pulled out my phone and tried to call the mystery number again.

No answer. But as I was about to hang up, voicemail kicked in. Just an automated voice telling me to leave a message at the tone, but the night before, I hadn't even gotten that much.

"Ruth Townsend," I said. "You called and messaged me yesterday, and I'm trying to follow up. If...this is Walt, I stopped by today, but you weren't in. I left two pecan logs inside your storm door. Give me a call to let me know you're okay."

I placed the phone on the coffee table and stared at it for a moment.

"You know, if you're worried about him, you could just contact Detective Webb. He'll probably be in the neighborhood himself tomorrow and he could do a health and welfare check."

"You're right," I admitted. "I was just reluctant to mention it because I didn't exactly tell him about the text message. Or the phone call."

He sighed. "Of course you didn't."

"Because I thought it might be Joe. Like you've said before, anyone can commit murder under the right circumstances. As much as I didn't—*don't*—want to think Joe actually killed Nathan, it looks bad. Maybe they argued and Joe snapped. I thought maybe Cassie and I could convince him to turn himself in."

Ed slipped an arm around my shoulders and pulled me toward him. "You do know that all cops aren't like Blevins, right?"

I raised an eyebrow. The comment seemed a bit like a non sequitur. "Obviously. You weren't corrupt when you were on the force. Neither is Billy, and Blevins's other deputy seems okay, too."

"True, but I'm thinking more of Steve's incompetence than his corruption. Webb will be questioning the neighbors if he hasn't already. One of them will likely show him your card and he'll know you were asking around."

"Well...I'm a reporter. It's what we do. I'm happy to dig for info online, but sometimes nothing beats good old-fashioned shoe-leather journalism."

He gave me a point-taken nod. "But you're also the ex-wife of an apparent suicide, who had keys to a house where a dead body was found. And to his office. You wouldn't be the first person to snap and kill a family member. Or an ex, in your case.... And yeah, I know you have a solid alibi, but how good is *Cassie's* alibi? You also wouldn't be the first mom to cover for her kid."

I hadn't actually thought about that. Not that I believed for a single second that Cassie could kill Nathan or Joe. "She might have had opportunity, but there's definitely no motive. Yes, she was gone for about three hours, off visiting friends from when she lived in Nashville. I'm sure they can vouch for her. And either way, I don't really think there would have been time for her to kill two people and stage a suicide. She didn't even have a car with her."

Ed leaned forward and planted a kiss between my

frowning eyebrows. "All of this is far-fetched, absolutely...but my point is that Webb didn't strike me as the type not to dig around a bit. He'll be doing some shoe-leather investigation, too. I just think you might want to be upfront with him to prevent those shoes from coming down on you or Cassie."

☆ Chapter Eleven ☆

I WOKE AHEAD of the alarm the next morning to the smell of coffee. The first thing I did, however, was rub the sleep out of my eyes and check my messages. Nothing from the mystery number, but Walt Petrie had sent me a text a little after midnight. That didn't fit with my knowledge of his daily schedule, but when I read the message, I found out that he was three time zones behind. He had gone see his daughter in California for spring break, as I'd suspected. Not just for a visit, though —he said was scouting out apartments so that he could move once the semester ended.

At some point, I'd need to call him and let him know about Joe. But that could wait until I had something more concrete to tell him.

As I trudged downstairs, there was only one beast underfoot. The fact that I'd abandoned him was apparently forgiven, if not forgotten. Cronkite's anger has a habit of melting away when hunger hits.

A note from Ed was propped against the coffee pot, and I read it aloud as Cronk rubbed against my ankles.

Don't let the little liar fool you. He's been fed. I thought you two might need some alone time to get back into his good graces and I have to dive back into my copy edits. Wish me luck.

Beneath his scrawled signature was a postscript. <u>Call Webb.</u>

Ugh. I didn't want to deal with that yet. Coffee first. And it was too early, anyway. I'd call him once I got to work.

Cronkite rubbed against my leg. "Don't even think about trying to scam a second breakfast. But I *will* give you a treat...and maybe we can do a bit of bird watching before I head into the office."

Fifteen minutes later, I was showered, dressed, and out on the deck wiping the morning dew off the picnic table. The air was a bit chilly and still smelled faintly of the previous night's fish. Cronk gave the grill a thorough sniff inspection before joining me at the table, clearly disgruntled that he hadn't found any stray tasty bits.

Bird watching is one activity we could never do when Owen was around. He seemed incapable of sitting still and watching. Cronkite, on the other hand, loved these mornings. He was a born bird watcher. A born bird catcher, too, when the opportunity presented itself, so I kept the feeder far away from the deck and made use of the binoculars I'd bought on a whim when I moved back to the mountains. Cronkite usually stared in the same direction I did, tracking his quarry with no apparent need for a visual aid.

"Well, look at that, Cronk. We have *feline* company this morning. Of a sort."

A gray catbird was perched in a tree near the feeder warbling away. It was hard to know which fragments of song were native to the bird. Catbirds are natural mimics, much like their cousins the mockingbirds, and they happily sing cover versions of tunes originally performed by almost every bird they encounter.

For the next twenty minutes or so, I tried to let my mind wander as I watched an array of other birds in the backyard and surrounding woods. I'd taken up this hobby in the hope that it would serve as a sort of meditation when I was going through the stress of my divorce. Most of the time, it worked quite nicely. That morning, however, my mind kept wandering off to our discovery of Nathan's body and Joe's note. And now that the shock had worn off, the latter was weighing more heavily on my mind, and I found myself remembering more of the good times than the bad. Joe had once been the center of my universe, and while I had no desire to go back to my life with him, the sad reality that he was either dead or in serious trouble kept circling like a shark in the water.

"Sorry, Cronk," I said after tipping back the last of my coffee. "I might as well head in to work."

He twitched his bushy tail, clearly annoyed at having our birding session cut short. Even though he could use the cat door and come out on his own, he rarely did. Maybe he'd begun to consider bird watching a group activity? I gave him another treat as an apology, poured the rest of the coffee into a travel mug, and piled into the Jeep for the short drive to the office.

I parked in the back lot and grabbed my laptop bag from the backseat where I'd left it overnight after our return from Nashville. I'd only taken a few days off, but there was still mail to sort through and a message on the answering machine from someone wanting to place a classified ad. By habit, I tackled these routine tasks first, transcribing the ad from the message and swearing for the gazillionth time that I was going to stop taking ads by phone. Everything was so much easier when they submitted them via the website. It was still a bit early to call them back to get their payment info, and definitely too early to call Detective Webb since Nashville time is an hour behind Thistlewood. Instead, I grabbed the computer bag so that I could start combing through the information that I'd emailed myself from Joe's office.

It wasn't until I began unzipping the bag that I realized I had Cassie's laptop, not mine. The bags are a slightly different style, but they're both black, and Cassie must have grabbed the wrong one from Wren's car. She didn't have to open The Buzz until ten, so I thought the odds were good that she wasn't awake yet. Cassie has always tended to roll out of bed a scant half hour before she's due at work. I sent her a quick text to tell her to bring the computer with her and then headed back into the press room to work on the galleys that I would print and assemble the next evening so that I could deliver the news to my subscribers bright and early Wednesday morning.

The edition had been almost ready to roll when I left. At first, I'd considered adding something about what had happened while we were in Nashville. Nathan's murder was news, and I was used to my investigations winding up on page one. But this was supposed to be the news from Thistlewood, not the news from two hundred miles away.

Joe was a different situation, however. He wasn't a resident, but he had spent time here on vacations and if his body turned up, I would pick a font and print his obituary next week. People would think it odd if I didn't.

When I took over the Star, I continued the previous owner's custom of printing each obituary in a special font selected from the massive collection of font cases that he'd purchased over the years. But what font do you choose for a man you once loved? Someone with whom you shared a child?

Thinking about preparing Joe's obituary is what finally broke me. I was wiping away tears when I heard a knock at the front door. It was still locked, and I hadn't flipped the OPEN sign yet, so I debated just ignoring it. But my desk lamp was on, which would give away the fact that I was here, and it was only a few minutes before nine. I'd need to open up soon anyway. Maybe it was the guy who'd ordered the classified ad coming by to pay up before he headed to work?

When I reached the front office, a man had his hand cupped to the window and was peering inside. He looked familiar, but I didn't think he was local. I opened the door and that's when I recognized him, more from his build than from his face. It was the guy I'd seen pounding angrily on the door at Joe's office as I drove away. The shiny blue BMW parked at the curb confirmed it.

"Keith Hanlon." The man extended his hand, as he flashed a smile that he clearly intended to be sympathetic, although it didn't quite work. "I'm a client of Joe's. A neighbor, too, as of a few months ago."

His voice was familiar. I couldn't be certain, but I thought it was the same guy who'd left the message on Joe's machine.

"I spoke briefly with you at a Riverfront Realty holiday party two years back," he continued. "You probably don't remember me, though. The place was pretty crowded. Joe really knows how to throw a Christmas bash, doesn't he?"

He was either wrong or just plain lying. Joe had never held Christmas parties for his clients when I lived in Nashville, and I certainly hadn't attended any party two years ago when we were in the middle of divorce proceedings.

"He does, indeed," I said. "What brings you to Thistlewood?"

"A fishing trip, actually. Joe always said Thistlewood was the place to go if you want to catch big-mouth bass."

I was fairly sure this was another lie. Fishing is the reason most people come to Thistlewood during the spring months, so it was the most logical excuse for the guy to offer. But fishermen generally don't show up in a sports coat, Dockers, and dress shoes.

"And while I was here, I thought I'd stop in and see if you or your daughter have heard anything about Joe. Because I have to tell you, I saw him Friday and he seemed perfectly okay. I mean, he was certainly fed up with that partner of his, and rightfully so." He stopped, as if weighing his words. "But, um, Joe didn't seem like the type to kill anyone, you know? And I'd never have imagined that he'd off himself like—"

"We haven't heard *anything*," I said firmly.

"Oh. Okay. Do you have any idea what's going to happen with Joe's business, though? I mean, he's missing, Nathan's dead. We were in the final stages of a major deal."

It was something that I actually hadn't thought much about, and something I really didn't *want* to think about. And it wasn't the kind of question that you expected anybody to start asking so quickly after a death. At least, not anybody with a shred of decency.

"I really couldn't say, Mr. Hanlon, but..." The name clicked right after I said it. The neighbor I'd spoken with had said Keith *Hanson* was the owner of the house that burned down, but that was only one letter off. "If you'd like to leave your card, I'd be happy to give you a call if we hear anything. When you're done with your fishing trip, that is. You'll be lucky if you get a single bar of coverage on the river."

"Sure, that would be great. But who do you think will be handling the business side of things? Because I need to get back with my partner within the next--"

"You *are* aware that we're divorced, right? I have absolutely no idea who will be handling my ex-husband's business affairs. So if that's all, I have work to do."

"Okay, well then perhaps I could speak with your daughter? I know she worked in the office from time to time, and I need someone to let me in so that I can get some paperwork. Doesn't she have a key?"

"Mr. Hanlon, I'm trying extremely hard not to be rude since you claim to be a client of Joe's, but you're making it difficult. My daughter is currently worried that her father might be dead. All she ever did was answer phones when her dad was shorthanded. She has no more idea about his business affairs than I do. Your partner will just have to deal with a delay, given the circum-stances."

Hanlon didn't respond or move toward the door. He

just tightened his jaw and stared back at me with a face that was growing alarmingly red.

I held his stare. "As I said, leave your card and I'll call you when I know something. But you *will not* bother my daughter with this. I went to high school with the local sheriff, and I'm sure it wouldn't take much for me to get him to issue a restraining order."

Well, the *first* part of that sentence was true. The last part, not so much. This guy and Blevins would probably hit it off instantly.

If Hanlon could tell I was bluffing, it wasn't apparent.

"I'll be in the area for a few days while I finalize some...travel plans. If you hear anything, I'd very much appreciate a call." The words were civil enough, but the clenched jaw and clipped tone suggested there was quite a bit of anger below the surface. He held my gaze for a moment, then reached into his back pocket. As he pulled out his wallet, the sports coat gaped open slightly to reveal a shoulder holster. He extracted a business card, slapped it down on the front counter, and headed back to his car without another word.

I would have sworn the car was empty when I looked out at it earlier. But as he screeched down Main Street, I spotted someone in the passenger seat. It might have been the woman I saw him with in the parking lot of Joe's office, but the car was gone before I could discern anything more than the fact that the passenger was probably humanoid. And even that was a stretch. It could have been a large dog. Or even a jacket slung over the seat. For the first time ever, I kind of missed the summer-time traffic. At the peak of tourist season, Hanlon would have still been at the curb, inching out until he found a kind soul willing to let him into the lane.

Why had he driven all the way to Thistlewood in search of information about Joe? I didn't believe for one second that the guy was here on a fishing trip, and he could have asked those questions over the phone. It was also a bit curious that he'd mentioned being Joe's neighbor but hadn't bothered to note that his house was the one that burned down the night of Joe's disappear-ance and Nathan's death. Hanlon knew I was in Nash-ville, so it stood to reason that he'd also know we were in the neighborhood when the fire department was putting out that blaze.

Of course, he might not know that I had any way of connecting him to the house. I'm certain he didn't see me when I was pulling away from Joe's office and he wouldn't know that a woman from his neighborhood had told me he owned the place. And technically, she *hadn't* told me that since she gave me the wrong name.

I decided I might as well get the call to Detective Webb out of the way before finishing up the paper, espe-cially since I now had a bit of interesting information to offer. Hanlon was clearly connected to Joe, he was acting suspiciously, and was probably someone Webb would want to follow up with. And given the way the man had just spoken about Nathan, he might even be a suspect.

☆ Chapter Twelve ☆

ED WAS WAITING on our usual bench with Owen
when I got to the park just after noon. The weather had
only recently begun to warm up, so there were just two
food trucks out—Dell's Tacos and Tennessee Pig—and
judging from the brown sack on the bench next to Ed,
he'd already grabbed our burritos.

Owen greeted me with his usual yowl and face
kisses, then sniffed the air, looking mournfully toward
the barbecue truck.

"Looks like someone isn't particularly happy with
our lunch decision," I said as I took the spot next to Ed.

Ed laughed. "Owen is clearly of the opinion that
veggie burritos, even with extra guac, can't hold a candle
to pulled pork. Dell tossed him a piece of tortilla, but
Darla usually gives him scraps from the grill, so it's hard
to blame him for having a strong preference." When I

reached for the bag, Ed held it just out of my grasp and said, "Did you call Webb?"

"Sort of," I told him. "I got his voicemail and asked him to call me back, because I actually have something worth telling him."

He raised his eyebrows for me to go on and I shook my head. "Food first."

"You wouldn't be so starved at lunch if you bothered to eat breakfast."

I stuck my tongue out at him as I fished one of the burritos out of the bag. "Or I could wait and eat at lunch when I'm actually hungry."

Between bites of lunch I told him about Hanlon stopping in at the *Star*, although first, I had to backtrack to tell him who Hanlon was and that I'd seen him outside of Joe's office. "He's super frantic for information on who's going to be handling Joe's business. He also didn't seem to like Nathan much and I'm not buying that he just happened to have a fishing trip planned here in Thistlewood."

"That *is* weird." Ed rubbed one hand along the edge of his jaw as he thought about it. "You wouldn't think he'd be talking trash about Nathan, however, if he'd actually killed the guy."

"Maybe. But he didn't strike me as the brightest bulb on the tree. And he kind of looked like he'd realized he let something slip after he said it. I'm just glad he hasn't bugged Cassie."

"You're sure he hasn't?" Ed asked.

I nodded. "I wasn't sure he'd listen when I told him not to bother her, but I stopped by The Buzz earlier to swap computers. We only got to talk for a second because she had deliveries coming in, but she said he hadn't been by."

"Would he have even known where she works?"

"Maybe not," I said. "I'm not even sure if Joe knew the name of the place. But this is *Thistlewood*. All Hanlon would have had to do is ask someone at the diner. Or pretty much anywhere."

As I was speaking, a motorcycle pulled up to the curb near the barbecue truck. The motor apparently needed a tune-up. It was belching smoke and the noise drowned out my last words. I gave the driver an annoyed look. He probably gave me one right back, behind his helmet, but at least he had the good grace to cut the engine.

"Ah, the first bikers are arriving," Ed said. "They're like bluebells. Thistlewood's harbingers of spring. One or two pop up, and then a week or so later the place is teeming with them."

He was right. The bikers, like the fishermen, started a bit before the main tourist season, and it wouldn't be long before the diner was packed with them on the weekends. "You might want to keep that bit of poetic imagery to yourself. I doubt most of the bikers would appreciate being compared with bluebells."

Ed shook his head in mock dismay. "So quick to stereotype. I'll have you know I once owned a motorcycle. Scraped up the cash to buy it used right after I turned fifteen and hid it in my best friend's barn." He chuckled softly. "And sold it at a loss six months later when my mama found out."

"Would you have appreciated being compared to a bluebell when you were a fifteen-year-old biker?"

"Nope. You win. Why did you have to swap computers with Cass?"

"Oh. She just grabbed the wrong bag getting out of the car yesterday, I guess. Which probably means she was more upset about Joe than she was letting on, since she didn't realize it until I showed up at opening time to swap them out. Usually she'd have at least checked email or social media--"

"Which she could do on her phone."

"Good point," I admitted. "Anyway, I told her to keep an eye out for a blue BMW with a jerk behind the wheel. And Dean was there, so he'll keep a look out while he's on his rounds. But I'll still feel better once I hand off that information to Detective Webb. He texted and said he'd call me around two."

"Not sure what Webb would be able to do from Nashville aside from calling it in to Blevins," Ed said. "I'm going to give Billy a call and have him drive past a few times during his shift."

"You don't need to do that," I said. "Hanlon is probably just a blowhard. The more I think about it, you were right with your first assessment. If he was involved in killing Nathan, he wouldn't be poking around here."

"Maybe. But don't discount your instincts, Ruth. They're usually darn good."

I took the compliment graciously, even though I could have given him numerous cases where my instincts had been wrong. For several minutes, we sat in companionable silence, focused on finishing our lunch. Just as I was tossing the last inch of my burrito to Owen, however, a voice called out from behind our bench.

"Sheriff Shelton?"

We both turned to see Olivia Byrne, a small, trim woman dressed in her usual grey skirt and pastel twin set. Like many Thistlewood residents, she still referred to Ed by his previous title. I think it was partly because old habits die hard, but the biggest reason was that many of the folks in Thistlewood were happier with the way the Woodward County Sheriff's Office was run when Ed was in charge.

Olivia eyed Owen cautiously, keeping the bench we were sitting on between herself and the dog. I don't think she was scared he would bite. Owen doesn't give off that vibe at all. But Olivia was all of a hundred pounds soaking wet, and it wouldn't take much for an exuberant dog his size to knock her over.

"I'm sorry to interrupt your lunch," Olivia said, giving me a brief smile. "I just wanted to check and see if you have any news about my quilt."

Ed colored slightly and shook his head. "I'm afraid I haven't had time to work on it, Miss Olivia. I've got the edits on my new book that have to be finished by the day after tomorrow, remember? Like I said before, just as soon as I get those turned in, I'll be able to devote my full attention--"

Olivia's face fell. "I don't *remember* you saying anything about edits, but...I'm a little more forgetful than I used to be. It's just that the conference begins on Thursday. And our delegation will be leaving for Nashville right after lunch on Wednesday."

"What conference, Miss Olivia?"

"The annual women's club conference. Our club was planning to enter my quilt in the statewide competition, since it won our local contest. Remember me telling you how jealous Lillian was that I won? I spent three years making that quilt. Back in the day, I could have made it in six months. A year, tops. But my hands shake a bit now, and I wanted each stitch to be perfect so I could have a shot at that trip to the conference. They're staying at the Opryland Resort, and I've heard such wonderful things about that place. I even bought a new suitcase for the trip. I'm planning to donate the quilt for our silent auction next week, and it will bring in a lot more for the scholarship fund if it wins a state ribbon. Our treasurer has it set up on one of those apps this year, so we might even get bidders from outside Thistlewood. But I guess now they'll have to pick one of the other two at tomorrow's meeting. Probably Lillian, although I really do think Roberta's quilt is better. And whoever wins will get to take the trip to Nashville, instead." Olivia sighed heavily as she opened her purse and began rummaging through it. "Maybe I can still return the suitcase if I can find the receipt."

Ed and I exchanged a look, and then he said, "All I remember you telling me was that someone, probably Lillian or one of her boys, swiped your quilt from the wall of the church. Then you showed me the picture that one of the other ladies made of a man's boot beneath the spot where it was being displayed. You said your quilt won first prize, but...I don't recall you telling me anything about taking it to the state conference this week."

There was a moment of silence, and then Olivia said, "I'm sure I told you, Edward."

I noticed with some amusement that it was *Edward* now, which I suspect is what she had called him back when she was his Sunday School teacher.

"Well, maybe you did," Ed replied. "My memory can be a little sketchy, too, especially when I'm working on a book."

This wasn't at all true. Yes, his mind occasionally wandered off during conversations when he was working out the details of a new mystery, but he really didn't become forgetful.

"So you'll talk to the women on that list I gave you?" Olivia asked.

"Yes, ma'am. I'll carve out some time this afternoon."

She gave him a wide smile. "Thank you so much, Sheriff. You always were my favorite. And now I'm going to head over to the library, so I'll let the two of you get back to your lunch."

Olivia began walking back toward Main Street. Once she was out of earshot, Ed cursed softly, and I couldn't help but laugh.

"If it's any consolation, I don't think you forgot. You told me about her showing you the picture and giving you a list of names the night after she showed up at your door to ask for help. If Olivia had told you about a conference and a contest, I think you'd have mentioned it."

"I know," he said. "I just told her that to make her feel better. Maybe I can get Sara to give me a few more days."

He'd already done this once, because a mild case of conjunctivitis the week before had limited his screen time. I knew he wasn't especially keen on asking his editor for a second extension.

"Or maybe you could give me the list of names and I'll do the sleuthing for you? I need something to keep my mind off everything else anyway. And Wren and I have been talking about joining the women's club—"

Ed laughed. "You are a dirty, rotten liar, Ruth Townsend."

"Yes, I am. Now give me the list. And don't think I'm doing this for free. The next loaf of banana bread Olivia delivers to you is *all mine.*"

"I knew there was a catch." He pulled two folded slips of paper out of his wallet. "But on the plus side, if you and Wren are interviewing members of the Thistle-wood Women's Club..."

He trailed off and I dug an elbow into his side. "You were going to say we'd stay out of trouble, weren't you?"

"I was," he admitted. "But then I remembered that I'm talking about you and Wren, and there are absolutely no guarantees in that regard."

"We mostly get into *good* trouble, though."

"Fair point. Do you want to risk dinner at Patsy's tonight?"

I grimaced. "I'll have to face the gossip mill at some point. But maybe it wouldn't hurt to put it off until tomorrow. Do you have ingredients for pasta Alfredo at your house?"

"Yep. Also some salad stuff that needs to be used."

"Good. I'll cook while you work." I gave Ed a kiss and Owen a scratch behind the ears. "And then I'll head straight home so you can keep right on working."

He groaned. "All work and no play..."

"Helps Ed meet his deadline?"

"Yeah. That's *exactly* what I was going to say."

Chapter Thirteen

ONCE I WAS SETTLED in at my desk with my own computer, I searched to see if I could find information about a memorial service for Nathan. I'd never met his sister, and I thought it quite likely that any flowers I sent would simply end up in the trash given the circumstances of Nathan's death. What would I even have the florist write on the note? *Nathan was a great guy. Sorry that my ex-husband might have killed him.*

When I found the information about the service, I discovered that they were requesting donations for St. Jude's Children's Hospital in lieu of flowers. Happy that I could do something in Nathan's memory that would actually do some good, I gave a hundred dollars and simply added my name and Cassie's.

Then I headed back to the press room to typeset the new classified ad. *Press room* was my grandiose label for the back half of the building that looked more like a garage than the massive press room at the *News-Journal*. During the first few months I ran the paper, Cassie frequently argued that I should move the *Star* into the current century. I do have an online edition, which is updated more frequently than the weekly print version, but I couldn't bring myself to shift to doing everything electronically. In part, it was because I'd feel like I was disappointing Mr. Dealey, who had owned the business when I was in high school and who taught me most of what I know about newspapers. But it was also because I enjoy the routine, the smell of the ink and newsprint, even the heat of the linotype machine and the smell of hot metal as it stamps out each line of type. Now that I have both machines in working order—the printing press (which Mrs. Dealey dubbed *Stella*, from that *A Streetcar Named Desire* movie, because he was always yelling at it) and the linotype machine (which he named Blanche, so he'd have a matched set)—I couldn't imagine doing it any other way. There's a certain satisfaction from knowing as I toss each paper onto the doorsteps on Wednesday mornings that it's something I've made from scratch.

I finished the classified section around one-thirty and placed it into the printing forme. With my official work out of the way, I pulled my laptop from the bag and navigated to Joe's EZBooks site. It didn't open, and I thought maybe I'd typed the username or password incorrectly, so I tried again. Still no luck. Then I checked my phone for the photo I'd taken of the password cheat sheet. The password was correct, and it had worked yesterday. But not now.

There was a button to retrieve a lost password. I was about to click it on the off chance that it would just ask for the answer to a secret question. When you were married to someone for nearly a quarter century, you generally know the make of his first car, the city where his parents met, and the name of his first pet. But then I noticed the sentence at the top of the dialogue box. *No account found under this email address. Try again?*

Whoa. Someone had wiped Joe's account. Which meant he was either still alive and kicking or someone else had access to the website.

With that avenue of investigation blocked, I started digging for details on Capella Holdings, LLC, the company that was the legal owner of the house that burned down. The owner turned out to be a second holdings company, Delana Holdings, which was in turn owned by another company. Which was owned by a subsidiary of yet another company. And another. I finally reached the end of the trail with a corporation in Delaware, which listed an attorney in New Jersey as the contact. No phone or email, just a physical address, which Google Maps showed as a tiny office wedged between a pawn shop and a tattoo parlor. Someone might be able to untangle the financials on this, but it wasn't going to be me. I'd be more than happy just to hand this thread over to Detective Webb when he contacted me. That was beginning to seem less likely,

however, since it was now nearly three and he still hadn't
returned my call as promised.

Frustrated at my inability to make any progress on
the real estate front, I decided to focus on the Mystery of
the Purloined Quilt. I pulled the papers Ed had given me
out of my pocket. The first sheet was a printout of a
photograph that one of the other club members took at
Shepherd's Flock Community Church, which was the
scene of the theft. It showed a muddy footprint on the
floor next to the wall. A boot print, to be precise. And it
was *probably* a male boot, judging from the style, but the
size was a bit hard to tell for sure from the picture.

The second sheet was a printout of the club
members' names and phone numbers. Many of the
names were familiar. Ed's sister, Sherry was a member.
The list also included D'Arcy Jones, an attorney who is a
friend of Ed's, along with a few local business owners.
Several older ladies were listed, including Olivia and her
cousin, Lillian. Jenny Blevins, Steve's wife, had the
words *Club President* penciled next to her name and a
typed version of those same words were marked through
next to the name *Verna Neilson*. Verna, the wife of our
local mayor, had rubbed me the wrong way several times.
My policy, which I'd carried over from Mr. Dealey, was
that the minutes from the club would be printed in full
the week after the meeting, *if* there was room. Actual
news, classified, and paid advertisements had to take
priority over long-winded minutes that were read only by
a handful of club members who felt important if they got

their name in print. If space was tight, the minutes would either be split between two issues or bumped to a week where there was space. Verna had objected to this on two different occasions since I relaunched the paper, clearly viewing the club minutes as frontpage news, so I'd been delighted to discover that Jenny Blevins ousted her at the January meeting. I don't know Jenny well, but despite her taste in husbands, she's surprisingly nice.

In addition to Verna's title, about a half dozen member's names were marked through, so it must have been an old list. Lucy McBride, Sally Blackburn, and Edith Morton, all of whom had died since my return to Thistlewood, were crossed out. Steve's mom, Bobbi Blevins, was crossed out because she moved to Knoxville four or five years ago, but her name was also scrawled across the bottom in pencil because she'd recently moved back. The one name that kind of surprised me was written just below hers—Elaine Morton, Edith's daughter-in-law. I wouldn't have pegged her as a clubwoman.

That was only about half the names, however. I recognized some of the others, but I couldn't say I actually knew them. In a few cases, I wasn't even sure I could pair the name with a face. Wren, on the other hand, had been back in Thistlewood a lot longer and she knew almost everyone in town.

I debated calling her, but it was only a few minutes' walk and I needed to stretch my legs a bit. Wren almost always had a pot of coffee this time of day, as well, and given her propensity toward stress baking, there was frequently the chance of a warm cookie to go along with the caffeine.

So I popped the *BACK SOON* sign on the door and headed down the sidewalk. As I reached Shepherd's Flock and was about to turn onto Wren's street, I spotted the motorcycle I'd seen earlier at the park. It was at the curb, and the biker, a pudgy guy of medium height, was standing beneath the awning of the old dollar store, which was currently vacant. The guy, who was still wearing his jacket and helmet, was talking to someone I couldn't see, and judging from his hand gestures, he was getting a bit frustrated.

I'm nosy enough that I tried to subtly peek back over my shoulder, and as a result I nearly collided with Wren's neighbor, Elaine Morton, who had just rounded the corner with the little beagle that she and Clarence adopted just after the holidays. Elaine was reading something on her phone and hadn't seen me either, so we both startled and then began laughing.

"I guess we both need to watch where we're going," I said. "And how is little Miss Delta doing?" The dog's tail, which was already wagging, kicked into overdrive at the mention of her name.

"She's doing a lot better," Elaine said. "Almost house trained, and she's only chewed up one shoe this week. Clarence grumbled about a dog being too much trouble, but you should see him now. He spoils her rotten. I was planning to call you later to say how sorry I was to hear about Cassie's dad. Have you heard anything?"

Ed was apparently right about the news spreading through the grapevine. "No," I told her. "Not yet. I'm really hoping it's a mix-up."

"Well, it's just awful. Are you headed to Wren's?"

I said yes and was about to make some excuse to get away, because Elaine will talk your ear off given the chance. But then I remembered her name at the bottom of Olivia's list. "You're a member of the Thistlewood Women's Club, aren't you, Elaine?"

She nodded. "Patsy's mom sponsored me to join last October. It was Clarence's idea, since I'm more or less retired now. His mom was a member, and he said they do a lot of good raising money for scholarships and so forth."

"That's what I've heard. I mean, I read the minutes from each meeting as I typeset them and...you said you need a sponsor to join?"

"You do," Elaine said. "But any member can sponsor someone. Why? Are you thinking of joining?"

"I am. Wren and I were talking about it recently."

Elaine's face split into a wide grin. "Don't think you can fool me, Ruth Townsend. You're trying to figure out who swiped Miss Olivia's quilt. We meet at three p.m., down in the basement." She nodded toward the church on our right. "And of course I'd be delighted to sponsor you both."

"That's really sweet of you, Elaine! Thanks so much. I can't wait to tell Wren the good news."

Wren, however, didn't consider the news to be at all good. I hadn't expected her to be excited about joining the club. She'd been back in Thistlewood for over a decade, and if she'd been interested in becoming a member, I was sure she'd have done so by now. But Wren was always up for helping me with investigations. In fact, she was usually more eager than I was, so I was quite surprised when she shook her head emphatically and said, "I have a viewing tomorrow for Mary Quinn."

"At seven thirty, yes. I typeset the notice. This meeting will be over long before that."

"Well, yes. But I'll have a hard time maintaining a calm and comforting exterior in the evening if I have to deal with that club. I heard enough about those women from Gran. And unlike her, I don't feel I have anything to prove."

I frowned, trying to piece together what she was talking about. Not *who* she was talking about—Gran Lawson had raised Wren and I'd spent many hours in her kitchen when we were in high school. But I didn't remember Wren ever saying anything about her grandmother and the women's club.

"It was after we graduated," she said. "The very next year, in fact. I think she was bored after James and I were gone, to be honest. And maybe she wanted to try and change things here in town, after what happened with James."

I had only recently learned the full story of what happened with Wren's brother that summer, and how it was connected to the disappearance of our friend, Tanya Blackburn. James had been gravely injured in a fight and

Gran Lawson decided it might be best for him to finish his last year of school with an aunt in Chattanooga. And it probably *was* better for James, who was an excellent student and had better scholarship opportunities at the new school than he'd have had here in Thistlewood. He was quite happy to leave this town in the rearview mirror, and after learning the full story of why he left, I really couldn't blame him.

"So...she thought she could change things by joining a women's club?"

"Apparently," Wren said. "She was the first black member. One of the teachers at the high school nominated her. While most of the members were cool with it, there were a few who didn't exactly go out of their way to welcome her. Bobbi Blevins, for example. She was the president back then, and she actually had the nerve to speak out against Gran joining, saying she was afraid she'd feel out of place. To be honest, I think it was just as much a class thing as a race thing. I mean, when are their meetings?"

"Um...the one tomorrow is at three."

"In the middle of a weekday, just like it was back then. Housewives and a few professional women. People who own their own business and can take an hour or two off, like D'Arcy Jones. There weren't too many working-class folks among their members back then, and I'm guessing there aren't now. Gran had to leave work early, using vacation time, during the two years she was a member in order to attend the meetings. She said they did some good things for the community, but she just couldn't take the in-fighting and backstabbing."

"That's okay, then. It would be a lot more fun with you, but it's just the one meeting. I can go by myself. It's not like I'm planning to remain a member. You know I'm not a joiner. Olivia just seems to have her heart set on entering her quilt in the state competition and winning the trip to Nashville, and the only way that's going to happen is if I can track the quilt down in the next two days. And all I have to go on is this. Do you think that's a man's boot or a woman's?"

I unfolded the sheet of paper with the boot print photo and held it out toward her. Wren gave me a perturbed look, because she knew exactly what I was doing—luring her in with clues and piquing her interest in the mystery. But she took the picture anyway.

"Hard to tell without knowing what size the tiles are," she said. "It would be easier if they were squares instead of hexagons. Finish your coffee and let's go."

I tipped back my cup obediently. "Where exactly are we going?"

"Next door to the church," she said with a grin. "I don't have to join their stupid club to help you solve this case."

"But Ed has had this photo for several days. I doubt the boot print will still be there."

"So do I," Wren said, placing her sneaker in the middle of a tile on her kitchen floor. "But they won't have swept away the tiles."

The church was open in the afternoons for a variety of club meetings. We headed downstairs to a standard church basement with white cinder block walls and long plastic tables with black fold-up chairs. Four rows of tables stretched the length of the room with little vases of yellow flowers that were too uniform to be real, placed about three feet apart. Two kids in Girl Scout uniforms who were apparently a bit early for their meeting gave us a quizzical look and then went back to whatever they had been giggling about when we walked in.

There was, of course, no handy sign to mark the spot where the quilt had been hanging, but aside from the rectangular tiles that hugged the wall, the hexagons were all the same. My size five-and-a-half foot nearly covered two of them. Wren's size ten was closer to two and a half, and the boot print in the picture covered three tiles, lapping over a bit onto a fourth.

"Definitely a guy's boot." Wren said as we headed back upstairs. "But who would have an incentive to steal a quilt? I'm still not buying that it was Lillian Autry, no matter how long she and Olivia have been feuding."

"Could just be someone planning to sell it on eBay," I said. "It would probably fetch a hundred dollars or so. Although apparently not as much as it would if it took a ribbon at the state convention. Olivia was planning to sell it at their silent auction next week and she said it would earn a lot more for the club's scholarship fund if she won."

Wren pushed the side door of the church open and

we stepped out into the afternoon sunshine. "I think the most likely thief is someone who thinks she has something to gain from Olivia being out of the running," she said. "So...who will be going in her place if we don't find it?"

I shrugged, deciding not to note the fact that Wren was now saying if *we* don't find it. "Olivia seem to think that would be determined at the meeting tomorrow. She was very worried that it would be Lillian, although she thought the other woman's quilt was better. Roberta, I think?"

Wren cocked her head to the side. "Um...pretty sure that's Bobbi Blevins."

"You're probably right. So...one of those two. I'll know which one after the meeting tomorrow."

She looked at me with narrowed eyes, and then laughed. "Oh, you are good, Ruth Townsend. You know what my curiosity is like. There's no way I'm going to sit over here waiting for you to come back and fill me in on the details. Guess I'll be going with you after all."

Chapter Fourteen

ED, who was thoroughly bored with editing, tried to convince me to stay for a bit after dinner, but I supplied his missing willpower and left as soon as we finished eating. I debated stopping by The Buzz on the way home to talk to Cassie, but in my twenty-four years as her mother I've learned that my daughter needs time to process her emotions. *Alone* time. That's a little tidbit I'd passed along to Dean early in their relationship when they had a minor squabble. Trying to get Cassandra Tate to talk before she was ready would just cause her to dig in her heels and drag out the whole process. I'd hoped that I would hear back from Webb so that I had an actual reason to contact her, although it had also occurred to me that any information the detective had to offer might be bad news. I'd settled for just sending her a text saying that I'd be at the house tonight and I was thawing out half of a fudge pie I'd stashed away after Valentine's Day if she was in the mood for comfort food. Cassie can't be *forced* out of a blue funk, but she can occasionally be lured out with chocolate.

And if not, I would curl up on the couch with Cronkite, a glass of merlot, and my Kindle. There were far worse ways to spend an evening.

I parked my Jeep in its usual spot and grabbed my computer bag from the backseat. The sky, which had been bright blue earlier in the day, had taken on clouds by the time I headed over to Ed's to cook and the air now had that heavy, expectant feel that comes just before a rainstorm. When I reached the front porch, I had my key out and ready, but then the motion sensor light flipped on, and I stopped. Dirt was scattered just to the right of the doormat and as my eyes traveled upward, I saw that the potted plant I usually keep on a wrought iron stand beside the door had been knocked over. I glanced toward the tree line, wondering if I'd had a visit from Remy, the not-so-little-anymore bear that I'd freed from barbed wire when he was a cub. It was warm enough now that he'd be out of hibernation, but he'd never come up onto the deck before. Raccoons were a possibility, too. They'd gotten into the trash on several occasions when I'd forgotten to strap the lid down. It could also have been Cronk, although I couldn't remember the last time he'd knocked something over without staring me in the eye to make it crystal clear that he *meant* to do that. For such a large beast, he is surprisingly graceful.

Then I noticed the footprint in the dirt. Definitely

human. And judging by the size of the footprint—something that was apparently a theme for my day—I was almost certain it was from a man's shoe.

Normally, I would have thought it might be Dean delivering the mail. But he'd dropped my business mail off at the *Star* during his regular rounds, and Cassie usually brought home anything sent to our address that wasn't junk mail. Maybe Ed had forgotten something here and then forgotten to tell me he'd stopped by? Except Ed would've cleaned the dirt up, or at least swept it over the side of the porch, and the plant was still lying on its side.

Alarm bells began to go off inside my head. Not loud, exactly, and they were accompanied by a voice telling me that I was overreacting. But they were there just the same, and I couldn't help remembering Keith Hanlon peering through the front window at the *Star*. He'd probably come by here before he went to the office and knocked the plant over while trying to peek into my front window. And he didn't even bother to pick it up. What a jerk.

The sky chose that moment to open up, without even a preliminary sprinkle to warn me. I quickly unlocked the door and Cronkite came bounding out. As I watched, he zoomed past my feet, into the yard, and back again like a possessed boomerang. Then he parked himself at my feet and yowled. This was a slightly more effusive welcome than I generally received, but then I was almost two hours late with his dinner. This heinous

offense, coming right on the heels of my recent abandon-
ment, might have wound him up more than usual. It
probably didn't help that he'd run out into a newly
arrived rainstorm.

"Come on," I said, stepping over the cat to enter the
house. He followed me inside but stuck so close to my
legs that I almost tripped twice on my way to the
kitchen. "I'm going, I'm going, okay? Calm down."

I flipped on the light, grabbed a can of his favorite
foul-smelling food from the pantry, and dumped it into
his bowl. He didn't tear into it as I'd expected, however.
In fact, he barely seemed to notice.

"Okay, Cronk. What's going on? How long are you
going to stay mad at me?"

Cronkite stared down the hallway that leads to the
guest room. The fur along his back was raised and his
upper lip was slightly curled. I followed his gaze and a
chill tracked down my spine as I remembered the
toppled plant outside the door.

"Is someone in the house?" I whispered.

Cronk said yes. Okay, *technically*, the noise he made
couldn't be considered an answer. It was just a hiss. But I
had absolutely no doubt what he meant.

I took several steps back toward the kitchen. The fireplace poker would probably make a better weapon, but
I'd have to cross back in front of the darkened hallway to
reach it. A knife would have to do. In my rush to get to
the knife block, however, my hip bumped one of the
kitchen chairs and it crashed to the floor.

Cronkite hissed again as heavy footsteps entered the living room.

"Ruth?" a voice called.

My shaking hand had just snatched the knife from the block, and I froze at the sound. I knew that voice. And a moment later, my missing, presumed-dead ex-husband rounded the corner to find me wielding a butcher knife.

I'm not sure I'd have recognized him in the dimly lit room if he hadn't spoken first. He'd put on around thirty pounds since the divorce, in addition to the fifteen that had taken up residence as he entered middle age.

My hand was still shaking, not from fear at this point, but from anger. "What are you doing here? Why were you hiding in my house?"

Joe stopped and held up both hands. "Whoa, Ruth. What the... It's just me. Put down the knife."

"I'm not putting it down until you answer my question," I said, taking a step forward. "What are you doing inside *my* house?"

Joe kept backing up as I advanced, probably because I was still holding the knife. Eventually, his legs collided with the edge of the sofa. "I'm here because I need your help. What is wrong with you?"

"What's wrong with *me*? Aren't you supposed to be dead?"

That clearly caught him off-guard. "Wow. That's an unbelievably cold thing to say."

"Yeah? Well, leaving a suicide note in your car for

your daughter to find was an unbelievably cold thing to *do*."

Joe shook his head. "I didn't have a choice. If that cop hadn't followed you to the reservoir, I would have told both of you then and there."

"How did you know about the cop?"

"I was watching from the woods. When I got to Percy Priest, I sat in the car for over an hour trying to decide what the hell I was going to do. I'd just gotten the motorbike out of the back of the truck and was about to leave. Couldn't risk going to a hotel, but I've got an empty listing a few miles away, so I was going to go there and sleep for a few hours. Then you guys showed up, so I pushed the bike into the woods and waited. Would you *please* put the knife down?"

I took two steps to the right and placed it on the dining room table. As soon as I dropped it, he started walking toward me.

"Oh, no. No, sir. You stay right where you are. I don't trust you. I'm not even sure I know who you are anymore. The man I knew would never have put Cassie through that."

His face fell. "I didn't know that she'd be the one to find the note! Like I said, I didn't have a choice. It was either pretend to be dead or *actually* end up dead like Nathan. And I thought you, of all people, would know that I wouldn't leave those two words as my suicide note, given how many times you heard me complain about it being unfair that my dad hadn't even tried to explain."

"I did think it was odd," I admitted. "But you don't generally expect rational actions from someone about to take their own life."

"As for why I'm here at the house," he said, "I was going to talk to you this afternoon at the park. But you were busy. Who's the elderly guy you were talking to?"

The *elderly* crack set my teeth on edge. Ed looks darn good for sixty-one. And aside from his hip injury, he's in better shape than the man standing there in front of me who was ten years his junior. "He's your replacement," I said levelly. "Ed Shelton. And he's a major upgrade." Then it clicked. "You were the guy on the motorcycle I saw when we were at the park. Where's the bike?"

"I parked it back in the shed," he told me, nodding toward the back yard. "And I didn't break in. I still have a key from when we used to come here on vacations."

Gloria Gaynor's "I Will Survive" instantly began playing inside my head. The song had run on a constant loop in my mind during the months after the divorce, and if I'd remembered Joe had a key, I would most definitely have changed the stupid lock.

"I'm afraid I scared Cronkite," Joe said. "He zipped out the door like a bat out of hell, which is why I bumped into the plant. You really shouldn't keep it so close to the door. He was friendly enough after I fed him, though."

Cronkite, who was now curled up in the recliner, pointedly ignored my dirty look. Although, to be fair, he hadn't eaten the second dinner I gave him. And even though it felt a bit like a betrayal, Cronk had lived in the same house as Joe for the first four years of his life. It wasn't even the first time Joe had fed him, although he hadn't made a habit of it. Joe is not a cat person. Or a dog person, really.

"But he gave me a wicked swat when I first came through the door," Joe added. "Cut clean through my sock and nicked my ankle." He pulled his pants leg up slightly to reveal a torn sock with a tiny bloodstain. "Guess he's not used to having a man around the place anymore."

"Or maybe he just doesn't like *you*."

"And then I crashed," Joe continued, without acknowledging my snarky comment. "I haven't slept more than a couple of hours since I woke up Saturday morning. I was going to take what used to be the guest room, but Cassie seems to have her stuff in there, so I moved down to your parents' old room. Next thing I know, I hear you knocking over the chair and I come in here to find you waving a freakin' knife around."

"You need to call Cassie. Right now."

"I already talked to her, okay? I apologized. And I asked her to check with you and see if it's okay if I stay here for a few days--"

"It's not. Which I could have told you if you'd bothered to stop by the office."

"I did. You weren't there. Anyway, Cassie was mad...*really* mad."

"Well, what did you expect? You scared her."

Cassie must have been the person he was arguing

with outside the old dollar store. I made a mental note to ask her why she hadn't called to let me know, but Joe answered the question.

"She said she wouldn't help me unless I came clean with you. Not just about faking my death, but about...the reason I'm in trouble. I got in with some bad people. A couple of deals that went wrong."

"You mean with Capella Holdings. Keith Hanlon."

He looked surprised. "So you *did* see my message! I knew your curiosity wouldn't let you leave town without searching the office. But then why didn't you—"

"You mean the text message? The one saying to get out of the house? Yeah, I got it. Right after we found Nathan's body. And I *did* call that number. Several times. No one answered."

"No," he said. "I mean, yes. I sent that message, too. But I'm talking about the one I left at the office. Inside the picture frame, with a different number to call."

For a moment I just stared at him, confused. Then I remembered the wedding photo.

"I saw the picture, yes. But why would you assume I would check inside a picture frame, Joe?"

He threw his hands out in a gesture of frustration. "Because it was *obviously* a message specifically for you. Otherwise, why would I put it there?"

"How on earth would I know? Did you kill Nathan?"

Joe stared at me for a long moment, mouth open, and then he shook his head in disbelief. "I can't believe you asked me that. Nathan was my friend for...what? More than ten years. My *best* friend until this thing blew up. Did you really think I could murder him...that I could murder anyone?"

I was tempted to fire back a sharp retort, saying that I didn't know what he was capable of anymore. But that wasn't entirely true. I had said more than once over the past two days that I didn't believe Joe was a murderer.

"No. I didn't actually think that. But between the body in your closet, the fact that he no longer works for you, and the suicide note, you have to admit it looks really bad."

"What makes you think Nathan wasn't working for me?" Joe asked.

"Why else would he clean out his office?"

"He was already over at the new location. We're..." Joe stopped and shook his head. "We *were* moving downtown. I just hadn't packed up my stuff yet. I took out a year's lease on an office I'll never be able to use now. And yes, it *does* look bad. I know that. That's why I need your help. Nathan never liked Hanlon. Neither did Cassie, for that matter. I should have listened. And then, when I found Nate's body, I just...panicked. Because I knew if I didn't get the hell out of there, I was next."

After making a second mental note to ask Cassie exactly what she knew about his shady business dealings, I said, "You should have called the police, Joe. Instead, you literally dragged trouble two hundred miles across the state."

"Yeah. Cassie told me Hanlon stopped by your office this morning. I swear, I didn't know he'd follow me. I'm not even sure how he knew where I went. I never told him about Thistlewood. Never told him where you worked. He asked at one point why Cassie wasn't filling in at the office anymore, and I said she moved over near Gatlinburg, because most people in Nashville have never heard of this place."

As angry as I was, I couldn't help but feel a tiny tug of sympathy. Twenty-five years of marriage gives you at least some measure of insight into what your spouse is feeling, and he wasn't lying about being scared. Or about not realizing Hanlon would follow him.

"Sit down," I told him, motioning toward the couch. "I'm not promising anything, okay? But I want you to tell me exactly what happened Saturday night. And then I'll decide whether I'm going to help you or whether I'm going to call Detective Webb."

"Do you have anything to drink? I ate one of your frozen dinners, but the only alcohol I could find was wine."

He made a face. Joe has never been a fan of wine.

"Wine, coffee, seltzer, or tea. I also have some Kahlua for the coffee. The bottle is in the cabinet over the sink. Those are your choices."

To my complete lack of surprise, he opted for the strongest option pouring nearly half of the small bottle of Kahlua into a coffee mug and adding a tiny splash of milk. While adding the milk, he spotted the fudge pie I'd left to thaw out in the fridge and helped himself to a hefty slice before coming back into the living room.

Then he shooed Cronkite and parked himself in the recliner. Cronk didn't exactly hiss, but his lip curled in a look that I've always interpreted as *I'd kick your butt if I wasn't such a nice kitty*. I tapped the sofa next to me, but the cat had clearly had enough of humans and stalked upstairs to Cassie's room.

"You remember when I started doing business with Hanlon, right?" Joe asked.

I shook my head.

"Seriously? It was the biggest deal I ever landed. About eighteen months before we split up."

"Joe, you came in every couple of months talking about some big deal you were working on. You described most of them as the biggest deal ever, and the details were usually the same as the *last* biggest deal ever. They kind of blurred together after a while. Do you remember the details of every major story I broke at the *News-Journal*?"

"Well, no, but...it's not like you got extra money for a big scoop. In fact, that usually meant you got *less* pay, at least in the short run, because you were putting in more hours for the same salary. And then they thanked you by giving you the boot."

His complaint wasn't entirely unjustified, although the offer of early retirement wasn't really the same thing as giving me the boot. Joe knows as well as I do that there are plenty of reporters who didn't even get that much consideration. Newspapers aren't exactly a growth industry in an era where half the people on social media imagine themselves as independent journalists because they hit record on their cell phones when driving past a wreck on the highway. But this had been a common refrain during our marriage. My job paid less, therefore it mattered less.

I was tempted to tell him that he was reminding me of all the reasons I really did *not* miss being married to him. But that would just prolong the agony of this conversation. "I don't remember you mentioning Hanlon, Joe. So just start from the beginning."

"Fine. I'd worked with him on two commercial deals, one for the Miller building and the other for that mixed-use development over near Gallatin about three years back. He made a lot on that deal. We both did. Then, about six months after it closed, Hanlon came to me with a plan. He was representing a consortium of buyers who wanted to start flipping houses on a larger scale and he wanted to pull me in as a partner. I'd find the properties and handle the sales, and he'd deal with getting financing from his backers. Said it was the same people who had helped him come up with the cash for the Gallatin deal, the family of this woman he started seeing a few years back. Her uncle, who is one of the backers, owns a chain of home improvement stores down in Texas. Said he could get us bargain basement prices for top-of-the-line appliances, etc. We'd grab foreclosures, update them with new fixtures and features, and flip 'em at a decent profit. Same kind of thing Nathan was already doing on a small scale."

A cloud passed over Joe's face as he mentioned Nathan's name, and then he continued. "Only Hanlon wanted a mix. Not just the little places like Nathan's, but upmarket, too. And you know how Nathan was. He was more into the fixing up than he ever was into the selling. So he started focusing on that end of the business. Had his sister helping out for a bit until she moved last year, and then we pulled in someone from the neighborhood. You remember Tammy Roscoe? She was looking for a job, and..."

"I already know you're dating her, okay? In fact, when I saw her at Nathan's yesterday, she informed me that you *started* dating her while we were still married, which explains a lot about the divorce. Guess it wasn't quite as out of the blue, as I thought."

"It wasn't like that, Ruth. I mean, yeah, I was seeing Tammy. Charlie, her ex, was in construction. She handled a lot of stuff for his business, so she had contacts with a bunch of electricians, plumbers, and so on, for the renovations that Nathan couldn't tackle because they had to be to code. It just sort of...happened."

His casual tone made me wonder whether it had *just sort of happened* with other women before Tammy. The possibility didn't sting nearly as much as I'd have imagined, however, and I wasn't going to give him the satisfaction of asking. And there was no way I was touching the first part about Tammy working with her ex-husband, since it was a not-so-subtle dig at me. Joe had said for years that I should quit my job and help him manage the business. That I'd have more flexibility and he could use the help. I'd never seriously considered it, because I'd have gone crazy and our marriage would have gone bust in a year or so if he'd been my boss.

"But I never planned to divorce you," Joe said. "Not until Cassie tipped me off about the money laundering and I realized both of you would be better off out of Nashville. Especially with you taking the early retirement because you'd have had way too much time on your hands, and you'd have started snooping."

"Wait a minute. *Cassie* tipped you off?"

"Oh, not directly. She just cracked a joke with Nathan about the renovations when she was filling in at the front desk. He was grumbling about the quality of some appliances he'd been shipped. Said the house he was working on already had better models than the supposed upgrades we were installing, that they weren't what we'd been promised, and asked how much we were paying for them. I told him I'd check with Hanlon. Cassie laughed. Told us it might be a scam and said we ought to watch this show called *Ozark*. You seen it?"

"Yes." I sighed. "Cassie and I watched it together. You gotta be kidding, Joe. You're laundering drug money?"

"I didn't know at first! Hanlon manages everything with his partners. All I did was find the properties and handle the sales. Nathan did the renovations. When our share of the money started coming in, it was more than either of us had expected, so it was clear Hanlon wasn't cheating *us*. If anything, I figured he was cheating his backers, because the expenses seemed too high. When I confronted him and said I wanted out, he said he promised his partners at least five years and pointed out that they weren't the kind of people who were accustomed to taking no for an answer. He also said there wasn't any real risk to us. His partners have a couple of police officers on their payroll. And I knew I couldn't tell you. You'd start digging around. So I did what I had to do. I knew you'd come back here when I told you I wanted a divorce. You'd said something about the *Star* being for sale after your Mr. Dealey died, and you had the cabin. Plus, Wren was here. I figured Cassie would move with you right away, but...at least me ending things abruptly ensured that she was angry enough she didn't come around much until she finally decided to make the move. I definitely didn't want her at the office anymore, so I trained Tammy to take over when I was between receptionists. Figured it was the only way I could be sure you and Cassie were safe until I got myself out of this mess. Then I could make it up to you. We could retire someplace nice. I mean, I wasn't a model husband, obviously, but you have your faults, too. And I love you anyway."

He obviously expected me to say something. Maybe to thank him for trying to protect us. But there were two big problems with that. First, I didn't entirely believe him. He could very well have been saying what he thought I wanted to hear in order to convince me to let him hide out here. Second, even if he had done all of this in some misguided attempt to keep me and Cassie safe, there was no way on God's green Earth that I was going back to him.

When I didn't respond, he chuckled softly. "I really didn't think you'd be inclined to put yourself back on the market at fifty. But I guess there are always a few lonely old men in little towns like Thistlewood."

Chapter Fifteen

I TOOK a deep breath and reminded myself that this was Cassie's father. If I killed him here in my living room, I'd most likely get caught, even though I was certain Wren would help me get rid of the body, probably singing that "Goodbye, Earl" song as we heaved his corpse into the river. If I was lucky enough to get a jury with a few women who had dealt with passive-aggressive, gaslighting ex-husbands, I might only get five or ten years.

Still not worth it.

"I'm mystified as to how you ever made it as a salesman, Joseph Tate. Because if this is your sales pitch for me doing anything aside from kicking your butt all the way back to Nashville, it's beyond pathetic. I get the point. You stupidly got yourself mixed up with money-laundering and even more stupidly opted not to go straight to the police. Could we skip to the part that explains how Nathan wound up—"

My phone was buzzing, so I pulled it out of my pocket. Detective Webb. I stared at the thing, debating whether to answer the call. I'd either have to tell him that Joe was sitting right across from me, or else lie when he asked the inevitable question of whether I'd heard anything from him. Because it was now abundantly clear that he wasn't calling to tell me that they'd dragged the reservoir and dredged up Joe's body.

It was after nine. A bit early for bed, but not so early that it would seem preposterous if I said I'd decided to make an early night of it. And I could always call Webb back at any point if Joe's answers to my next questions were less than satisfactory. So I ignored the call for the time being and returned the phone to my pocket.

"That was the detective in Nashville who's working the case of your disappearance. I still haven't decided what I'm going to tell him."

"You can't tell him I'm here," Joe said. "Please. For all I know, he's one of the cops Hanlon's friends are paying off. Heck, they could have killed Nathan."

I sighed. Webb had come across as a very straight arrow, and I couldn't really see him being on the take, but I didn't want to go into that with Joe right now. "Like I said, I haven't decided yet. A lot is going to depend on your explanation for how Nathan wound up dead in your closet and you wound up here in Thistlewood."

"Well, you know the housing market kind of tanked,

right? We were able to turn the houses around in a matter of months this time last year, so Hanlon's partners were getting their clean cash back on a regular basis. Now we've got eighteen properties we're having trouble moving, and I think they're wishing they'd stuck with fast-food franchises and bars, although those businesses don't move as much cash these days since most people pay with credit or debit cards. Two of Hanlon's backers got into some legal trouble after a drug raid. They've got expenses, I guess, and their patience is wearing thin. The partner with the home fixtures and furnishings outlet started jacking the prices up and Hanlon ordered *way* more than we needed for renovations. The higher prices didn't hurt Riverfront's bottom line, since the purchases were being made by Hanlon with the money from the consortium, but it made Nathan nervous and he started complaining. I just wish he'd left well enough alone. Like I told him, let Hanlon deal with his people and if every-thing went south, we'd have some deniability. Nathan calmed down for a bit, but then the most expensive of the properties, a place we sank nearly two and a half million into, had a gas leak about a month ago and blew up. No one was in it, but a fifteen-year-old boy who was out walking his dog got hit by the debris. He made it, but it was touch and go there for a while. Nathan didn't believe the explosion was an accident, and yeah...he *was* going to quit. But he changed his mind when I covered the cost of the kid's hospital and rehab. There's no way Riverfront Realty could have been held legally responsible, but a sign with my face on it was in a couple of the pictures that popped up in the news. There was going to be publicity either way, and footing the expenses made it positive rather than negative. Plus...it just seemed like the right thing to do, you know?"

I nodded, glad to find that doing the right thing was still at least a tiny factor in his moral calculus.

"Anyway, Nate had calmed down a bit. Mostly he was focused on getting things set up at the new office, and interviewing candidates for receptionist since Tammy was going to come onboard as a selling agent as soon as she passed her licensing exam. I did take your advice, you know. Lowered the company's share of Nathan's commissions to twenty-five percent rather than forty-five at his last annual review."

"Good. He'd more than earned it." I wondered how much that decision had been in recognition of Nathan's hard work and how much was simply to buy his silence. But I didn't see the point of diving into those waters and it was all a bit moot now that Nathan was gone.

"But Hanlon ordered another delivery of appliances," Joe said. "A hot tub and four washer and dryer sets with all the features, even wifi."

"Wifi? For what?" I asked, as lightning lit up the sky outside the cabin.

He shrugged. "So you can start the machine while you're at work, apparently. Yeah. Sounds stupid to me, too. Anyway, Hanlon said they got a good deal on them. Then, Nathan starts digging around online and finds out

about a series of thefts fifty miles or so from this ware-
house that's been shipping us the appliances. Over a
million dollars' worth, swiped out of model homes in the
Dallas-Fort Worth area. He puts two and two together
and says he thinks they're delivering us stolen goods.
Which I'd kind of figured as soon as I started putting the
pieces together, but apparently Nate didn't consider that
aspect. He totally lost his cool in our weekly meeting
with Hanlon. Said the hammer was going to hit him
twice as hard because he was storing the inventory. I
thought Hanlon and I had managed to talk him down
again, but when Tammy was over at the new offices on
Friday night dropping off some boxes, she said she over-
heard Nate on the phone with someone, probably his
sister, saying he was thinking about calling the police
before he got in any deeper. I thought about it long and
hard, and I realized he was right. Maybe they'd go easy
on us, since we didn't know what we were getting into."

"But you said you'd known for nearly two years..."

"Well, not really. We didn't suspect anything at the
beginning. And even after that, we didn't know for sure.
Plus, we could claim we were just too scared to say
anything. Go state's evidence. We'd have to turn over
some money and I thought there was a decent chance
we might have to go into witness protection, but maybe
that was better than the alternative. And I knew if Nate
was getting out, I pretty much had to do the same. So
first thing Saturday, I shoot him a text. Ask him to come
over to my place that afternoon, once we finished up

with the clients we were meeting with that morning, so we could discuss how to go about getting out of this mess. He calls back and asks if I'm sure. When I tell him I am, he says he should be done by three. I was late getting back to the house, though. It was closer to four and I figured he'd be there already. He had a key from watching the place when we were out of town. But there was no sign of him. I tried calling, but no luck. Even called his sister and asked if she'd seen him. Finally, I gave up. It was almost time to meet Cassie at the restaurant, so I went upstairs to change. When I opened the closet..." He shuddered, shaking his head. "They must have had either my place or his bugged and heard our conversation that morning. Anyway, I panicked. Grabbed a bag and shoved some clothes into it. Stopped by Walmart and bought a couple of burner phones, and withdrew as much cash as I could from the ATM. Then I went to the office and grabbed the cash we had on hand in the safe. When I was sitting out at Percy Priest about to write that suicide note, I was seriously considering following through with it. But then it occurred to me that I had the text. It would back up the fact that we were planning to turn ourselves in. And if I could just find a way to prove Hanlon killed Nathan, I could testify against him."

He got up from the recliner and went to the kitchen, where he poured the rest of the Kahlua into his glass, dispensing with the fiction of milk. At this rate, his blood was probably pure sugar and alcohol. To his credit, he did put the plate in the sink, which was a radical departure from his married-life habits.

"How do you know it was Hanlon?"

"Well for one thing," Joe said as he settled back into the recliner, "I'd been ignoring texts from him all day. He was really pissed, so either Nathan said something that tipped him off or more likely, they were intercepting our communications. I used the first burner phone to call you, but you didn't answer. So, I left you the message in the picture frame that you *didn't get* telling you to keep an eye out for an overnight package I really thought would have arrived by now."

"Probably not if you mailed it on Saturday. Why were you sending me a package?"

"A longer suicide note, with details I was certain you would know were bogus in case the police didn't release specifics of the one they found in the truck. Printouts of the financial information I wiped from my computers, so you could investigate. Plus, my bank account info. My will. Insurance policies, and so forth. Just in case Hanlon caught up to me, I didn't want all of that on my person."

"You could have left it in the safe."

"That Tammy knows the combination to. And...she wasn't entirely happy about me deciding to go to the police. We talked for a long time Friday night. I said I'd pay her ten grand as a bonus, and that maybe we should stop seeing each other. It would be easier on her, and...I didn't want to keep stringing her along. So anyway, I shoved my papers and the cash from the safe into an overnight envelope, addressed it to you, and dropped it at the post office. Then I went to Nathan's to get his motorbike. Only I couldn't lift it into the truck bed, so I had to grab the tabletop he was refinishing and use it as a ramp. Nearly wrecked my back trying to load the thing. Then I headed out to Percy Priest."

"But wait...when did you send the text warning us about the fire? I thought it might be Walt at first, but..."

"He's in California. What fire are you talking about?"

"Your text said to get out of the house."

He ran one hand through his hair. "Because there was a *dead body* in the closet! And Hanlon could still have been around. When I stopped at the reservoir, I saw Cassie had messaged me again on my iPhone. This time she said she was at the house waiting for you and Wren. Your number was already in the burner phone, so I texted you to get out. Are you saying our house caught fire?"

"No. Not *your* house. The one at the end of the cul-de-sac. Hanlon's according to one of your neighbors. I thought you knew about the fire."

"Hanlon stayed there occasionally when he was in town, but it was one of the Capella houses. And no, I had no idea. Although...maybe that's what Nathan meant on the phone. I thought he was just talking about the stolen appliances, but..."

"What did he say?"

"That he thought they were going to do it again."

I shook my head, not following his train of thought.

"The gas leak at the other property? Maybe Nathan saw something that led him to believe they were going to settle for the insurance payout on that place, rather than having us lower the price again. If he confronted Hanlon, maybe the guy snapped and killed him."

"And he left the body there to frame you?"

"Yeah. Also to deliver the message that I'm next if I start making waves."

I sighed. "So you lured him to where our daughter lives."

"What do you want me to say, Ruth? I'm sorry. I already told Cassie that. I'll tell her again when she gets home if you like."

"Pretty sure she's staying at Dean's."

His eyebrows shot up. "You let her stay overnight?"

I laughed. "Cassie just turned twenty-four. All I can do is tell her to be careful. Dean's a nice guy. Maybe she'll introduce you at some point once you're no longer a fugitive. She's as safe with him as she'd be here. And Ed said that he'd call Billy, his former deputy, and ask him to keep an eye out for Hanlon in case there was any trouble."

"Ed...is a cop?"

"Former sheriff. Okay. You said you need help. I agree. You're in major trouble. But what exactly do you want me to do, Joe?"

"You're a reporter. Find evidence that Hanlon killed Nathan. Dig up something on his partners. Then, like I said before, I can go state's evidence or whatever, but until we have some way to pin this on Hanlon, I need people to think I'm dead."

"What are you planning to do in the interim?"

He shrugged. "The only thing I *can* do. I'll just hide out here."

I stared at him for several seconds. Joe had never been particularly supportive of my career. In fact, he'd often been downright dismissive. Now he wanted me to use my skills as a reporter to clear his name? While he just lounged around inside my house?

My first inclination was to tell him to kiss right off. But he was Cassie's dad. And even if he hadn't been, I didn't like the idea of him going to prison for something that he hadn't done. Most of all, I didn't like the idea of Nathan's killer going unpunished.

A glance outside told me that the rain hadn't let up. I couldn't exactly kick him out in the middle of a thunderstorm, so he would have to stay at least until morning. But I didn't have to stay here with him.

"Fine. You can sleep here tonight. I'm going to Wren's. Please feed Cronk in the morning. *But*," I said as I headed up the stairs to get a change of clothes, "as soon as the rain stops, I want you out. There's camping gear in the shed. The key to the lock is on the hook next to the fridge."

"Camping?" He followed me to the base of the stairs. "You've got to be kidding..."

Turning back, I glared at him. "I'm most certainly

not kidding. That's my offer. Take it or leave it. You shouldn't have any trouble getting a campsite this time of year."

"What if they ask for ID?"

I hadn't thought about that. He was right. They'd probably ask for a credit card or some sort of identification to reserve a campsite. "Then you camp in the woods. I've got nearly five acres out there. Pick a spot and pitch the tent. And you might want to keep an eye out for my bear."

☆ Chapter Sixteen ☆

WHEN I WOKE the next morning, Wren was already up and at the small desk between the kitchen and living room. Her apartment isn't large, and aside from the two bedrooms and baths it's one open space. The atmosphere is cozy and comforting, which should have been hard to pull off given that there was a funeral home just below us and a morgue in the basement. I was even fairly certain there was a body in the morgue since she had a viewing this evening. But Wren has a knack for decoration. I needed to get her to come give the cabin a makeover at some point.

"You're awake early," I said, peeking over her shoulder. "What are you up to?"

She flipped the screen of the laptop down. "None of your business, Miss Nosy. And I'm not awake all that early if you check the time. You have maybe fifteen minutes to shower and dress if you don't want to keep Ed waiting."

Wren was right, both about the time and about the fact that I *am* Miss Nosy. I reached past her and flipped the screen back up to reveal the familiar layout of the *Thistlewood Star Online*. That's all I could tell, however, before she slapped my hand away.

"Go," she said. "I'll tell you all about it when we get to the diner. Otherwise, I'll have to say everything twice because we need to fill Ed in, too."

"What? Oh...the quilt. I'd almost forgotten."

"Well, it's not like you have anything else on your mind. How could something as earth-shattering as a missing quilt be forgotten in the midst of your presumed-dead, apparently felonious, and admittedly cheating ex showing up at your door? Have you decided which font to use for his fake obituary? Personally, I think you should go with whatever one you use for the rest of the paper."

"I thought about that," I said. "But I hate to break with tradition."

Wren snorted. "Except Joe's not actually dead. And even if he was, I think Mr. Dealey would agree the lying, cheating scumbag doesn't deserve a special font to commemorate his departure."

I had phoned Wren as I left the cabin the night before, giving her only the barest of summaries—Joe was alive, he was in deep trouble, and could I crash at her place? The question was a formality, because the one thing about being friends with someone for nearly four decades is that you know you don't need to ask. It had been well after ten when I arrived, and she was already in her jammies and tucked in with a book and a cup of Sleepytime tea. She had a ton of questions, but it must have been clear that I was exhausted, because about twenty minutes into the conversation, she made me my own cup of tea, pointed me toward the bed, and said we'd talk over breakfast in the morning.

"Joe showing up at my *door* wouldn't have been so bad. I was worried enough that I might actually have been glad to see him. Showing up in my living room uninvited, however...that's another matter entirely."

"True. Now would you *please* go shower? We have a busy day ahead and I don't know about you, but I'm in desperate need of at least two cups of coffee and a big fat waffle. The only question is whether I want pecan or blueberry."

"We'll go halfsies and you can have both." I said as I grabbed my shower kit from Wren's spare room. I showered quickly, applied a few blasts of the blow-dryer to my curls, and pulled on one of the new outfits I'd purchased in Nashville. Wren scanned me, gave a quick nod of approval, and we headed out into a clear, if still slightly damp morning.

"So...does Ed know that Joe is at your house yet?"

"He does *not*. That kinda seemed like something I should tell him in person. That's why I asked him to meet us at Pat's for breakfast."

"Mm-hmm. That way you can bat your eyelashes and look all hurt if he gets upset. Good call."

"I do *not* bat my eyelashes, Wren Lawson. But, yes, that's one reason I told him to meet us at the diner. There's a limit to how loud he can yell with everyone listening. Not that Ed really *yells*, but...he's probably going to be annoyed that I didn't call him last night when it happened. And that I didn't call Detective Webb back. Making a breakfast date also forestalled the possibility that he'd decide to show up at my place."

"Ooh. That might have been fun to watch, though. Even with his bad hip, I think Ed could take Joe."

I rolled my eyes. "No one is going to fight. There's nothing to fight *about*. I had no interest in Joe before he turned up on my doorstep, and that goes double now that I know what he's been up to."

"Still, I wouldn't be so sure that *no one* is going to fight. First, he cheats on you and divorces you without the slightest warning, then he has the nerve to break into your house and ask for your help. *And* he drags poor Nathan's killer along with him all the way from Nashville to Thistlewood. I've half a mind to drive over to your cabin and kick his sorry butt myself."

I laughed. "That's a fight I would pay to watch. You could definitely take him."

Once we turned onto Main Street, we picked up the pace a bit. We were supposed to meet Ed at eight and it was already a couple of minutes after. I'd also texted

Cassie the night before to ask if she wanted to join us, but she hadn't responded. No big surprise there. This was well before her usual wake-up time and I suspected that she was also putting off talking to me about the current situation. She'd clearly been keeping a few secrets that were now out in the open. On the one hand, I understood her reluctance to talk to me about Joe. During and just after the divorce, I hadn't been particularly interested in hearing his name. But Joe had hinted that Cassie had at least an inkling that he was involved in something questionable even before I left Nashville. I didn't like thinking she'd have kept that kind of secret from me.

When we reached the diner, there were a few people at the tables and a small line at the register, where folks were grabbing their breakfast sandwiches and coffee before they headed off to work. *Good Morning America* was chattering away on the small TV behind the counter.

Much to my dismay, Jesse Yarnell was seated on his usual stool, a plate of eggs in front of him, staring at the screen. The *other* reason I'd suggested meeting for breakfast was that it was a bit early for the hardcore gossip crew. Jesse, who was retired aside from occasional side gigs, usually didn't show up until a bit after ten, mostly because Patsy let the B-team run breakfast until the tourist season picked up and he preferred to be at the diner when Patsy was here. His usual schedule was to drink coffee and shoot the breeze until it was time to order lunch, and then head home for a snooze before coming back in for dinner.

I cursed softly under my breath. It wasn't that I disliked Jesse. Aside from the fact that his tongue was loose at both ends, he was a decent enough guy, although I'd often wondered if his gossipy nature wasn't the main reason Patsy kept him around. She's a savvy business owner who doesn't want to seem too intrusive, because that might tick off the customers, but gossip might as well be a standard menu item at Pat's, served up free with any order, just like the beverage refills. Everyone knows Jesse doesn't have a filter, and he spends most of his spare time with his ample belly up to the counter, sharing rumors, jokes, and half-baked observations with anyone who drops by and cares to listen. And most people do.

Plus, it wasn't quite tourist season yet. Gossip was darn near the only game in town.

Jesse glanced toward the door when we entered, and I expected him to start peppering me with questions as Wren and I headed toward the back, where Ed was waiting at our usual booth, beneath one of the large photographs of a 1950s sock hop. But Jesse just gave me a sullen look and returned to watching the TV.

Ed caught my expression as I slipped into the booth next to him and grinned.

"Yeah, I wasn't too pleased to see Old Motormouth, either. He's in early because he's supposed to be down at Jolly's Marina at ten to do some odd jobs. I already told him you weren't in the mood to talk. Still..." He tapped the stack of quarters next to his coffee cup.

This was our standard course of action whenever Jesse was in the diner. The guy's hearing still seemed fine, but he wouldn't be able to decipher much of what we were saying over the music, especially if we talked softly. I dropped several quarters into the little jukebox at the end of the table and queued up our playlist. The first two, as always, were "I Heard it Through the Grapevine" and "Harper Valley PTA," two songs that were the auditory equivalent of a middle finger in Jesse's direction given their emphasis on gossip.

Marvin Gaye's mellow voice soon flowed through the speaker, but at about half the usual volume. Jesse turned slowly toward us and grinned. "I told Patsy it's awful hard to hear the TV over the music, so she cut the volume a bit. I'm sure you folks won't mind. I think it's important to keep up with what's goin' on in the world."

Wren cursed under her breath. "Score one for Jesse, I guess."

"Sleeping with the proprietor seems to have a few perks," Ed mumbled.

"We'll just stick to talking about the *local* issue," I said, raising my eyebrows at Wren to let her know I was going to wait until after we left to tell Ed about Joe. "I mean, even if Elephant Ears picks something up, the missing quilt is last week's news."

"Not to Miss Olivia," Ed said. "She was waiting outside her house when I walked Owen this morning.

The only thing she said was hello—well, that and a brief comment about the weather—but she clearly wanted to make sure that I hadn't forgotten about her."

"Not to worry," Wren said. "We're on the case. There are only two people with motive...the other two quilters. And one of them will be heading to Nashville in Olivia's place if we don't figure this out. I was thinking about it this morning, and I had an idea. But first, Ruth... are you still wanting to get rid of that crystal lamp?"

The lamp in question is nice enough, but one of the few household items I packed into the jeep when I left Nashville was a custom lamp with autumn leaves pressed into the shade. The wife of one of my coworkers at the *News-Journal* made the leaf lamps by hand, and I loved that it helped me keep my favorite season alive year-round. It fit perfectly in the spot next to the sofa when I moved in, so I really didn't have anywhere else to put the crystal lamp. It was pretty, but it looked a bit like a chandelier, with hanging pendants, and I'd never thought it fit well with the rest of the décor in the cabin.

"Yes. I stashed it in the room where J—" I caught myself before spilling the beans, but Ed still gave me an odd look. "Where my parents used to sleep. Why?"

"Elaine was outside with her puppy and she yelled across the fence that we should bring something for the silent auction they're having next week over at the high school. But, as you know, I cleared out pretty much all of my old junk at the yard sale a while back."

I shrugged. "Sure. I'll go grab it from the house at lunchtime."

"I've got an appointment at noon," she said. "Should be done by one-thirty or so. Wait until then and I'll drive you. And after that, we need to take a short ride to the sheriff's office."

Ed frowned. "Why? Olivia said she didn't want to get Blevins involved."

"I just want to see if the shoe fits," Wren said with a little smile.

"You mean Blevins?" I said. "You actually think he took the quilt off the wall?"

"Yes, because as we discussed yesterday, his mama is one of the remaining two women who were in the running for the trip," Wren said. "Olivia's cousin Lillian being the other. Even if you ignore the footprint, it was almost certainly a man who removed the quilt. I checked the picture in the *Star* from two months back when they announced the winner and the article said that it would be hanging on display in the church rec room until the statewide contest. Here, I saved it on my phone."

She pushed the picture across the table toward me and Ed. I vaguely recalled posting the photo for the online version. I hadn't bothered with it for the print edition because I don't print in color and it wouldn't have been very distinctive in grayscale. The most striking thing about the quilt was the interplay of shapes and rich jewel-tone colors. It reminded me a bit of a stained-glass window.

"See?" Wren said, tapping the screen. "Whoever hung it used a ladder. You can tell how high it is off the ground by counting those cinderblocks. Each one is about a foot high. In order to lift the pole that's holding the quilt off those hooks, a person would need to either be at least six feet tall or they'd need to haul in a ladder."

"Or a chair." Ed nodded toward me. "Shortcake here might not be able to reach it from a chair, but you could."

"True," Wren admitted. "Only they'd have had to drag one of those in, too, unless they were stupid enough to try and balance on one of those...*folding chairs.*" A sly grin spread across her face and she raised her voice a bit. "Sometimes Jesse's gossip comes in handy."

"What do you mean?" I asked, but then we had to table the conversation because the morning waitress was there with the coffee pot. Marva is a tiny thing, painfully shy, and she's never interacted with the customers as much as Patsy or her mom. But Patsy said she was a steady worker, always willing to take an extra shift on the weekends when the high schoolers she hired part-time usually wanted to take time off.

"Y'all ready to order or do you need a minute?" Marva asked, after filling our cups.

"Ruth and I are having waffles," Wren said quickly, probably worried that I'd changed my mind about sharing. "Blueberry for her, pecan for me. Eggs scrambled, both with bacon, extra crispy."

I was tempted to protest at having my free will usurped, but she was completely right.

Ed laughed and ordered his usual breakfast platter. "You two must have been really hungry to plan all that out in advance."

"We needed comfort food," Wren said. "Ruth will explain once we're out of here."

The waitress was walking away, but Wren called her back. "Marva, do you remember which day last week Patsy had that sinful mocha cheesecake on the dessert menu?"

Marva tilted her head to the left and considered the question for a moment. "I *think* that was Monday. It's not on the menu today. We've got a key lime pie, though..."

"Oh, no! I don't think any of us is going to have room for dessert after breakfast. Just needed to give my memory a little jolt."

"I think she's right," I said, as Marva headed off to the kitchen with our order. "Ed and I were in here that night and were going to split a piece after you raved about it, but it was gone. Why?"

"Because when I was in here that afternoon, Jesse was telling everyone that Jenny Blevins was just about at her wits' end dealing with Steve's mom. His buddy told him Bobbi took a fall the night before and banged up her hip. Said Jenny was having to wait on the woman hand and foot. Remember?"

"I remember you mentioning it to Steve when he pulled us over—"

"When did he pull you over?" Ed asked.

"Coming back from Nashville. Some nonsense about Wren's taillight blinking on and off, but I think he mostly just wanted to jab at me and Cassie about Joe." I turned back to Wren, remembering the look on her face when she mentioned the folding chairs, just before the waitress came over. "You think Bobbi tried to get the quilt down herself and the folding chair collapsed on her. And then Steve..."

"Yep," Wren said.

Ed shook his head. "I detest Blevins as much as anyone in town. Heck, more than anyone in town, except maybe for you two and Cassie. But I can't see him stealing a quilt off the wall of the church recreation room."

Wren sniffed dismissively. "I wouldn't put anything past him. That trip to Nashville would be three nights his mama wasn't in his house, and I'm guessing Jenny hasn't been in the mood to give him any lovin' at all since Bobbi moved in. Or maybe he offered to steal the quilt in exchange for her packing up and moving back to Knoxville. Ruth saw his face when I asked how she was settling in."

Ed pointed out that even though Blevins tended to assume he was above the law in most cases, there was an election coming up. Currently, his only opponent was likely to be a guy who had once been a deputy two towns over. Everyone knew he'd moved to Thistlewood only because he was eyeing the sheriff's job, and he'd left his previous position under a bit of a cloud. As much as

Blevins was disliked, it was a pretty safe bet that he'd beat the guy in November.

But if there was even a hint of scandal, that could change. And Blevins was savvy enough to know that if Billy Thorpe, his head deputy, decided to run, there was a decent chance that he'd win. Personally, I thought it was close to a sure thing, especially given that Ed would throw the considerable weight of his reputation behind Billy, who had not only been his own head deputy when he was sheriff but was also his friend. But Billy would have to quit his job as deputy to throw his hat into the ring, and he had a wife and two kids to consider. He still hadn't decided for certain, but he told Ed he was leaning toward waiting until four years from now, when their youngest was a little older and his wife would be working again.

Wren countered that Steve Blevins had never been one to think things through and that he probably believed no one would suspect him. "Plus," she said, "he's been scared to death of incurring his mama's wrath since we were in school. I'm sure Ruth remembers the story about the dictionary."

I hadn't actually remembered until she mentioned it. "Yeah," I said, laughing. "He came to school with a weird bruise on his forehead. Word got around that his mom hurled a dictionary at his head because he got home after curfew. And it wasn't one of the paperback varieties, but one of those that came with the encyclopedia sets that used to be on everyone's bookshelves. If he wasn't such a total jerk, I'd have felt kind of sorry for him. These days, someone would have called the Department of Children's Services on her for something like that, and rightly so. But back then most people viewed it as *tough love*."

"If she'd thrown it a little harder maybe she'd have knocked some sense into his head," Ed mumbled around a bite of the toast that Marva had just placed in front of him. "Anyway, you said there are still two people in the running, so there's no guarantee his mom would win. And even if it was a sure thing, I'm not convinced he'd take that sort of risk."

To be honest, I wasn't convinced either. Wren had already admitted that she didn't like Mrs. Blevins, and I couldn't blame her for that. I had only spoken to the woman in passing, and I didn't like her. I certainly didn't like the way Wren said she had treated Gran Lawson back in the day, so I was doubly sure that Wren resented her for that. Bobbi Blevins simply wasn't very likable and all of us disliked her son. It would be way too easy for us to overlook other clues—and the other suspect—simply because we wanted Wren's theory to be right.

For the next few minutes, we mostly focused on eating. The diner was beginning to get a bit more crowded, and the noise was now at the point where Jesse would have had a tough time hearing anything we were talking about over the chatter of patrons and the clatter of forks and plates.

While we were waiting on the check, Ed asked, "So,

are you just going to ask Blevins if he swiped the quilt? Because I don't see that going so well."

"Of course not," Wren replied. "We're going to compare footprints first. And then we're going to get Bobbi to confess and give it back."

I held up a finger in the middle of that sentence to shush Wren, but it was too late. Teresa Grimes, Patsy's mom, was at the booth behind ours refilling coffees, and her eyes shot straight toward us when she heard the name.

"Oh, dear Lord," Teresa said. "I told Olivia it was Bobbi, but she's bound and determined that Lillian took the darn thing. Plus, she said she didn't have any evidence and it would be un-Christian to speak ill of the woman without proof...not that it stopped her from accusing Lillian."

"Why do you think Mrs. Blevins took it?" Ed asked.

"Because Roberta has been stealing stuff since we were in high school. Stupid stuff. She was Bobbi Jeter back then, and she swiped an English Literature book from Evangeline Peters and Bobbi wasn't even taking English Lit. I shared my book with Vangie for at least a month and then one day we walk into class and, lo and behold, the book has miraculously reappeared under Vangie's assigned chair. The stuff Bobbi takes is never anything she actually needs and always, always from people she knows. She gets a weird kick out of it. See that booth over there? The one with the mismatched salt and pepper shakers? We had to set out one of the old ones after the last time Roberta Blevins stopped in for lunch. No one saw her take it, but I know darn well both shakers were there when she sat down and the next customers who came in told me they had to borrow the salt off another table. Anyway, next time I saw her, I told her if she couldn't keep her sticky fingers honest, she could just take her business elsewhere."

"What did she say?" Wren asked.

"Oh, same thing she always does. She denied it, of course. Acted all insulted. Said she'd rather get coffee over at The Buzz anyway. You should probably tell Cassie to keep an eye on her when she's in the store, although...like I said, she generally only pulls that crap on people she's known forever."

"Kinda weird that no one ever reported her," Ed said. "I mean, it might be awkward now, but there weren't any reports when I was sheriff."

"Just Bobbi being Bobbi. You don't report someone you've known all your life over a saltshaker," Teresa said, looking a little embarrassed. "But she's getting kinda brassy. Lida considered reporting her last month, when she walked off with a box of fudge from the candy shop, but someone must have told Jenny about it, 'cause Lida found an envelope with twenty dollars stuck under the windshield of her car the next day. But taking Olivia's quilt was just plain mean. Olivia worked hard on that. I hope you get it back."

When Teresa walked away, Ed gave a Wren a little

nod of admission. "Apparently, your instincts were right."

Wren didn't exactly look pleased, though. "Proving it, however...when she's the sheriff's mom? That's going to be tough."

As soon as we'd paid the bill and were outside, Ed said, "So spill. Why did you need comfort food? Did you and Cassie find out something about Joe?"

"Sort of..."

Wren squeezed my arm. "And that is my cue to leave. See you around one."

Chapter Seventeen

THE MESSAGE LIGHT was flashing when Ed and I entered the office, but I decided it could wait. Ed had work that he needed to get back to, and I didn't want to keep him here while I took orders for classified ads or whatever.

"So, Joe's not dead..." Ed prompted, as he parked himself in the office chair near the spare desk.

"He is not. And...he's at my house. That's why I stayed with Wren last night," I added quickly. "It's kind of a long story, so you might want to settle in."

He tugged the bottom drawer of the desk open a few inches so that he'd have a spot to prop up the foot on his bad side. "I'm settled."

For the next fifteen minutes, I rehashed the story that Joe had told me the night before. The only part I didn't go into was Joe's suggestion that he wanted to patch things up between us. For one thing, I didn't entirely believe it. For another, I didn't want to seem like I was trying to make Ed jealous. But most of all, it didn't matter *what* Joe wanted, because I didn't want him.

When I reached the end, Ed leaned back in the chair and exhaled. "Okay, then. What are you going to do?"

"I don't know. He's Cassie's dad. I don't want him arrested for a crime he didn't commit. Joe's going to be in enough trouble for all of the stuff that he *did* do without adding murder to the list. And what if he's right? What if Hanlon is planning to kill him, too? And what if Webb is one of the cops they had on their payroll?"

Ed shook his head. "Admittedly, I didn't talk to Webb for long. But he didn't strike me as a bad cop. I've got a decent sense for those, otherwise I probably wouldn't have figured out what Blevins was up to when he was my deputy. Did Joe say specifically that they had a detective on the payroll? Because that would narrow it down. Metro Police, as you well know, is a big department. At least a thousand officers."

"Closer to fifteen hundred," I said. "Or at least it was a few years back. And no. He just said police officers. I had some decent contacts within the department back when I was doing investigative work, but I was on mostly editorial duties for the last decade I worked at the *News-Journal*. And you walk a fine line when you go in suggesting that one of their fellow officers might be involved in something illegal. Not exactly something you want to broach unless you really know your source."

"Do you even know the cop story is true?" Ed asked.

"Maybe Hanlon just told Joe and Nathan that so they wouldn't be as worried about Nathan's place getting raided."

"You're right," I admitted.

"So, let's say you wait on telling Webb the truth. I don't like that, but let's say you do. You show him this more detailed suicide note, if it arrives, and you write up an obituary. Joe hides out for a bit. What's the game plan for investigating? Joe has to know you're not a forensic accountant. Figuring out how to expose Hanlon is way outside your area of expertise. Mine, too. And you're four hours away from the scene of the murder. Does he expect you to go to Nashville to investigate?"

"I don't know what he expects. My goal last night was getting out of there because I was about ready to throttle Joe for bringing all of this down on us. But I hashed out a rudimentary plan as I was trying to fall asleep after I got to Wren's house. Hanlon left his card, demanding that I call as soon as I heard anything about Joe. I'm thinking I'll call and schedule a meeting with him." I recognized the look on Ed's face. It was the exact look I had expected, so I barreled ahead without even pausing for breath. "I'll tell him about Joe's longer suicide note, and maybe take a page out of the info Joe mailed to me and see if I can get Hanlon to slip up and confess to at least the financial side of it, if not to Nathan's murder. I'll record the conversation and then turn everything over to Webb. Hanlon didn't seem all that sharp to me, so he might fall for it. Maybe I could tell him I have Joe's

account information and I'll give it to him in exchange
for a cut. Of course, all of that's assuming he's still here in
Thistlewood. Otherwise—"

"Pretty sure he's still here," Ed said, still wearing
the look that said he didn't think much of my plan.
"Billy spotted the BMW outside Mountain View. The
clerk said a man matching Hanlon's description
checked in, along with a woman, so you were right
about someone being in the passenger seat. But you
think this guy killed Nathan and might be planning to
kill Joe...and now you want to *meet* with him? I don't
like the sound of that, especially since I'd be your only
backup. We can't pull Billy in on this if you're keeping
stuff from Webb. That's too big of a risk for me to ask
him to take, especially when he's still weighing
whether or not to run against Blevins in November's
election." He pressed his lips together and gave me a
long look. "I don't suppose you'd be willing to take a
pistol?"

"You know the answer to that question already, Ed
Shelton."

Ed had been trying to put a gun in my hands since
the incidents surrounding Edith Morton's death. He had
not been successful, much to his chagrin. As I'd told him
a few days later, I'd seen too many deaths from gunfire as
a reporter to ever want a gun of my own. I don't have an
issue with other people keeping them, including Ed, and
I'd even be willing to live in a house with his guns if we
ever get to that point in our relationship, although they'd

definitely have to be under lock and key if Cassie decides
to make me a grandma at some point.

"I'll carry my pepper spray—"

"Which will be useless if he has a gun."

"I'm not carrying a pistol," I repeated. "I can have
him meet me in a public place, though."

"Still don't like it," Ed said. "But he's staying at
Mountain View, so I suppose you could have him meet
you in the restaurant. Since Hanlon doesn't know me, I
can just sit a few tables over. Or see if Larry will let me
hang out in the kitchen and watch from there."

I couldn't remember if Larry was the chef or the
owner of Mountain View. Ed had a vast array of contacts
in the area after several decades of law enforcement in
Woodward County, and I was just beginning to get the
various names attached to faces, after having spent over
half my life in Nashville. Mountain View Grill was a
standard fixture in Thistlewood, but the hotel was newly
acquired and renovated. The hotel had been owned by
one of the chains but closed a few years back, probably
because it's really hard to keep any year-round business
going here in the mountains. In the past, the restaurant
had only been open on weekends this time of year, but
having the hotel up and running again meant the owners
had an incentive to keep it open for those guests who
didn't want to trek all the way into town for their meals.

My feelings were decidedly mixed about meeting
Hanlon at Mountain View Grill. It was the restaurant
where Ed and I had our first date, just over a year ago,

and where he'd taken me again for a combination birthday and anniversary dinner a few weeks back. I kind of thought of it as our place, and the idea of sullying that through association with Hanlon and this whole sordid mess annoyed me. But the only other viable options within a reasonable distance that would be open this time of year were The Buzz, Pat's Diner, or an open-air venue like the park. The first was out of the question due to the fact that it was Cassie and Dean's workplace, and the other two seemed a little *too* public. Mountain View was a few miles out of town, so it generally wasn't very crowded, especially if I set up the meeting outside of the lunch or dinner rush periods.

"The grill works," I said. "Hopefully, Hanlon will still be in town by the time I get the packet Joe mailed to me. He implied that he was looking for a place to lay low for a few days, something about having to work out travel plans. So, if you think you'll be done with edits by tomorrow afternoon..."

"I'll be finished," he said, leaning forward to look me in the eyes. "Do *not* go without me. And I hate to ask this, but..." He stopped, clearly trying to think of how to phrase the question. "Do you trust him, Ruth?"

I gave him a quizzical look. "Hanlon?"

"No," he said. "I'm talking about Joe."

"In what sense? I mean, if you're asking whether I trust him to tell me the truth...no, not really."

"I mean in terms of your safety. I don't want you to get hurt. Not just physically, although that does worry me because from what you've said he sounds kind of desperate right now. But I know he blindsided you with the divorce, and..." He shrugged. "Just worried about you."

"Don't be. Joe won't hurt me physically." I rolled my chair toward Ed's, angling up next to it so that I could take his hand in mine. "But I *will* be careful. Wren will be with me when I stop by the cabin. I told Joe to get his butt out of my house and pitch a tent in the woods, but I'll be staying at her place again tonight, just to be on the safe side. And as for hurting me emotionally? There's no way he could do that. Joe Tate doesn't hold any piece of my heart." I pressed a soft kiss against Ed's lips. "You finish up your work, okay? There should be enough of the pasta left over from last night for your dinner, if you need to work straight through. And I'll see you bright and early tomorrow morning when I deliver your copy of the *Star*."

"You're not planning to toss it into the bushes again, are you?"

I laughed. "I have never even once tossed your paper into the bushes and you know it. But..." I ran one finger gently along the inside of his arm. "If I make your place my very last stop, I suppose I *could* take a few extra minutes and deliver it right into your hands."

"Hmm, I don't know," he said with a slow grin. "Not sure I'll be up that early."

"I can come in and wake you up, if you'd like."

"Oh, I would like that a *lot*. Can't think of any better

incentive to keep my nose to the grindstone today." He kissed me again and then got up from the chair. "I'll call you after dinner. And since Wren seems to have taken the lead on this quilt thing, try to keep her out of trouble, okay? Blevins isn't above finding a flimsy excuse to arrest someone."

"We'll be good," I told him. "You focus on edits. Wren and I will focus on finding Miss Olivia's quilt. After I write an obituary for my not-dead ex."

"Have fun with that. The good news, given the divorce, is that nobody will be surprised at all if you keep his obit short and not-so-sweet." When Ed reached the door, he turned back. "Oh. What are you going to tell Webb?"

"I guess I'll tell him that Joe still hasn't called me. That's true. I'll also mention that Cassie and I were talking, and she remembered Joe saying something about Capella Holdings. And a guy named Hanlon. Maybe digging into that will keep him busy."

"You need to call Cassie and make sure you have your stories straight. Because his very next call after he hangs up with you will probably be to her."

Chapter Eighteen

I DECIDED it might be best to talk to Cassie face to face, but when I walked down to The Buzz a few minutes later, the person opening the door was Ed's niece, Kate. Her long blonde hair was pulled back into a neat bun, so I almost didn't recognize her at first. She'd been clerking at the bookstore and learning some of the management tasks since January, on some sort of work training program with the high school, but she usually came in after lunch.

"They're going to call the truant officer on you, young lady. Or do they even have those anymore?"

Kate laughed. "Pretty sure they just call family services on your parents if you miss too much. I usually have computer programming this period, but the teacher said I could make it up since Cassie called and said she needed me to open the store this morning. The other clerk can't make it until eleven thirty and she said things are taking a little longer than she thought they would in Nashville." Her smile faded. "I hope she's able to find out more about what happened to her dad and his friend."

I nodded, choosing to pretend that I knew exactly what she was talking about rather than admit that Cassie hadn't told me she was leaving town.

"Did you want something from the café?" Kate asked. "It will only take me a couple of minutes to get everything set up."

"Oh, no, that's fine. I needed to ask Cassie something and I thought she would be back by now. I'll just send her a text."

"Okay! You and Uncle Ed should come out to the house soon. Daniel told me last night that he'd like another playdate with Owen."

Ed and I had gone to dinner at his sister's house a few weeks before. Daniel, Kate's border collie, and Owen had gotten along quite nicely, although Daniel hadn't been too happy about Kate paying attention to Owen. The dogs had chased each other around the property, and Owen had been so worn out that he hadn't even begged Ed for his evening walk that night.

"I'm sure Owen would like that, too," I told Kate. "I'll have Ed check with your mom so we can find a good time."

As I walked back to the office, I pulled out my phone and sent Cassie another message.

Where are you? Why aren't you returning my texts?

Then I called. Still no answer. My panic level began to ratchet upward, so I reminded myself that she was an adult. And she was with Dean. There was nothing to be worried about.

But of course I was still worried, and my uneasy feeling carried over to the tasks I needed to get out of the way. I checked the blinking message on the office phone, and discovered that it was another message from Webb, who must have decided to try the office number on the card I'd given him when he didn't get me on my cell. I needed to call him back, but as Ed had pointed out, I really couldn't do that until I got my story straight with Cassie. Why wasn't she answering?

I resisted the urge to call again and flipped open my laptop. After about ten minutes at the keyboard, I came up with a short, perfunctory obituary for Joseph Adam Tate.

Now I just needed to pick a font. I was tempted to follow Wren's advice and leave it in plain old Times like the rest of the articles. The whole point of the obituary, however, was to provide some cover, so I didn't want to break with the tradition. But what font to pick for a not-really-dead ex who cheated on you?

Personally, I have nothing against Comic Sans. It's a

perfectly serviceable font, clear and legible. But when I typed up a note for Cassie to give to the attendance office in her senior year, she'd wrinkled her nose in distaste. "Comic Sans, Mom? Really..."

And so I changed the font of those two paragraphs to the pariah of the graphic design world. I'd agreed to write his fake obituary, but I hadn't promised to give the matter any dignity. Joe probably wouldn't get the joke if he ever saw it, but Cassie would.

I published it to the online version and then printed it out so that I could tackle the more time-consuming job of typesetting. When I finished, I rearranged the stories currently inside the printer's forme for page seven and pulled out a fluff piece I was using as a spacer. Then, I added Joe's obituary next to one for Mary Quinn, the woman Wren was holding the visitation for that night. I hadn't known Mrs. Quinn, so I'd had to go on the information provided in the obituary. I'd chosen Century Schoolbook Light for her final remembrance, both because she was a teacher and because her last name began with Q. I've always loved the quirky capital Q in Century Schoolbook.

I went back out front and retrieved the card that Keith Hanlon had slapped down on the front counter. My first instinct was to call him, but I'm only a mediocre liar and my voice might give me away. I decided a text would be better because I could craft my words more carefully.

———————————————————

Mr. Hanlon—Have received information that convinces me Joe is indeed dead. I also now have a better understanding of exactly why you were looking for him. He cheated me out of a good deal of money in the divorce. Would like to discuss a mutual arrangement that could keep you out of trouble and me out of debt. Tomorrow 2pm at Mountain View Grill.

I ADDED a link to the obituary in the *Star*, one of the pictures I'd taken of Nathan's storage area, and an image of a file I'd downloaded while at Joe's office that included the name Capella Holdings.

He responded almost immediately, saying that we could meet in his room at the Mountain View Lodge. I replied to that with a simple no. He then answered that the grill would be fine, but he wasn't sure about the time and would get back with me.

I rolled my eyes. Did he really need to check his schedule while hiding out a hotel room? I suspected it was just a power play leading into the negotiations. I'd set the place, so he had to stay on equal footing by setting the time.

Cassie *still* hadn't called me back. While I had the phone in hand, I tried again, and then decided to call

206 C. RYSA WALKER

Nirvana, the metaphysical shop in Nashville where
Cassie had worked before she moved to Thistlewood.
She had been roommates with Bella, the owner of the
shop, and she'd said on several occasions that she needed
to take Dean to Nashville at some point to meet her old
friends. I thought it entirely possible that they'd stayed at
Bella's place rather than getting a hotel.

The phone was answered by a girl with a smoky
voice. "I'm Leann, and you've found Nirvana. How may
I help you?"

I asked for Bella and was told that she was visiting
her family in New Jersey but would be returning on
Monday.

"Oh. When did she leave?"

"Last Wednesday, I believe. May I take a message?"

I debated asking if the girl knew Cassie and whether
she had been in but told her no thanks and hung up.
That was weird. I'd asked Cassie how her visit with Bella
went, and she'd said Bella was doing fine. One more
thing that she had lied to me about.

Worried Mom merged with Annoyed Mom at that
point, so I pulled out my phone again.

Cassandra, you need to call me right now. I
already know you're in Nashville and I need to
talk to you. It's urgent. CALL ME.

Using her full first name seemed to do the trick, because my phone rang a couple of minutes later.

"Well, I *was* going to wait and call you back once I had more than two bars of coverage, but if you're willing to deal with the call dropping, fine."

This might have been true. But since it was also an excuse Cassie had used on several occasions when avoiding returning a call, I had my doubts.

"Thank you," I said. "After my conversation with your father last night, which I really wish you'd warned me about, I have to call Detective Webb."

"To turn him in, right?"

"No!" I said. "Or at least, not yet. But Webb called me. I have to return the call and tell him *something*, so we need to get our stories straight. I just published a brief, bogus obituary for your father. Your dad said that he mailed me some papers, and I'm going to tell Webb there was a note in it that convinced me he actually went through with it. And, assuming those papers ever arrive, I'm hoping I can find a few details to offer up that will pull at least a partial confession out of Hanlon."

"Um...I have those papers. And it's not just papers. He sent about twenty thousand bucks through the freakin' mail."

"What?"

"I'm sorry I didn't tell you!" she said. "Dean said there was an express mail package for you. I told him I'd take it to you, but it was Dad's handwriting on the front. I wanted to see what was in it, to see if my suspicions

were right. I knew as soon as I read the note that Dad
had faked his death. Some garbage about how he'd hold
our family memories from some cruise to Alaska —a
place we've never been, and where I don't particularly
want to go—as the final thought in his mind. And then he
shows up at The Buzz, on Nathan's motorbike, of all
things...and I kind of forgot about everything else."

"You didn't tell him the envelope arrived?"

"No. He actually asked about it. But I figured I'd let
him sweat it out a bit. How stupid can you be sending
that much cash through the mail? Someone could have
stolen it. I didn't want to leave an envelope full of cash at
The Buzz given that we still just have a lockbox rather
than a safe or leave it at the house while we were away.
It's here in my computer bag."

I didn't think it made any more sense to carry it with
her to Nashville, but she'd already admitted that she
hadn't been thinking clearly. It was hard to fault her for
that given the emotional rollercoaster Joe had sent her on
over the past few days, and I couldn't blame her for
wanting to get a little payback by letting him worry about
the package.

"I'll stop by and get the envelope this afternoon," I
said. "But why didn't you tell me you were going out of
town? I was worried, Cassie. I even called Bella's store, to
see if you were staying with her, but they said she's been
in New Jersey for the past week."

There was a long pause, and then Cassie said, "I
didn't *say* I visited Bella. You asked how she was. I told

you. We *do* talk on the phone. We even Skype from time to time."

"You definitely implied that you saw her. And isn't that what you told Detective Webb, as well? I mean, he asked where I was that afternoon. I'm sure he asked the same of you."

"No. I told him the truth. I had a meeting with one of my professors, talking to him about the possibility of lining up an internship this summer. Hopefully a virtual one, so that I can stay in Thistlewood."

My mouth literally dropped open. I'd been trying to get Cassie back into college for well over a year. "One of your...professors?"

"Yes," Cassie said. "I started taking online paralegal classes in January. I didn't tell you, mostly because I wasn't sure I was going to stick with it. Let's say it was a trial balloon. I talked to D'Arcy Jones about the possibility of becoming a paralegal and she helped me find a good online program."

That triggered a memory. D'Arcy had mentioned something along those lines at the *Star*'s Christmas party the previous year, but we'd been in the midst of trying to solve a murder on the set of the movie that was filming in Thistlewood, and the whole thing had kind of gotten wiped from my mind. Cassie had idly mentioned going back to school several times, and I hadn't wanted to push, because she was right...it's all too easy to get my hopes up on that particular subject. I really want her to finish her education.

"Oh. That's nice," I said, deciding to play it cool. She clearly hadn't planned on telling me yet, so I'd wait and let her come back around to the subject in her own time. No pressure. But inside, even with everything else on my mind, I was doing cartwheels. I don't really care what my daughter decides to do with her life. If she's happy working at The Buzz, that's great. I just want her to get an education so that she'll have options if, as so often happens, life throws her a curveball. "So, why are you back in Nashville?" I asked.

"Well technically, we're not *in* Nashville. We're on our way home. Should arrive in Thistlewood by one thirty. Maybe two."

I waited to see if she'd answer the next logical question, but clearly, I was going to have to drag each and every word from her lips. "Okay. Why *were* you in Nashville?"

Cassie gave an audible sigh. "To see if I could pick up any sign of Nathan. I was annoyed at myself for not screwing up the courage to try and find him before we left town. I owed it to him. Nathan wasn't just a friend. You know that. He was almost like family. And...Dean realized how much it was upsetting me, so he suggested we take a road trip."

I paused for a moment, not wanting to sound like a scold, or an overprotective mom. But I kind of *am* the latter, and she knows that I am, so in the end I just blurted it out. "Why didn't you tell me, Cassie?"

"Because you would have said I shouldn't go."

"Yes," I admitted. "Because you *shouldn't* have gone."

"Maybe. But I *had* to go. I knew I wouldn't have a decent night's sleep until I found him. The other ghosts I've encountered were acquaintances or people I didn't even know, and I still risked a lot to help them find peace. How could I do anything less for someone I actually cared about?"

She was right. I'd heard her toss and turn at night on several occasions in the past year and a half. Even though both of us tended to view it as a mixed blessing, Cassie's gift was undeniable. If she thought there was any chance that she could help Nathan, she wouldn't have been content until she at least tried.

"Okay. You're right. I'm just worried about you ending up on the wrong side of the law by entering the house. It's a crime scene, after all."

Cassie snorted at that comment, which was fair. I'd entered crime scenes on numerous occasions, and I was pretty much permanently on the wrong side of the law here in Woodward County.

I ignored her unspoken commentary. "Did you find him?"

"Not at Dad's house," Cassie said. "Not at the house that burned down, either. I picked up...someone in the neighborhood, but it wasn't Nathan. Then I remembered that his fish might need feeding. I'm sure his sister will be coming down to handle his affairs and everything, but the fish might not make it that long. So we stopped at the pet store and bought one of those extended feeder things. And...yeah. Nathan was there. On his back porch."

"But...that's nearly ten miles from your dad's house. How did he get all the way over there?"

"I don't know!" Cassie said. "A ghost taxi, or maybe that Harry Potter night train thing. I didn't ask him. Nathan was still pretty freaked out about being dead. And no, he doesn't know who killed him. They came up from behind. He was on the couch, waiting on Dad, and...next thing he knew, there was something around his neck and he couldn't breathe. He was killed right there on the couch where I've slept countless times, and..."

It was clear from her voice that she was on the verge of tears. "Oh, sweetie, I'm sorry. I know that wasn't easy. Did you tell him we're going to find his killer? Because we are."

"Yeah," she said. "But...that's not the only thing you need to know. Remember the shed you mentioned with all of the appliances and home renovation stuff? Well, someone removed the door. And, aside from some tools and an old gas can, the place is empty."

☆ Chapter Nineteen ☆

IT WAS CLOSER to one thirty when Wren tapped on the back door. I unlocked it and then went to clean up. Ink has a way of getting on my hands in the press room even when I'm not actively printing out the news. I'd finished the final layout for the next day's edition, so when I got back from our afternoon's adventures, all I'd need to do is ink up Stella, crank out the copies, and put them into the automatic collator, which Mr. Dealey had dubbed *The Collector* after yet another character from *A Streetcar Named Desire*.

While I scrubbed up, I filled Wren in on my morning, concluding with the call I'd placed to Mark Webb after I hung up with Cassie. And Ed had been right. Cassie texted me ten minutes later to say that the detective had called to ask what she knew about Capella Holdings.

"She fed him back the story we agreed upon," I told

Wren, "so I'm hoping he'll focus on that until I can come clean with what I know."

I grabbed a towel to dry my hands. Wren was hunched over the forme for page seven, laid out with the others on the worktable, squinting at the obituary I'd written for Joe. The page I'd printed off from my laptop was still next to the linotype machine, so I handed it to her.

"Here. This will be quicker than trying to read it backward."

"I can still read backward just fine, thank you very much." There was a hint of sass in her voice, but she still took the printout. "Skills like that don't tend to atrophy and I spent almost as much time in this place during high school as you did."

That was true. Mr. Dealey had never had a problem with Wren and Tanya keeping me company when I was working. That was especially true before he bought The Collector, since two extra pairs of hands made collating go a whole lot faster.

She glanced down at the page and laughed. "Oh, girl, you did *not*. Comic Sans. That's some serious shade you're throwing. Although, I'm guessing there are only a few readers who will get the joke."

"That's okay," I said. "Cassie will understand. And she'll think it's entirely warranted. She's as annoyed at Joe as I am. Maybe even more so."

I locked the place up and caught her up on the morning's events as we headed out to her car. Once we were out on the highway, she asked if I thought Joe would still be at the cabin.

"Hope not," I said. "I told him where the tent was, and there are plenty of woods for him to pitch it in. If he's nice, I'll let him come in and take a shower. Might not be necessary, though, if I give him a bar of soap. I checked the weather and there's a chance of more rain overnight. Not a gusher like we had *last* night, but enough that he should be able to lather and rinse."

"Are you going to feed him?" Wren asked with a touch of amusement in her voice. "Or do you plan to let him tap into his inner Euell Gibbons and find out how many parts of a pine tree are edible?"

"Whoa. You had to reach *way* back for that reference. And believe me, Joe can afford to miss a few meals." I stopped, thinking about how that sounded. "God. I'm being awful, aren't I? I should just tell him to stay in the house. He's Cassie's dad, after all. Poor Cronkite won't be happy, though. He never much cared for Joe."

"Personally, I think you're being too kind even letting him sleep in your woods," Wren said. "And I'm with Cronk on this one."

"You liked Joe well enough when we were married."

"I liked Joe well enough when he made you happy and he was good to Cassie. But I always thought you could do better. And lo and behold, you've done precisely that. Proving that life is better after fifty."

We clinked imaginary glasses on that one, but I

couldn't help thinking that it really wasn't true for Joe. The odds seemed solid to me that he'd be spending at least a few years in prison for this disaster. Although, to be honest, he probably wouldn't get as much time as some kid Cassie's age who got hauled in for simple possession. White collar crime never seems to be taken quite as seriously, especially in a state like Tennessee.

"You could tell Joe to sleep down in the basement," Wren said. "Toss him a can of insect spray, just in case he runs into that big spider we saw when we were putting away your Christmas decorations. At least then you'd have a little deniability if the cops decide to check your place. You can say he broke in and has been hiding out in the cellar."

She had a point, although I doubted that I'd have much cover, whether he was in the guest room, the basement, or camping on my property. If Webb called the local sheriff and said he was suspicious of the story Cassie and I had told him, and that he thought we might be harboring a wanted man, Steve Blevins probably wouldn't even knock before he kicked down the door to my house. And he'd be more than happy to search every nook and cranny.

"Hopefully, Joe is already out in the tent, but I kind of doubt it. Either way, is it okay if I stay in your guest room again? If all of this isn't over by tomorrow, I'll go to Ed's, but he needs to work tonight."

"That room is yours anytime you need it," Wren said as she turned into my drive. "Now let's grab that lamp

and get out to the sheriff's office. I'd actually rather deal
with Blevins than with Joe Tate right now."

Joe was, as I expected, still in the house. I could
hear the TV before we even reached the porch. A soap
opera, judging from the music, which was weird
because he'd always sneered at anyone who watched
them. Well, that answered my question about whether
I was being too harsh by not letting him stay in the
house. Anyone who stopped by would realize someone
was home. And if they peeked through the curtains, as
I did while unlocking the door, they'd see a man in the
recliner. They might not be able to make out his
features well enough to make a positive ID, but that
would definitely be enough for Blevins to justify
breaking down my door. And Joe made a perfect target
if Hanlon decided to just shoot him through the
window and confirm that he'd gotten the right guy
later.

Joe looked up when we entered. Cronkite, who was
at the top of the steps, zoomed down and began rubbing
against my ankles, meowing loudly.

"Hi, Wren. Not sure why Ruth would pull you into
this, but...good to see you." Joe turned toward me. "Are
you too broke to afford cable? All you've got are the
Knoxville channels and they keep doing this weird pixi-
lation thing."

"Cable is a waste of money for people who have lives
and relationships," Wren told him. "She's at Ed's most
nights anyway."

That wasn't true, but Wren was clearly enjoying twisting the knife a bit.

"The controls to the Roku are right there next to you," I said. "But you won't be needing them because you'll be *inside the tent.*"

He rolled his eyes. "I can't believe you're serious."

"Oh, I'm serious. Are you a total idiot? This is a small town. Cassie and I are almost never here during the day. You claim you're scared Hanlon is going to kill you, and yet you're sprawled out in clear view of the window, with the volume up high enough that I could hear you as soon as we got out of the car."

As I was speaking, Wren slipped out of the room and headed toward the back of the house where the lamp was.

"I saw you pull into the drive," Joe said. "It wasn't Hanlon's car. Not a police cruiser, either. Then I saw you and Wren through the windshield. Otherwise, I'd have had plenty of time to turn the TV off and get out of sight."

He was probably right, but it didn't negate the point that he'd ignored my instructions.

"What I told you to do, however, is get out of my house. You didn't. Did you even bother to feed the cat?"

Cronkite meowed even louder at this point.

"No. Because he hasn't been downstairs until now. Anyway, at some point during the night, he ate the extra dinner you put in his bowl. Remember?" Joe gave me a look that was far too smug given his current situation.

"You are not staying in the house. I'm taking a big enough risk as it is." I pointed toward the kitchen. "Grab some food and a few bottles of water from the pantry. You can put them in one of the grocery bags. Take a book if you'd like. The tent and sleeping bag are in the shed. I think there's one of those big flashlights out there, too."

Wren came back with the lamp. She glanced toward the door, but I shook my head.

"Not until he's out. I need to lock up." I turned back to Joe. "I want your key before I leave because you're staying out there until this is...over."

Joe pulled his buzzing phone out of his pocket and glanced at the screen. Then he entered a single keystroke, and quickly tucked it back inside.

"I was going to say that I really hoped that was a wrong number," I told him. "Since you're supposed to be dead and all, based on the obituary I just posted. But since you responded, I'm going to go out on a limb and say no."

He colored slightly. "I'm surprised the message came through. I keep having to walk around the house in order to get even two bars here. You'd think that would have improved over the past few years. But yeah, I didn't think it was fair for Tammy to keep believing I was dead. At a bare minimum, I owe her the ten grand I promised."

"Were you planning to pay it out of the cash you mailed?" I asked.

"So the envelope arrived?"

"It did. Not exactly the safest way to send cash, Joe."

"Hey, I didn't have a choice. Most of what I have is about to get tied up in court. I wanted Cassie to have money for school."

"She told you she's back in college?"

"Yeah, she mentioned it. Said she was majoring in fifteenth-century French feminist literature, of all things. I didn't even know she spoke French."

I had to bite back a laugh. Since Cassie was about eight, Joe had been telling her he'd only pay for college if she picked a practical major, which basically meant business or nursing, since his mom had been a nurse at one time. I've told her she can study whatever she wants, because the contributions came mostly from my salary, not Joe's. Around the time she entered high school, she began responding to all questions from Joe about college or future plans with some wild, impractical major just to watch him sputter and fume.

"I put about half of what was in the safe into the envelope and kept the other half," he said. "I'll pay Tammy out of that."

"Depending on how much that stuff in Nathan's shed was worth, you may not owe her anything."

He looked confused. "You didn't tell me the shed had been cleared out."

I started to say that I hadn't known until this morning, but then I'd have had to go into Cassie and Dean's trip to Nashville, and I really didn't want to drag the conversation out any longer than I had to. "Guess I forgot."

"I doubt that was Tammy," he said. "She'd have had to hire movers. More likely Gina, Hanlon's girlfriend, called her uncle when she heard about Nathan and he sent some of his guys over. Anyway, Tammy's not going to say anything. She was over the moon to find out I'm okay. Given that she kept quiet for this long about the deal with Hanlon, I think she can keep her lips zipped a few more days. And I didn't even tell her I'm here if that's what you're worried about. Told her I was staying with a college friend up north of Nashville and she could meet me there once my name is clear and I can come out of hiding."

I was tempted to remind him that he'd said just the night before that he didn't think it was fair to keep stringing her along. But that might have given him the impression that I was jealous, and that wasn't at all true.

"Good," I said. "But it wouldn't exactly take a rocket scientist to guess that you might have come here, would it? That's all the more reason that I want you out of the house. You got me and Cassie into this mess and you're going to make at least some effort to give us cover in case this all goes south. I'm doing my best to keep you from being pinned with Nathan's murder, Joe, but I'm not going to jail for you. Understood?"

Joe grumbled and took a good ten minutes getting his stuff together. I opened a can of food for Cronkite...way early, but he'd no doubt consider that much better than way late. Then, I grabbed the key to the shed's padlock from its hook in the kitchen and herded Joe out the door.

It took a bit of time moving things around inside the shed, but I eventually found the tent, a sleeping bag, a lantern, and a large plastic canister.

"What's that for?" he asked.

I shrugged. "It's a bear canister. You could also hang your food from a branch, but since you don't have to hike all that far to pitch the tent, this will be easier. There's a little clearing through that gap in the trees, where Cassie had her play fort when she was a kid. A hundred yards in, maybe a little more. The brush has grown up, but you can probably still make out the trail." I locked the shed and then held out my hand. "Your key, please."

He peeled it off the ring and dropped it into my palm. I tucked both keys into my pocket and looked up to find Joe staring at me with a perplexed expression. "You really are not the same woman I was married to. When did you get so hard, Ruth?"

I glanced over at Wren, who was leaning against the side of the shed. She'd given me and Joe a wide berth since we arrived, something I suspected was due more to her lingering desire to punch him than to privacy concerns. I turned back to Joe with a tight little smile and repeated the words Wren had said to me a few days back in Nashville. "You're right, Joe. I'm *not* the same woman. This is Ruth 2.0. If you're not happy with our arrangement, I could axe the plan to confront Hanlon. I'll just call Detective Webb back and we'll see how you fare with the justice system."

He sighed and closed his eyes briefly. "No. I'll be fine

in the woods. Were you serious about there being a bear on your property?"

Wren laughed. "Oh, she's serious. And you'd best hope Remy doesn't have some sort of sixth sense. Black bears are usually kind of mellow, but Remy gets riled up at people who aren't nice to his foster mama. He left some wicked grooves in the last guy who gave her trouble. And he was just a yearling back then."

I fought to keep from laughing at Joe's expression. Although everything Wren had said was true, I thought it was quite likely that Remy was no longer in the area. And even if he was, he'd probably steer clear of Joe. But I didn't see the point in clarifying all of that at the moment. Maybe it would do Joe good to lie awake, worried about a little bear vengeance. Maybe he could use a sleepless night or two, as he stared at the inside of the tiny tent and thought about all the stupid things he'd done that landed him in this situation.

"Stick close to the tree line," I told him. "I'll stop by tomorrow morning to feed Cronkite and give you an update."

"You mean, you're not going to even be here, and you're still making me..." He trailed off, probably because my raised eyebrows reminded him of my previous threat to call Webb. "Okay, okay. Guess I'll see you tomorrow." He hoisted the tent bag and bear canister over his shoulder and began trudging off toward the woods.

Wren and I made it back to her car before she burst out laughing. "Oh my God." She put the lamp in the backseat and then got behind the wheel. "His expression was absolutely priceless. How much you want to bet you come back tomorrow morning and find him sleeping on your deck because he's too spooked of the bear to sleep in the woods?"

"Not taking that bet," I told her as she pulled back onto the road and turned toward the sheriff's office. "I think your comment about Remy pretty much guarantees he'll either be on the deck or under it. But this at least gives me some deniability since I'm not hiding him inside my house."

The Woodward County Sheriff's Office had once been downtown, but they relocated to a new building about five miles out of town a few years before the accident that forced Ed to resign. In the summertime, when the area was packed with tourists heading down to the campgrounds and various attractions along the river, traffic was horrible on the two-lane streets running through Thistlewood. Relocating put them a bit closer to the river and nearer the turnoff for the road that led up to some of the tiny communities in the mountains, cutting down on the time it took to reach both areas in case of an emergency.

Wren skipped the first entrance to the parking lot, which avoided her car passing directly in front of the building. She pulled up beneath a large maple near the side entrance, just two parking spots away from the police cruiser marked *Sheriff*.

"So...are we just going to waltz in and ask him for his foot-o-graph?" I asked as we got out of the car.

She rolled her eyes. "That was a truly horrible pun. And no. We're going to get it from that path across the lawn, which should still be muddy from last night's rain."

I frowned. "But there's a sidewalk. How do you know he won't use that?"

Wren smiled. "Because we share a lawn service. Dave Weaver has been cutting my lawn since I bought Memory Gardens and we chat from time to time. He has the contract for landscaping the various county properties, including this one, and he dislikes Blevins as much as I do. A few weeks back, Dave put down some seed on the front lawn where we've had trouble getting the grass to grow. He thought it would take, as long as I kept people off that section of lawn for a bit. Said the only place he hadn't been able to get it to take was at the sheriff's office because Blevins couldn't be bothered to use the darn sidewalk."

"Well, that bit of chatter came in handy," I said. "Jesse needs to watch out or you'll steal his job as curator of the town's grapevine."

There was indeed a well-worn path between the door and the sheriff's reserved parking space. It saved, at most, ten steps. Unfortunately, the path didn't seem to be damp.

Wren sniffed in annoyance and went back to her car. I followed, but before I could get in, she pulled out her travel mug of coffee and a bottle of water from the back floorboard. Then she headed back to the path.

"There," she said, as she poured both onto the dirt near the sidewalk.

I glanced toward the door. "We could be waiting here a long time for him to come out, though. It's two forty. And we're due at the church for the club meeting at three."

"He'll be out within five minutes. And we'll make it to the meeting in plenty of time."

I raised an eyebrow. "How can you be so sure?"

"Have you ever known Elvis to be late for his afternoon milkshake?"

"Ah. *Very* good point."

Patsy had started calling Blevins *Elvis* when we were back in high school, partly because he'd thought he was all that and a bag of chips when he was younger and sporting a full head of shoulder-length hair. Mostly, however, the nickname was because of his addiction to peanut butter and banana milkshakes. Ed told me Blevins had vehemently opposed moving the sheriff's office from the courthouse, and he thought it was mostly because Elvis could no longer just stroll across the street to the diner. The five-minute drive from the new facility made it less convenient, but it certainly hadn't stopped him from getting his three o'clock fix.

The door opened less than a minute after we were back inside the car. Blevins frowned slightly as his eyes adjusted to the light, then he pulled a pair of sunshades out of his pocket. As predicted, he ignored the sidewalk completely, strolling right through the muddy patch. Instead of heading to his car, however, he walked straight toward us.

"Uh-oh," I said. "Think I may have spotted the flaw in this plan."

Wren just smiled serenely and pulled a sheet of paper out of the center console as Blevins wrapped his knuckles on the glass. She rolled the window down and said, "Good afternoon, Sheriff. I was just about to head inside to let you know that I took the car in to the garage and had that taillight inspected as you suggested. Everything checked out fine."

"Okay," he said, looking confused. "You didn't need to drive all the way over here to tell me that."

"Well, I didn't want there to be any doubt. After all, I wouldn't want you to have to write me up. Should I give this to the secretary or..."

"I didn't even give you a written warning," he said, shaking his head as he turned toward his car. "You're good to go."

"Thank you," she said cheerily. "Enjoy the rest of your day."

She was laying it on a bit thick, and I half-expected Blevins to turn back and ask what we were up to. But the lure of his milkshake must have been too strong, because he hopped into the cruiser and screeched out of the lot without even looking back.

"You paid to have your taillight checked just so you'd have an excuse?"

"Ten dollars well spent," she said. "You can add it to my bill."

As soon as Steve's car was on the highway, we got out and checked the small patch of wet soil. One full and one partial print. I snapped a picture of the prints with my phone, but Wren was already shaking her head as she put her foot next to them.

"It's not him. The other foot was narrow. A bit longer, too. Steve's foot is as fat as his head."

Chapter Twenty

THERE WERE ALREADY six or seven women inside the basement of Shepherd's Flock Community Church when Wren and I entered ten minutes later. Most were gathered around two long tables pushed against the far wall, on which they'd placed a variety of items. Six chairs were lined up next to the table to serve as makeshift displays for two quilts, which were neatly folded and draped over the back. The one on the right was a basic square pattern, similar to the "memory quilt" currently on the bed in Cassie's room, which my grandmother had made from scraps of clothing she'd sewn over the years. The other, in various shades of blue, was a bit more complicated, in a sunburst pattern. While I'd only seen the photograph of Olivia's quilt, it was abundantly clear that neither of these could hold a candle to her work.

Elaine wasn't among the early arrivals gathered around the table, so Wren and I stood awkwardly near the doorway, with our sacrificial lamp for the silent auction. After a moment, Jenny Blevins spotted us. She finished writing something on a tag that she taped to the edge of a picture frame, and then came over to greet us. Bobbi Blevins followed close behind.

"Ruth!" Jenny said. "I just wanted to extend my condolences about Cassie's father. And Wren! It's so nice to see both of you." There was a slight hint of a question in her voice, so I stepped into the breach.

"Thanks, Jenny. I was talking to Elaine Morton the other day, and she mentioned the silent auction, so we decided to bring this by. And then she got to telling me about all the community service projects the club does and offered to sponsor Wren and me if we'd like to become members. But Elaine doesn't seem to be here, so..."

Jenny laughed, dismissing the comment with a wave of her hand. "Elaine will be here eventually. She tends to wander in about halfway through the business part of the meeting. We're delighted that you're interested in joining us."

Bobbi cleared her throat softly. "I'm afraid Elaine may have overstepped. The bylaws clearly state that any member in good standing may nominate a new member for consideration. A new member. Singular, not plural. And from everything that I've heard about these two, they're a package deal."

The words were innocuous enough. But there was

something about the elder Mrs. Blevins's tone that didn't sit well with me.

Jenny turned her infinitely patient smile toward her mother-in-law. "You're *technically* correct, Roberta. But that's not a problem in the slightest. Elaine can nominate Ruth. I'll nominate Wren. That way, we've followed the rules, and everyone is happy."

Bobbi looked like she was going to say something, but Elaine breezed in at that moment. Her face was flushed, and she was slightly out of breath. "I'm so sorry! I'd planned to be here early, but Delta was digging a hole in the back yard again and I had to get her inside."

Wren and I exchanged a look. Judging from the twitch of Jenny's lips, she was also thinking about what was found the last time someone went digging in Clarence Morton's back yard. Elaine, however, was totally oblivious, and proceeded to tell Jenny that she'd offered to sponsor us for membership.

"We were just talking about that," Jenny said. "And Roberta helpfully pointed out that we'll need to split the nominations up, since you can only propose a single candidate. If anyone was inclined to be a real stickler for the rules, that is. But I'm sure Ruth and Wren want to be certain the club is a good fit for them, so we'll just consider them our special guests for today's meeting and take up the membership vote next month. That's usually how we handle new arrivals, so would that be okay with y'all?"

Wren and I both nodded. In truth, it was more than

acceptable to me. If we could locate the missing quilt, I could go back to my introverted, club-free existence.

Now that the formalities were over, we found a spot for the crystal lamp among the auction items. Then we joined Elaine at the second table. I looked around for friendly faces, hoping that I'd see Ed's sister or D'Arcy Jones, but they seemed to have skipped the meeting. There were eleven women in total, and one thing hadn't changed over the years. Wren was the only person of color in the room. Jenny introduced us to the others as guests, and more than a few, including Olivia's cousin Lillian, cast knowing looks in our direction. Apparently, Elaine wasn't the only one to find our sudden interest in the club a bit on the suspicious side.

After ten minutes or so of approving the minutes and dealing with unfinished business, Jenny moved on to new items on the agenda. There was some discussion about the upcoming auction, and a report from the treasurer about the website where she'd be posting the items and a reminder that we all needed to fill out full information on our donations and tag them before leaving, so that they could be transported over to the high school for the event. Next, they briefly discussed ideas for their summer fundraiser. Most seemed inclined to stick with the usual concession booth in the park on the Fourth of July, but the previous president, Verna Neilson, noted that the revenue had fallen sharply since the city had started allowing food trucks to set up along the perimeter of the park.

Wren and I had sat silently during the rest of the meeting, so I was surprised to see her raise her hand with a suggestion. "What about setting up a karaoke booth? It's not that expensive, and most people would be willing to cough up five or ten bucks as an entry fee if you offer a prize. Oh, and you could let people buy tickets to get various town leaders to sing. Tell them if you raise a hundred dollars, you'll draw one of the tickets and the winner can decide what song Mayor Neilson or the city council members or Sheriff Blevins has to sing."

One of the women said she didn't think town leaders would agree to something like that, but Jenny and Verna both laughed.

"They definitely will," Jenny said. "It's an election year. I like that idea, Wren. Could you email me information?"

Wren nodded, and I whispered, "Thought you were just here to solve the mystery."

"Shh," she hissed. "I want karaoke in the park."

Jenny looked down at her papers, and then glanced nervously around the room. "Those of you who read the agenda I sent around may recall that our final business item is selecting a new winner of the quilting contest, given the unfortunate theft that occurred last week. My inclination, as most of you are aware, was for Olivia to take the trip anyway, as planned. You all saw how excited she was when she won. It's only fair, in my opinion, given that we declared her the winner. Olivia, however, has declined. She told me that she is confident that the thief will be found and brought to justice, but if not, she doesn't want the club to be without an entry for the state competition. Even when I offered to cover her expenses —personally," she added quickly, "not out of the club accounts, she was adamant. I was hoping that she would be here today so that you could help me convince her that we're far more concerned about the loss of her quilt than we are about the state contest."

I scanned the faces in the room as she spoke. All of the women were nodding, including Lillian, who really was as ancient as Wren had said, and Bobbi Blevins. It seemed to me that Mrs. Blevins was smirking slightly, though. It was an expression I recognized instantly because I'd seen it so often on the face of her son.

"But Olivia said that she was certain some members wouldn't think it was fair for her to go to the conference," Jenny continued, her tone growing dark. "Apparently, this was based in part on an anonymous note *someone* mailed to her house earlier this week, stating that she'd never have lost the quilt if she hadn't been so prideful, leaving it on display. I'm sure that couldn't possibly have come from anyone in this group." Her eyes traveled around the room, lingering briefly on Lillian and even longer on Bobbi. "Since Olivia is not here, however, I guess we'll have to pick an alternate from the other two entries. You've seen both of them before, but I asked Lillian and Roberta to bring them back in today so that you could refresh your memory. They're on the chairs against the wall. Once you've made your decision, jot the name down on a slip of paper and drop it into the purple vase at the end of the table."

Wren and I were guests, and therefore not voting, but we headed over with the others to check out the quilts. As I was pushing my chair back under the table, my phone vibrated with an incoming text.

It was from Hanlon.

Leaving town tomorrow morning. Can you meet tonight at eight instead?

Not exactly what I'd hoped for, but I texted back a quick yes.

"What's wrong?" Wren asked.

I showed her the text. "Ed and I were hoping to set it up for tomorrow, after he finished his edits."

She frowned. "I'd offer to go with you, but I have the Quinn visitation."

"Oh, that's okay. I'm sure Ed can take a late dinner break." Even if Wren hadn't been busy, I was reluctant to pull her into this. She owned a pistol, and thanks to her time in the military was a decent shot. But Ed had connections that would make it far less likely that he'd face any sort of legal complications if he had reason to draw the weapon.

"Don't even think about going alone," she said with a stern look. "And yes, I most certainly *will* call Ed to make sure you don't."

I really wasn't intending to go alone, but I stuck my tongue out at her for good measure, and then we went over to look at the quilts.

Given Olivia's statement about the two other contestants, I expected the simple quilt to have Lillian's name on it. But it belonged to Bobbi Blevins.

Wren pulled me off to the side. "I thought Olivia said..."

"She did," I whispered back. "That has to be a really deep rivalry for her not to admit Lillian's quilt is a clear second. And...it kind of messes up our theory about the motive."

Wren huffed. "Now we need footprints from Lillian's sons, and I'm pretty sure one lives in Maryville."

"What are you two whispering about?" Elaine said from directly behind us.

"Nothing at all," Wren said. "Just admiring the craftsmanship. They're both really nice."

"Well, I voted on Lillian's quilt," she said. "It's clearly the best now that poor Olivia is out of the running. Do you have any idea who—"

I made a little kill motion to cut her off, since I could almost see the ears of the other women straining to pick up what we were saying. She grinned and pantomimed zipping her lips, and then hurried back to the table.

When the votes were counted, no one was particularly surprised that Lillian was the winner. She clapped her hands happily, and everyone, including Bobbi Blevins, congratulated her. Lillian pulled herself up with her walker and stood next to Jenny, who handed her a print certificate, while I snapped a picture for the next week's edition of the *Star*.

"I'll call the hotel this evening and transfer the reservation into your name," Jenny told Lillian. "And we'll cover your meals, as well, of course. You and Verna can work out what time she'll pick you up."

"Oh, no," Lillian said, laughing nervously. "I can't make a trip like that at my age. As much as I'd love to go, I'm just not up to the hotels and it's *such* a long drive. So just go ahead and put the reservation in Roberta's name. I asked her if she'd mind taking my place and present my quilt for the competition if I won. She said she'd be more than happy to. Wasn't that sweet of her?"

"Well, you know Bobbi," Jenny said between clenched teeth. "Always so considerate of others."

If Bobbi detected the sarcasm in her daughter-in-law's words she didn't let on.

"But," Jenny continued, "I'm not sure that the judges will allow that. We should probably call to check."

"Oh, it's fine!" Lillian's eyes darted over to Bobbi, and she said. "I called and checked yesterday just in case I won. Since...Roberta had offered to go. If I won, that is."

The two of them had clearly cooked the entire thing up together. I exchanged a look with Wren and could tell that she agreed. Proving it, however, would be next to impossible given the deadline we were under.

"It's truly my pleasure," Bobbi said. "All I need to do is jot down a few notes about Lillian's pattern and her process in case the judges have any questions. And Verna, you won't even need to pick me up. I can just ride with Jenny and Steve."

Jenny made a noise that was almost a growl as her mother-in-law walked off. Wren also looked like she was one step short of throttling the elder Mrs. Blevins, so I decided that it might be a good idea for us to clear out, now that the meeting was adjourned and most of the other women were leaving. But when we reached the door, I remembered that I'd forgotten something.

"I need to fill out the information about the crystal lamp for the auction website," I told Wren.

"I'll wait outside." She sniffed and wrinkled her nose. "After the load of manure those two just dished out, I could use some fresh air."

Jenny was at the table talking on her cellphone while I filled out the form. "Except, you were supposed to be here already, Derrick. Have her put your coffee in a to-go cup. Or pour it out. I don't care which, just get your butt over here. We're supposed to have everything at the school by four thirty and there are a lot of items to transport."

I slipped the pen back into the clipboard and was about to join Wren outside, but some instinct made me turn back. "Did you need help moving the auction items? My jeep is parked behind the *Star* and I'd be happy to lend a hand."

"Well...I guess you could help me box some of the donations up if you're sure you don't mind. Derrick is right around the corner at The Buzz, though. Probably chatting with your daughter. Guess they just lost track of time."

I didn't correct her, but if Derrick was at The Buzz, I was quite certain that Cassie had not lost track of time. She was most likely watching the clock, counting the minutes until he finished his coffee and got out of her face.

"He's home from college and hasn't started working yet. I told him he needs to do something to earn his keep." Jenny laughed after the last bit, but there was a tiny bit of tension in her voice.

She pulled two boxes from under the table and we began placing the smaller items inside. I felt a slight pang as I attached a tag to the base of the crystal lamp. It almost seemed as if the thing was watching me—reproachfully—as I helped Jenny box up the other items. Had there been a reason my mom kept it in the living room, despite the fact that it clashed with the décor? Had some family member given it to her? Was there a story behind it? I wished I'd been able to ask her, although it wasn't likely that the subject would ever have arisen in casual conversation, even if she hadn't died so suddenly. And if I used that logic, keeping every item because it might have some sentimental attachment, even though I had no clue what it might be, I'd never change anything at the cabin. I wouldn't even be able to empty out the junk drawer. It would always be my parents' house, and never my home.

"I'm really glad that you and Wren came today," Jenny said after a few minutes. "And we'd be delighted to have both of you as members if you're still interested in joining our group. I don't know if you're aware, but Ed's sister is a member. We had several people absent today, probably out of sympathy for Olivia, since she sent around an email saying she thought it would be best if she just stayed home today. They're a great bunch, for the most part." She frowned toward the table where Bobbi and Lillian were chatting and lowered her voice. "Just a few bad apples. If you're over at Ed's and you happen to see Olivia out in the yard, please tell her that my offer still stands. There's room for one more in the car, or she can ride with Verna. And I will *gladly* cover her expenses."

"That's very kind of you," I said. "I'll be sure to let her know."

Derrick Blevins was coming out of the elevator when I left the recreation room. He ignored me, and didn't bother to hold the elevator door, which was fine with me. I'd never even considered using the elevator, given that it was only one flight of stairs.

When I got outside, Wren was crouched down, staring at a patch of grass a few feet from the curb where Derrick's burgundy Dodge Charger was parked.

"What are you looking for?" I asked, thinking maybe she'd lost an earring.

"A footprint, but there's too much grass. And it's too springy. By the time I got over here, I could barely tell where he'd stepped." Her eyes scanned the side of the church, landing on the hose coiled up near the corner of the building. "But I've got a better idea."

"You're kidding?"

"Nope. Second time's the charm. Unless you wanna help me cart over some dirt. But we probably don't have much time, and I think that would look kind of suspicious."

"And water won't?" I glanced up at the almost cloud-less afternoon sky.

Wren ignored me and hurried over to the faucet. "Keep an eye on the door, okay?"

I moved toward the edge of the building so that I had a clear view of the side entrance. No one was coming. Yet.

Behind me, Wren grunted. "I can't get the darn thing to turn. What I need is a pair of pliers."

"I have a toolbox in my jeep, but..."

"No," Wren said through clenched teeth. "I think I've got—" She yelped and sprang away from the wall, running into me and nearly sending us both crashing onto the lawn.

Water spewed from the side of the hose, which appeared to have a leak at the base. It wasn't a mere trickle, but more like a geyser that arced over the side-walk leading from the church and all the way out to the street.

Wren's pants were completely soaked.

"Turn it off," I said. "Hurry." To me the sound of the water was thunderous. Half of Main Street was prob-ably staring at us by now.

I didn't turn around to check. Instead, I flattened

myself against the wall as best I could and moved toward the source of the calamity, a fine mist already lashing at my face from several feet away.

"Oh, jeez," Wren breathed as she inched back toward the faucet, trying to avoid the spray. When her hand finally grasped the handle, she twisted. "It's stuck again!"

Of course it was.

Several seconds passed. Finally, with a squeak from the faucet and a curse from Wren, the stream of water reversed course across the sidewalk and vanished into the wall.

"Well, it worked. The sidewalk is wet."

"So am I," Wren said. "Not sure it was worth it."

"Shh." I yanked my head back from the corner. "Derrick's coming." We had three seconds, maybe four, before he'd spot us.

I grabbed Wren's arm and pulled her toward the large brick sign engraved with the church's name. Derrick rounded the side of the building and headed for his car, carrying a large box. He stopped, staring down at the wide expanse of wet concrete, then tilted his head back to check out the mostly blue sky.

I had to bite the inside of my cheek to keep from laughing.

Derrick shrugged and popped the trunk of the Charger, leaving a healthy set of wet footprints behind as he carried the box to the car. All we had to do now was stay out of sight until he went back inside, and then we could compare his prints to the one in Olivia's photo.

Except, much like his father, Derrick Blevins seemed to enjoy taking his own sweet time. When I peeked around the edge of the sign to find out what was taking so long, I saw that the trunk wasn't empty. He'd had to set the box down to make room. A flash of color caught my eye as he tucked a large black trash bag around something. He then shoved the bundle to the back, put the box of auction items at the front, and headed into the church, leaving the trunk wide open.

"Let's go," Wren said.

"You check the footprint. I need to check the trunk."

She gave me an odd look, and then nodded. We headed in opposite directions, Wren toward the sidewalk and me toward the curb. When I got to Derrick's car, I glanced behind me to see if anyone was watching from Main Street. There were two people on the sidewalk, but they were engaged in conversation, and apparently hadn't noticed the two crazy women on the church lawn. If anyone happened to spot me, I'd say a squirrel ran into his trunk. Or something.

I reached inside for the edge of the garbage bag. Based on my suspicions of Steve Blevins's son, there could also be drugs in this trunk. Or, for that matter, a body. I was still fairly certain he was guilty not just of the hit-and-run that injured Ed, but also of accessory to murder.

But when I tugged the plastic up a few inches, I

could see that the bag was covering exactly what I'd suspected when I saw that flash of color. Olivia's quilt was wadded up beneath it. I stepped back, pulled out my phone, and snapped two quick photographs. Then I hurried over to Wren.

"It's him!" she said, nodding down at a long, narrow footprint on the sidewalk. "I'm almost certain."

"I'm *completely* certain." I snapped a shot of the footprint, then swiped the screen to pull up the previous picture of Derrick's trunk.

"Great!" Wren said as we moved away from the wet patch on the sidewalk and back toward Memory Gardens. "We've got the thieving little rat." Then her face fell. "But if we call it in, I seriously doubt Steve will arrest his own son. More likely, he'd charge you with tampering with Derrick's car. What are we going to do?"

I glanced toward the building. Through the glass door, I could see several people just past the elevator. Jenny, who was carrying my lamp and the picture frame, was next to Lillian. They were moving slowly down the hall toward the exit in deference to Lillian's walker. Bobbi and Derrick were just behind them, and Derrick was carrying another large box. Several other boxes were stacked against the wall.

"I think *you* should go upstairs and change," I told Wren, glancing down at the front of her linen pants, which were completely soaked. "Otherwise, they're going to know you sprayed the sidewalk. And while there's no law against that, I'd really rather have them think I saw this accidentally."

She started to protest, but I shooed her on. "Go! You can watch from the window. And I'll give you full details in five minutes, tops."

Wren heaved an exasperated sigh. Then she scurried off across the wide lawn, pushing through the low hedge of azalea bushes that separated the two properties. The door of the funeral home had barely closed behind her when the side door of the church opened.

I waited until Jenny had helped Lillian down the single step and Derrick had headed back inside to get another box. Then I tapped Jenny on the shoulder and motioned her to the side. "I believe I've found Olivia's quilt."

"Really?" A smile spread across her face. "That's wonderful! But..."

Her smile faded as I showed her the picture on my phone. She glanced first at Bobbi and Lillian, who were sitting on the bench near the azalea bushes, then at Derrick, who was now coming down the sidewalk with the remaining boxes.

"Thank you, Ruth. I'll take care of this." She handed the phone back to me and marched toward Derrick's car. "Hold up. I need to double check something in one of those boxes before you close the trunk."

Derrick stepped away from the car. Jenny made a pretense of looking through one of the boxes and then nudged the plastic aside to reveal the quilt. "Oh my goodness, Derrick! You must have grabbed this by accident when you were packing up the first batch of auction items last week."

"What first batch of..." He trailed off as he realized Jenny was tugging the quilt out of its hiding place.

"This wasn't supposed to be packed away," Jenny said. "Everyone assumed it had been stolen. Didn't you hear your grandmother and me talking about the missing quilt? We were discussing it at the dinner table just the other night."

He shook his head. "Guess I wasn't paying attention."

"Guess you weren't," Jenny said flatly, staring her son directly in the eyes as she refolded the quilt.

"Nana said she was going to give it back," Derrick said, apparently deciding that the clueless act wasn't going to cut it. "It was just a practical joke, Mom."

Jenny didn't respond, but just held his gaze a moment longer, her eyes still blazing. Then she turned to her mother-in-law. "Derrick is going to drive you home, Roberta. I'll wait here until Lillian's son arrives to pick her up. Derrick, you drop her at the house and then meet me at the high school so we can unload all of this. And no side trips. You'd better be there by four-thirty. Understand?"

"Yes, mom." He heaved an exasperated sigh that sounded more like a kid in middle school than a guy in his mid-twenties. "Come on, Nana."

I could feel Bobbi Blevins's eyes on me as she headed

toward the Charger, so I turned and gave her a tight little smile, to make it completely clear that I knew this wasn't just a mix-up or a joke. She and I were never going to be friends, anyway, but I suspected this put her firmly in the enemy category. Derrick glared at me, too, so I seemed to have won the trifecta by being on the enemy list of three generations of Blevins's.

Lillian's ancient face was squinched up in a tight angry bow. Jenny gave her a disappointed look and then came over to where I was standing. "I'm going to drive this quilt over to Olivia as soon as I'm done here. And I guess I need to call Verna and let her know she'll have a passenger after all."

She paused for a moment, watching as Derrick's car pulled away from the curb, and then lowered her voice. "Ruth, I hate to ask this, but is there any way we could keep this between us? Roberta was kind of put out when I told her that Steve was going with me to the conference. He's taking a few days off because we really haven't had any time together since she moved in. I'll be busy during the day, but we both just needed to get away. His mom is perfectly okay by herself, especially with Derrick there, but she got it into her head that she was coming, too. I told her that there really wouldn't be room in the car for all of us, let alone in the hotel room. Steve actually backed me up for once, probably because he needs the time away from her. She and Lillian cooked this up thinking they'd kill two birds with one stone—Roberta would be able to ruin our trip and Lillian would be able to gloat because she kept Olivia from going. I'm planning to have a long talk with both of them...and with Derrick. His grandma spoils him rotten, so I'm sure all she had to do was offer him a few bucks to take the quilt off the wall and stash it in his trunk. Or maybe he just didn't want to have to watch her this weekend while we're gone. He probably *did* think of it as a practical joke, though, and... given Steve's position..." She gave me a hopeful smile.

"Wren already knows," I said. "She just had to get back home. I'll have to tell Ed, because he's the one Olivia asked to help find the quilt in the first place. We only offered to assist because he was busy today. And...I really don't think it's fair to Olivia not to tell her the truth."

"Oh, no! I definitely wouldn't want you to lie to any of them. I'm planning to tell Olivia exactly what happened. I only meant..." She glanced down at the phone. "The photo that you took for the paper. I didn't know if you intended to run a story about all of this."

"Absolutely not. As far as the readers of the *Thistlewood Star* need know, there was never any winner aside from Olivia."

She sighed. "All three of them are lucky that Olivia didn't call this into the sheriff's office. She would have been well within her rights to do so, and Steve would be livid if he knew."

"Well, my lips are sealed," I said, "although I can't speak for Olivia."

Jenny nodded. "I'll talk to her when I drop off the

quilt. Thank you, Ruth. I really hope that all of this hasn't scared you and Wren away from joining our group. It's not always this much of a soap opera, and we do a lot of good in the community."

I smiled and said we'd think about it. But I already knew the die was cast. Wren was going to make sure there was karaoke in the park this Fourth of July, so I was quite certain she'd be joining. And that meant I'd be joining, too. Because as Bobbi Blevins had said earlier, Wren and I are a package deal.

Chapter Twenty-One

WREN OPENED the door of Memory Gardens before I even reached the steps. She was still in her wet clothes, so I suspected she'd watched everything that transpired from the windows that overlook the front lawn.

"I need to cut down that hedge," she said as I followed her upstairs. "I could hardly see anything."

While she changed, I filled in the details. When I reached the part where Jenny asked me to keep the matter private, Wren frowned.

"So Bobbi kind of got away with it."

"Not entirely," I said. "Olivia will be going on the trip, not Bobbi. Like you said earlier, there really wasn't much chance that Blevins would arrest his own mother. That goes double now that we know his son was involved. And I have a feeling Jenny isn't going to let either of them off scot free."

"Maybe." Wren grabbed a sweater from the closet and tugged it over her head. "But I plan to keep my eye on that woman. Teresa said she does this kind of thing all the time. Sooner or later, Bobbi Blevins is going to cross the wrong person and the fact that her son is the sheriff isn't going to protect her."

"I look forward to the day," I said. "Listen, I need to run. I still have to get the package Joe sent from Cassie and figure out a strategy for getting Hanlon to 'fess up for the recording. I'll message you as soon as I'm out of the meeting—"

"Which you will not be attending without Ed."

"Which I will not be attending without Ed." I repeated and gave her a mock salute as I closed the door behind me.

When I entered The Buzz a few minutes later, Cassie was behind the bar with her back to the door, washing out one of the blenders at the small sink. Her laptop was open at the far end of the counter. A familiar masthead was at the top, but it wasn't the *Star*. It was the *Nashville News-Journal*. She must have been searching to see if there was anything new about Nathan's murder.

There were only a few customers in the shop—one in the small seating area off to the right of the café, and two more on the lower level, browsing through the used books. There were probably a few more on the upper level, which held the e-sports room, but Dean had been smart enough to spring for decent soundproofing, so I couldn't tell for sure.

"I'll be right with you," Cassie called out as I approached the bar. When she finished giving the blender a final rinse, she turned around wearing her best customer service smile. It promptly faded when she saw me.

"Well, that's a wonderful greeting for your mother."

"You're mad at me. And I don't want to hash through everything while I'm at work. It's only me and Dean from now until closing time. So can we do this later?"

"I'm not mad at you." That was actually true. I was a little disappointed, yes. And maybe a little sad that she was hiding things from me, but heaven knows that's par for the course with children, especially adult children. "I was *concerned* when I couldn't get up with you. But I do understand you wanting to know more about what happened to Nathan. If I had your gift, I'd likely have done the same thing. I just wish you'd been able to get a little more information." I lowered my voice, even though there didn't appear to be anyone within earshot. "Aside from the shed being empty, we don't know much more now than what I learned from talking about all of this with your father last night."

"Why are you going along with his scheme?" Cassie's tone was sharp, and it took me a little aback. "You should have told him no."

"All I'm doing is helping him get some evidence against Hanlon before he turns himself in."

"By *faking* his death. I've already seen the obituary.

Comic Sans was kind of fitting, but you should have told him to pound sand."

"It's only for a few days. I'm not even letting him stay in the house, Cass. I gave him a tent and pointed him toward your hideaway back in the woods. And I'm meeting Hanlon in a couple of hours, so we may even be able to wrap this up sooner."

She shook her head. "Hanlon gives me the creeps. You shouldn't go. And Dad shouldn't have asked you."

"I thought you'd *want* me to help him. I'm going to record the meeting. That's why I need the envelope your dad sent. He said there was some financial information in there that I could use to sort of...prime the pump, so to speak." I lowered my voice. "Not the cash. He said that's yours, for your degree in French feminist theory or whatever."

She snorted. "I don't want his money. There's enough in my college account already. You keep it. Or give it back to him. He's going to need it for his legal bills. And you might, too, if you get mixed up in this."

"Well, I'm not taking it. If you want to give it back to your dad, fine. I'm only going to let Hanlon know that I'm aware of his partnership with Joe. I'll tell him I want in. Then we can—"

"You need to call Detective Webb. Let him handle this, Mom."

Cassie's sudden tilt toward obeying the letter of the law was a little odd. She was usually more than willing to bend the rules a bit in service of solving a case. Maybe the paralegal training was giving her a new respect for toeing the legal line? That still seemed off, though, given that earlier in the day I'd been the one cautioning her about running afoul of the law when snooping around in Nashville.

"This is no more dangerous than dozens of stories I worked on at the *News-Journal*, hon. I'm not going to help him cover up his financial crimes if that's what you're worried about. But I really don't want your dad to end up in prison for a murder that he didn't commit. Do you?"

"No," she admitted. "But he got himself into this. He knew there were risks. And what if *you* end up in prison for obstructing justice by trying to help him? Just give whatever evidence you have to Webb." She shook her head and flung the dishcloth into the sink.

"I will. After I actually have something substantive to give him. Ed is going with me."

"Fabulous. Now he'll be at risk, too."

The bell over the door sounded and two teens headed toward the espresso bar. Cassie sighed and reached under the counter for the envelope. She pushed it toward me but kept a grip on one edge as she stared me directly in the eyes. "I told Dad last night that he needed to get back on Nathan's motorbike and turn himself in to the cops. Nathan would probably be alive today if he'd had the guts to turn himself in as soon as he figured out what was going on. I specifically asked him not to pull you into this mess. So if you're doing this for me, *please don't.*"

"I'm not." I could tell from her expression that she knew that wasn't entirely true, but at least the words gave her some emotional cover. "You said you'd have felt bad if you didn't use your ability to try and help Nathan. Well, I feel the same way, okay? Despite everything he's done, it feels wrong not to help your father. But I'll be careful. And I'll give you a call when the meeting is over."

Cassie rolled her eyes and headed to the other end of the bar to take the new customers' orders.

I had no desire to take the money with me. I opened the express mail packet and found a manilla folder with the printouts Joe had mentioned. When Cassie came back to start the order, I pushed the envelope with the money and Joe's other documents toward her.

"I've got what I need for the meeting. You should put this in the safe. Or give it to your dad. It's up to you."

She snatched the envelope and put it under the counter, then went back to preparing the drinks. It was a clear signal that our conversation was over, so I left. We could talk it all out later.

Once I was back at my office, I thumbed through the printouts and entered a few bits of info into my phone—dates, prices, and property addresses. I took a photograph of several emails, along with partnership papers bearing the signatures of Hanlon, Nathan, and Joe. Then I stashed the envelope into the filing cabinet. As I closed the drawer, however, I realized it was the first place Hanlon would look if he broke in searching for it. So I pulled the envelope back out and headed down into the "morgue" in the basement where we keep old copies of the *Star*. I tugged one of the volumes off the shelf and stuffed the folder between the pages of newsprint. Then I headed back upstairs to call Ed and make sure he could still provide back up, given the change in times.

Ed said that he could definitely take a break. That he *needed* a break come to think of it and was pretty close to being finished. It might even have been true, although it was a little hard to tell over the phone. He agreed to pick me up at seven-thirty and said we'd grab dinner at Mountain View. It wouldn't be a romantic dinner, since we'd be at separate tables across the room, but the food would be a nice change of pace from our usual options.

It was a little after five, which left me with about two hours to kill. I shot a quick text to Wren to fill her in, and then spent the remaining time inking up the press and printing off the interior pages. Out of habit, I always printed the inside pages first. In Nashville, the reasoning for that had been clear. Big events frequently altered the planned headlines only a few hours before we went to press. Breaking news was a rarity here in Thistlewood, but Mr. Dealey had always followed the same rule. As he noted, you never knew when someone's cow might die and bump the town council meeting right off the front page.

When I finished the interior, I put the stack of pages into the Collector and checked the time. I'd have to wait and print page one later, but I went ahead and inked Stella up a second time and ran a galley for a final proofread. That way, I'd be all set to finish the job when Ed and I returned from Mountain View and could hopefully get out of here at a decent hour. I didn't like the idea of stumbling into Memory Gardens at midnight, and not just because I'd have to wake Wren up. Plus, I'd need to be back in the office by around five the next morning in order to start my deliveries.

I finished my proofread, fixed one spacing error, and then spent a few minutes at the sink trying to remove most of the ink from my fingers and fingernails. Once they were reasonably close to their normal shade, I ran a comb through my hair, applied a dab of lipstick, and then went out front to wait for Ed. When I'd gone back into the press room earlier, there had still been quite a bit of daylight, so I hadn't turned on the overhead light. Now the room was mostly dark, and as I reached for the switch, I had the eerie sensation of being watched. I jerked my head toward the front window and was startled to find a large man peeking through. Too large to be Ed. Larger even than Hanlon. His bulk was silhouetted by the twilight sky and lit windows on the other side of the street.

Even before my fingers flicked the light switch, I realized it was Jesse Yarnell. What the heck did he want?

Comic Sans for the Ex   259

I went over to unlock the door, still trying to get my heart back to its normal rhythm.

"Jesse," I said. "You startled me."

"Oh. Sorry," he said. "Patsy's mom wanted me to come over and ask where you found Olivia's quilt. She's thinking it must have been inside the church, since a bunch of people saw you and Wren sneaking around outside the building."

"We weren't sneaking around. Just leaving the place after the Women's Club meeting."

I suspected that it was mostly Jesse who wanted to know about the quilt, but he wasn't telling a complete lie. Teresa Grimes, who was watching from her cashier stand across the street at the diner, gave me a little finger wave. She clearly wanted to find out whether her tip about Bobbi Blevins had paid off, and I hated to disappoint her. But I'd promised Jenny I'd keep it private aside from Ed and Wren. Telling Jesse and Teresa would be pretty much the polar opposite of keeping it private.

"The quilt got packed away," I said. "In a trunk."

"How'd you find it?"

I shrugged. "Just a matter of getting people communicating with each other."

Jesse was clearly disappointed by my answer. Teresa probably would be, too. But they'd no doubt find something else to chatter about within the hour.

"Oh," Jesse said. "Almost forgot. Some guy came into the diner a little while ago. Asked how long it had been since we'd seen your ex here in Thistlewood. It has to be three years. Maybe four. Anyway, he was talking about him like he was in the present tense, so I'm guessin' he doesn't think the guy is dead. You didn't decide to get a little post-divorce revenge while you were in Nashville, did you?"

"You're not funny, Jesse."

He grinned. "Of course I am. But mostly I just wanted to let you know someone is pokin' around in your business. I told the guy if he had any questions about your family, he'd have to ask you."

I started to say something like *yeah, sure*...because it was hard to imagine him passing up the opportunity to spread a bit of gossip. But then I realized he was serious. Jesse would have been happy to chatter about my business non-stop with his buddy Mack or any of the other regulars. But Hanlon wasn't from-here.

Technically speaking, neither was I. Oh sure, I'd lived here from age thirteen to eighteen, but then I'd moved off to Nashville. And while my parents had remained here and I'd visited frequently in the summers, when I first moved back, it had been abundantly clear that I was still not-from-here.

Apparently, I'd paid my dues in the past eighteen months. I'd probably never be considered from-here in the same way as those who shared a crib in Sunday School and could swap anecdotes about their first day of kindergarten, but I was from-here enough that Jesse and the Gossip Gang were willing to circle the wagons to protect me from a nosy outsider.

I smiled. "Thanks, Jesse. I appreciate that."

Ed's truck pulled up to the curb at that point. "Hey, Jess. You making moves on my girl?"

"Wouldn't think of it." Jesse gave me a wink and added, "Don't worry. I won't tell Ed about your green-eyed side guy."

The words were in a stage whisper, but still plenty loud enough for Ed to hear. Jesse walked away, chuckling to himself.

"What's this about a side guy?" Ed asked as I slid into the truck.

"Hanlon apparently stopped into the diner to see if any of them had spotted Joe lately." I shook my head and laughed. "Town gossips have impressive powers of observation. I'm a trained journalist, and even I hadn't paid any attention to the color of Keith Hanlon's eyes."

"Once you get the *Star's* circulation up a bit, you should hire Jesse as a reporter."

"Sure," I said. "Right after I treat us to a trip around the world and buy a swanky vacation house in Florida. Did you finish the edits?"

"This close." He held up his hand showing his forefinger and thumb barely apart. "Another hour. Maybe two. How about you?"

"Same. I just need to print the front and collate."

"After your date with your green-eyed side guy."

"Hey, I've got to have someone waiting in the wings in case you fail to pay up for me solving the quilt mystery."

"What? You found it? Why didn't you tell me?"

"Sorry," I said. "I thought I'd let Olivia break the good news. Jenny was taking the quilt over to her house after the meeting. Olivia didn't stop by?"

"She might have," Ed said. "Owen barked at someone, but they didn't ring the bell. Probably because I had the sign up."

The sign was a door hanger that I'd bought for him on Etsy a few months back. *Writer at Work. Do Not Disturb.* Owen's vocalizations rendered it much less effective, but Ed said he found it easier to get back into the flow if it was just the dog barking rather than him answering the door and having a conversation that didn't revolve around his characters' discussions of murder and mayhem.

I filled him in on the details as we headed up the mountain.

"So Teresa was right, more or less," he said.

"Yes, although Wren would be quick to tell you that she had it solved first, even without Teresa's firsthand experience with Bobbi's larcenous nature. And she's not particularly happy with the fact that, once again, the woman is basically getting a slap on the wrist. Olivia was sort of right, too. Lillian and Bobbi were definitely in cahoots. Lillian wanted bragging rights and Bobbi wanted the trip to Nashville, at least in part so she could mess up Steve and Jenny's romantic getaway."

Ed chuckled. "A romantic getaway to a women's club conference. Steve Blevins is living the life."

"I think he's getting the better end of the deal, since he's lucky enough to be spending the time with Jenny and I cannot fathom what she sees in him. And the Opryland Resort might not be Paris, but I'm sure it will be infinitely more romantic for both of them *without* Roberta Blevins tagging along."

Chapter Twenty-Two

MY PHONE WAS in plain sight, face up on the table. If Hanlon wanted to check to make sure I wasn't using it to record, I'd be happy to let him. Hopefully, he wouldn't ask to check beneath the napkin on my lap, where Ed's phone was hiding, with the recording app open and waiting.

Like the app, I was also waiting, and my patience was wearing thin. Even though Ed had set the phone's timeout for five minutes, I'd still had to tap the screen twice to make sure it didn't shut down. In another minute, I'd need to tap it yet again.

I glanced across the restaurant at Ed, who was sitting near the hostess station at a small table beneath a framed mountain landscape. It wasn't a bad painting, but the view from my table was much better. The restaurant is set at the very edge of a cliff, and each of the tall windows that lined the back wall of Mountain View

Grill offer a stunning view of the valley. Tonight, the tree line was illuminated by faint streaks of color from the last remnants of the sunset, while a few early evening stars twinkled in the darker sky above.

Ed had called his friend—the manager, not the chef, as it turned out—and let him know what we were planning a few hours before we arrived. He'd parked the truck at the far end of the lot, out of view of the hotel. We entered the restaurant separately, about ten minutes apart, just to be on the safe side.

"Are you ready to order, ma'am?" It was the second time the waitress had asked, so I suspected the manager hadn't filled her in on why we were here. "Maybe a drink? We have a wonderful selection of wines."

It was tempting. But I needed a clear mind when Hanlon finally decided to make his entrance.

"Not yet," I told her. "But maybe a cup of coffee?"

The waitress bowed her head and then vanished into the kitchen.

While I waited on my coffee, I sent Hanlon another text. I'd sent the first one after I was seated to let him know I'd arrived. When he didn't respond, I'd assumed he was on his way over from the hotel next door. Then I'd assumed that he had a phone with lousy reception in the mountains. I was now moving on to the next assumption...that he wasn't coming.

Ten minutes later, with the coffee cup now empty, I looked over at Ed and shrugged. I tucked a five under the saucer and headed over to the hostess station. Ed followed. At this point, Hanlon either knew I'd brought backup to the meeting and had bolted or there was some other issue.

"Excuse me," Ed said to the hostess. "We were supposed to meet someone here about thirty minutes ago. I don't suppose you have any messages from a Mr. Hanlon?"

The girl, who looked to be in her early twenties, shook her head.

I gave her a brief description of Hanlon—tall, pale with dark hair and a husky build—and asked if she'd seen him.

"Oh, yeah. They're staying over at the hotel. He and his wife were in for dinner last night and I delivered room service to them right after I came on shift this afternoon. He might have...um..." She was clearly about to say something but decided it wouldn't be appropriate.

"We're actually kind of worried about him," I prompted gently.

"You could check over at the hotel. Maybe they'll ring up to the room. It's possible he fell asleep or he's...indisposed."

I had a feeling there was a story behind her last comment, but the girl's lips were now pressed firmly shut, as if they'd revealed too much and she was wishing for a zipper.

"We'll do that," Ed told her. "Thanks for your time."

I handed back his phone as we walked into the parking lot.

"What do we know about the woman Hanlon is with?" Ed asked.

"Not much. Joe said he was dating the niece of one of the guys in the drug ring. I only caught a brief glimpse of her when Hanlon pulled into the parking lot. Dark hair. Attractive. Thirty-five, maybe forty."

"Is she actively involved in all of this?"

"No clue," I said. "Joe only mentioned her in passing. He might know more. Should I call him?"

"Maybe. Let's see how this goes first."

The newly renovated Mountain View Lodge sits right next door, and like the restaurant, it hugs the rim of the cliff. It isn't very impressive from the front—just a narrow, three-story structure, with one row of rooms per floor. Each room has a tiny, enclosed balcony that juts somewhat precariously over the edge.

"I'm sure the view is fabulous," I said, "but those balconies look like they're about to slide off and tumble down the mountain."

"They're sturdy enough. But there's a reason they're enclosed now. In the early 1990s when I was a deputy, they were open. This was a Holiday Inn back then, and everyone swore the place was haunted." Ed pointed to one of the rooms on the top floor. "The sheriff, Charlie Pitt, referred to that as the suicide suite."

He was about to say more, but something off to the right caught his eye. I followed his gaze and saw a thin woman with light brown hair pushing a housekeeping cart toward the dumpster on the side of the building.

"That's Billy's cousin. Pretty sure you met her at one of our poker games. Kyla? Kayla?" He snapped his fingers a couple of times, trying to kick his brain into gear.

"I'm thinking maybe that's her daughter's name."

"You're right," he said. "Oh, well. I'll wing it. Come on."

The woman unloaded several bags of trash and turned the cart around. Ed gave her a wave and we picked up the pace a bit.

"Hey, girl!" Ed gave her a broad smile. "I didn't know you were working here. How's your old man? You remember Ruth, don't you?"

We exchanged greetings. Then she and Ed spent a minute or so in idle small-town chitchat, talking about Billy's kids, her own son who was a pitcher on the high school baseball team, and other points of commonality.

"Listen," he said, "we were supposed to meet a contact over at the Grill for a story Ruth's investigating, but the guy didn't show. He's not answering his phone or texts, and he has a heart condition. Any chance you could stop by with some fresh towels or something and see if he's okay? I could go the formal route and call Billy, but...seems like a waste of his time."

"Yeah," I said. "It's entirely possible that the guy is ghosting me because he's changed his mind about the interview, and if that's the case, we'll leave. But I'd hate not to check just in case there's something wrong."

"Sure," she said. "I can do that. Do you know what room?"

Ed and I exchanged a look. "No," he said. "That may be a problem."

The woman chuckled. "Probably not. It's early in the season. We've only got five rooms occupied tonight. If you describe him, I can probably figure it out."

I gave her the same description I'd given the hostess at the restaurant. "He might have green eyes, too, and he's here with his girlfriend."

"Don't know about the eyes, but we've got a couple up on the second floor with a guy who matches that description. I remember because he called down to Dale at the front desk to order ice and got his nose bent out of shape when Dale told him there was an ice bucket in his room and an ice machine in the stairwell. I need to drop the trash cart off first, but if y'all want to wait down in the lobby, I'll check on him."

She pushed the cart through the side door as Ed and I walked back around to the main entrance. Something occurred to me at that point. "Hold up," I told him, and then jogged over to the far side of the building to look in the parking lot.

"He may have left already," I told Ed when I got back. "The BMW is gone. Don't know why I didn't think to check that in the first place."

"Well, that's easy enough to find out."

Dale, the guy at the front desk, didn't even have to consult the guest list. "They didn't check out. The woman took the car about thirty minutes ago. I saw her drive past and it was definitely just her. She's probably heading to the package store. They seemed a bit annoyed that we don't have a bar on the premis...es."

His last word was punctuated by a scream, high and loud, from the floor above us. I took off across the lobby and up the stairs. Ed followed at a slower pace, taking the steps with a grunt and a curse that was barely audible over the fresh screech that echoed off to my left when I reached the landing. It was coming from about halfway down the corridor. A thin sliver of white light spilled out into the hall from an open door. I ran toward it, turning into the room and nearly running smack into Billy's cousin. My arms reached out and caught her before we could fully collide. She was trembling and with a thrust to the side, popped out of my grasp like a cork from a wine bottle and ran toward Ed.

I let him deal with her and stepped into the room. The bathroom door was open, giving me a clear view of the interior. Hanlon's lifeless body was half-propped against the bathtub. He was fully clothed, thankfully, and the cord from a window shade dangled from his neck. As with Nathan, his eyes were wide open.

"Ruth," Ed said from beside me. "We need to get out of here. This is a crime scene. Let's go."

"Right," I said, allowing him to pull me away. When we reached the door, however, I turned back and took a few steps toward the bathroom. I didn't really want to see the body again, but I needed to double check something.

Ed cleared his throat.

"I'm coming. His eyes are *brown*."

He gave me a baffled look and then realized what I was talking about.

"But I have seen someone with green eyes recently," I said. "Mark Webb."

Billy's cousin was sitting on one of the sofas when we reached the lobby. The guy behind the desk was standing next to her with a bottle of water. "Here, Leslie. I called the police."

She stared at the bottle as if she had no idea what it was. "Thanks, Dale."

"Leslie," Ed said, clearly glad to finally have her name. "Are you okay?"

She shook her head. "Not really. I've never found a dead body before. I've seen dead people at the funeral home, but that's different." She looked over at the staircase. "I mean that was *dead* dead... Maybe even murdered. It's different."

Definitely murdered, but I didn't correct her. Most people are lucky enough never to actually stumble across a murder victim. I'd seen more than my share during my years at the *News-Journal*, but I had naively thought that type of reporting was in my past when I took over the *Star*.

"What time did the woman leave in the BMW?" Ed asked.

Dale scratched his head. "Thirty minutes ago? Maybe a little longer."

"Can either of you describe her?" I asked, since I'd

only seen her through the window of the BMW, from the neck up.

"Yeah," Leslie said. "Your age, maybe a little older. Blond hair. Average height. Slightly above average weight, although that was mostly..." She cupped her hands about eight inches out from her own breasts.

Oh, crap.

"We have to go. Right now." I grabbed Ed's arm with one hand and pulled out my phone with the other.

Tammy Roscoe had killed Nathan, And now she'd killed Keith Hanlon, too.

I had a sinking feeling that Joe was next.

And worse yet, if Tammy wanted to lure him out of hiding, the perfect bait was currently behind the espresso bar at The Buzz.

Chapter Twenty-Three

I CALLED Cassie as we walked back to Ed's truck. Her phone sent me straight to voicemail. Same for Dean's, which doubled as their business line since they still needed to cut corners as much as possible. They were the only two working this shift so that wasn't too surprising. I left a terse message, then tapped out a text to Cassie, telling her to call me immediately, emergency, all caps, double exclamation point. She ignored phone messages all the time, and texts always seemed to get through more quickly.

When we reached the truck, I clicked my seatbelt into place and started scanning through my recent messages for the burner phone Joe had used. It took a minute to find, partly because I kept glancing back up at the road each time I spotted headlights. Ed knows these roads well, and I was sure that he'd driven them at high speed plenty of times when he was sheriff. But my heart was already in my throat and narrow mountain roads always make me edgy at night. It didn't help that the light drizzle forecast for this evening had now begun.

"You're sure about this?" Ed asked as he screeched out of the parking lot.

"Sure that Tammy is planning to kill Joe? No. Not at all. But I am fairly sure that she killed Nathan. She was at his place snooping around the next day. And Joe said she wasn't happy about his decision to follow Nathan's lead and go to the police. So I don't think it's an unreasonable assumption that she killed Hanlon, given that she was apparently there when it happened, and she's taken off with the guy's car."

"Another possibility," Ed said, "would be that someone else killed Hanlon and Tammy took off because she was scared that she might be next. You said Hanlon seemed worried about his partners, and while they might not get involved directly in this sort of thing, I'm sure they're not above hiring someone to handle it. Maybe they got tired of waiting for their money."

"If that's true, then the same partner killed Nathan. And are drug lords generally fond of garroting people? I'll admit I haven't known many firsthand—"

He gave a short chuckle. "You haven't known *many*?"

"Okay, *any*. But I investigated a few at the *News-Journal*, and I've seen plenty on TV. They tend to prefer guns to extension cords."

"True. Joe's not answering either?"

"Nope. His burner phone must be T-Mobile,

because he was griping about dead zones when Wren and I stopped by this afternoon. I'm really hoping for his sake that he wasn't lying when he said he told Tammy he was staying with a friend up north of Nashville. Maybe she headed in that direction."

"Let me call Billy," Ed said. "He might be able to get over to your place faster and it might be easier if he's the one telling Blevins why we left Mountain View before he could take our statement."

"Except, Billy's headed up to investigate Hanlon's death. We'll probably pass his cruiser any minute now."

"It's an election year. Steve's not going to let Billy take the lead on a murder investigation."

"No, but assuming everything went according to Jenny's plan, Blevins is in Nashville by now."

Ed cursed softly. "Well, this is a first. Can't believe I'm actually a little disappointed to learn Blevins is out of the county. Maybe Billy can send Mason."

When he got Billy on the phone, however, we learned that Deputy Mason, whose services they shared with a neighboring county, was at least twenty minutes away.

"Why does Ruth think the woman is heading to her place?" Billy asked.

Ed shot me a quick look out of the side of his eye, clearly debating how much he should tell Billy about Joe. "Um...just a hunch, really. It's also entirely possible that she's headed for the interstate, so you might want to get Sheila to put out an APB on that blue BMW. Might also want to check and see if he had a gun in the room. Ruth spotted a shoulder holster when he stopped by the *Star* yesterday. So if it's not in the hotel room, you can assume she's armed. Anyway, we'll check Ruth's place and downtown. I hated leaving before you arrived, but...Cassie could be at The Buzz or at the cabin. If the woman is looking for Tate, I'm guessing she'll start by seeing what his daughter knows. Give me a call when you're finished up at Mountain View and we can meet somewhere for you to take our statements."

"Okay. Call me if the situation changes. I mean, from what you said, the guy at Mountain View ain't going anywhere."

"Yeah, and if you peel off from a murder investigation on what could well be a wild goose chase, Blevins will have your head. I'll call if we need you." Ed ended the call and then flipped on his wipers since the rain was beginning to pick up a bit. "Looks like we're on our own. No officers in the vicinity."

"Based on what Jesse told me, I'm pretty sure there was a cop in the diner asking questions a few hours ago. I've got Webb's card so we could call him. Unless..." I stopped, not really wanting to voice my next thought.

"Unless what?" Ed prompted.

"Unless your bad-cop radar doesn't work so well over the telephone? Webb *could* be the cop Hanlon's partners had on their payroll, in which case, what you said earlier about Tammy being on the run from the killer rather than *being* the killer seems a bit more plausible. I mean, how common is it for a detective to drive over three hours one way to follow a lead?"

Ed shrugged. "Wouldn't say it's *common*, but it's definitely not unheard of. I took a few road trips in my day. Even a couple on my off-duty hours, following up on hunches. But you're right. You should probably hold off on calling him. Maybe Wren could run over and check on Cassie?"

"She's got a visitation tonight. Hold on, though." I pressed the button on my phone. "Call Pat's."

A cheery voice answered a few seconds later. "Pat's Diner. We can still do takeout if you hurry, but we close at nine."

"Patsy, it's Ruth. Is Jesse there, by any chance? I don't have his number and I have a favor to ask. It's kind of urgent."

"Does it have anything to do with the murder up at the Mountain View?"

I shot a look over at Ed. How the heck did they find out so soon?

"Indirectly," I told her. "Sort of."

"Well, that's no answer at all," she grumbled.

"Could I speak to Jesse?"

"Sure. Hey, Jess!"

A second later, Jesse was on the line. "What's up? If you're looking for your green-eyed lover boy, he ain't been in since I talked to you."

"No. I need a favor. I can't get through to Cassie or Dean. Wren's in the middle of a memorial service--"

"Yeah," he said. "Mary Quinn. She went kind of fast, didn't she? I was talking to her cousin Bertie this morning and--"

"Jesse," I said, trying to keep the impatience out of my voice. "Cassie's not answering her phone. I need someone to run down to The Buzz and tell her to call me immediately."

"Why don't you just run down and tell her yourself?"

"Because I'm still about ten minutes out of town."

"Then who was over at the *Star* just a minute ago? The light was on and I saw someone walking around. Kinda short, so I thought it was you. Maybe it was Cassie?"

"Maybe." I said, although I couldn't think of any reason Cassie would have gone to my office. "How long ago was that?"

"A couple minutes ago. Right, Mac?" A male voice in the background agreed.

"Was there a blue BMW parked at the curb?" I asked.

"Not that I noticed. But I *have* seen a blue BMW driving through town the past few days."

"Could you get the message to Cassie for me? I'd *really* appreciate it."

"Sure," he said, a little begrudgingly. I could hear him getting off his stool at the counter. "Patsy ain't gonna like it, though. She may have buried the hatchet with

Cassie and Dean, but I'm not supposed to step foot in The Buzz."

"Tell her it's a personal favor to me, Jesse. I owe you big."

After I ended the call, Ed said, "You don't think that was Cassie in your office?"

"I don't know."

"You think Joe might have mentioned to Tammy that he mailed some cash to Cassie for college? If so, that could be what she's looking for at the *Star*."

"Joe was dumb enough to mail it, so he might have been dumb enough to tell her. He said Tammy knew the combination to the safe at his office. I'm guessing she also had a decent idea of how much money he kept in it. He apparently told her he was staying with a college friend up north of Nashville, but I have no idea what else he might have said. When I spoke to Tammy at Nathan's house, she was pretty upset. Seemed to blame me for Joe's apparent suicide. Maybe she decided she was owed more than whatever Joe had promised her. Either way, if she's looking for the money, she didn't find it. I stashed the papers inside one of the binders down in the morgue, but I left everything else with Cassie."

My phone rang. Dean's number popped up on the screen. "Hey, Ruth. Sorry I didn't answer earlier. Had a customer come in and then I had to run upstairs and give the gamers the ten-minute warning that we're about to close. Not used to running the place on my own."

"On your own? Where's Cassie?"

"She drove over to your place. Things were slow, so she decided to take a couple of sandwiches over to her dad. And she...um...had something else she wanted to talk to him about."

Probably chewing him out for getting me and Ed involved in all of this, I thought.

"I've been trying to call her for the past ten minutes, Dean. Keith Hanlon is dead. Strangled, like Nathan. And we're thinking maybe Tammy Roscoe killed them. That's the woman that Cassie's dad—"

"Yeah. Cassie thinks Tammy may have killed her husband, too. Why is she in Thistlewood?"

"I'm not sure. Why does she think Tammy killed her husband?"

I realized the answer even before Dean began explaining. When she called me on the way back from Nashville and I asked whether she'd located Nathan she mentioned finding *someone* in the neighborhood, but it wasn't him.

"Did Cassie say if he was strangled?"

"No. Blunt force to the side of the head. Cassie said she'd seen him before. First time was back when she was in middle school. He was one of the first ghosts she sensed, even before her grandparents. Freaked her out because the guy was pretty messed up. She said she just avoided the area after that. Yesterday was the first time she'd been on that side of the street since she was twelve."

"So that's what she meant by *the bad side of the street*. Huh."

The first time Cassie had mentioned seeing ghosts was at my parents' funeral, where she'd very nearly passed out. My mom and dad died in a car accident when Cassie was thirteen. For several years before that, she'd been odd about going near graveyards or even hospitals, but she'd never explicitly said she'd seen anything out of the ordinary. I'm sure she was scared that we'd think she was just imagining things, and we probably would have. Cassie had a really vivid imagination as a kid and would come downstairs in the mornings to tell me about the crazy dreams she had the night before, some good and some not-so-good. But apparently when the nightmares followed her into the daytime, she'd just withdrawn. I felt awful that she'd seen something that had to have been traumatizing but hadn't been willing to tell me.

Ed's phone buzzed with an incoming text. He flipped it around so he could read it but didn't try to respond since he was driving.

"Cassie didn't connect the dots until a few hours ago," Dean continued, "when she tracked down a wedding picture of Charles and Tammy Roscoe in the online archives of the Nashville paper. She debated for a bit, and then decided she had to go talk to her dad. Even though she was sure he wouldn't believe her, that he'd think she was making all of it up, she said she had to try. And now I'm worried...you said she's not answering?"

"No. But you know Cassie. She's almost as bad as I am about plugging in her phone. It's probably charging in the car. I'm sure she's fine." I said the words almost as much to calm myself as to calm him.

"I'll kick the customers out now. Heading that way..."

"We're closer, Dean. We'll be there in three minutes. And I'm sure she's okay. Jesse said he saw someone inside the Star not much longer ago than that. Is it possible that Cassie stopped by there first?"

He thought for a moment. "It's possible, I guess. She didn't say anything about that though, and I saw her drive out of the parking lot about a half hour ago. So unless she circled back around..."

"That means it was probably Tammy, then. Which is good because it means she can't have been at the house long. I'll call you back."

"The message was from Billy," Ed said after I ended the call with Dean. "No gun in the hotel room. But he did find extra ammo and the shoulder holster. So we have to assume she's armed. Billy's on his way, but maybe you should call Webb. I think the odds of him being on the take a pretty slim at this point."

I nodded, pulled up Webb's number from my recent calls, and dialed it again.

And was instantly kicked to voicemail.

I cursed and smacked the dashboard with the palm of my hand. "What is it with the stupid phones today?

What's the point in even having the darn things if no one answers?"

So I left a message, telling him that Tammy had killed Nathan, Keith Hanlon, and quite possibly her ex-husband about a dozen years ago. That she was armed and dangerous, most likely holding hostages, and while the local police were on their way, we could use backup. Then I texted him my address—729 Mountain Ridge Rd.

The light from my cabin was just ahead. My driveway is fairly long, with a buffer of trees that keep me from having to stare out at traffic. There's just one thin spot as you approach from the west and I managed to catch a quick glimpse of the yard as we passed it.

"Two cars," I said. "Cassie's Honda and the blue BMW. Joe is supposed to be in a tent out in the woods. There's a clearing almost directly opposite the shed and we should be able to pick up the trail that leads down to the remnants of the old playhouse my dad helped Cassie build. There's a unicorn flag, or what's left of it, hanging from one of the branches. But Wren was telling Joe stories about Remy when we were here earlier, so I wouldn't be surprised if he pitched the tent on the deck or maybe under it, given the rain."

"I'll check there first." Ed cut the lights and the engine as he turned into the drive. The Silverado coasted along for a few yards due to the slight incline. He tapped the brakes about twenty yards from the BMW. It was a dark night, with just a sprinkling of stars and a tiny sliver of moon mostly hidden by the cloud cover, and we were still just inside the buffer of trees. Even from the front porch, his dark green truck shouldn't be visible.

He flipped the dome light override switch so the car wouldn't light up when he opened the door. Then he opened the glove box and pulled out his pistol. "Okay. I'm going to work my way around to the back using the tree cover. You need to stay here."

"No way, Ed. I'm going with you."

"If you were armed, I would agree. But—"

"You need another set of eyes."

"Ruth, right now, my primary goal is to protect Cassie. Protecting Joe is a very secondary goal, and only it doesn't interfere with keeping Cassie safe. If you're here in the truck, I can focus on that objective. But if you're out there with me, in potential danger, I won't be able to concentrate on Cassie. So, please. Promise me you'll wait in the car."

I wanted to argue with him. It would rip my insides to shreds waiting here, knowing that he and Cassie were in danger. Every second would seem like an eternity. But he was right.

"Okay, under one condition." I dialed his number from my phone. "Answer that. I'll put mine on mute. Stick it in your pocket and don't hang up. If I hear that you're in trouble, I'm coming in."

"Agreed." He answered the call and then stuck the phone into the breast pocket of his jacket. Then he reached into a small box beneath the seat and pulled out a second pistol. "This is my Glock. It's point-and-shoot, kind of like your Nikon. The safety is in the trigger, so you don't need to fumble around trying to find it. Hold it tight. Both hands. Point and shoot."

I recoiled automatically when he placed it on the console between us.

"Just a precaution, okay? If it's you or your ex's crazy girlfriend, you'll be glad it's here." He leaned over and kissed me. "But I don't think you're going to need it. I'll be back with our girl before you know it."

Chapter Twenty-Four

EVERYTHING ED HAD JUST TOLD me made perfect sense. He was an excellent shot and had the marksmanship trophies on his mantel to prove it. Even though the hip injury might slow him down a bit, there was no doubt in my mind that the odds of getting Cassie back safely were better if I stayed behind, given that I'd resisted his repeated efforts to put a gun in my hands.

My only question now was whether that had been a mistake? If Tammy killed Cassie or Ed—or Joe, for that matter—my moral stance on weapons was going to be very cold comfort.

The flat black pistol on the console taunted me. I hated feeling useless. My nerves jangled at each crack of the branch that I heard on my phone as Ed moved slowly through the underbrush and into the woods. After a couple of minutes of anxious watching, I picked up a slight movement inside the tree line parallel with the back deck of the cabin and then Ed stepped briefly into view. The deck was apparently empty, because he stepped back into the trees and I once again heard the rustle of his footsteps on the leaves and pine needles as he headed back toward the clearing, but then he was gone again. I took deep breaths and dug my nails in my palms.

Despite all of this, I fully intended to wait. To keep my promise. But just as Ed stepped back into the trees, I spotted an arc of light from the corner of my eye. Looking toward the cabin, I saw it again. A flashlight, inside the house. This time, the swoop of light swept past a window, and I picked up the silhouette of Cronkite, perched on the picnic table on the side deck where we birdwatch.

My first thought, fueled mostly by sheer hope, was that it could be Cassie inside the house. Maybe the power was out? But I knew that didn't make sense. I could see the glow from the lights on the back porch. And Cronkite was outside. Even if you ignored the fact that he doesn't like rain, if Cassie was in the house, Cronk would be right there with her.

This was confirmed a moment later when Tammy Roscoe stepped out onto the front porch with flashlight in hand and scanned the yard. She started close to the porch and I crouched down out of instinct when the beam began moving toward the truck. It might have remained hidden in the dark, but the flashlight would definitely reflect back.

I unmuted my phone. "Ed, Tammy was *inside* the house. She's outside now and she's spotted the truck. I ducked down, though, so I don't think she spotted me."

"I'm coming," he said in a low voice. "I can see the unicorn flag, but there's no tent here. He wasn't on the deck, though, and..."

Ed was still talking, but I didn't hear what he said because the flashlight came back around for another pass, lingering on the truck. It wasn't any brighter than before, however, and the beam seemed the same size when it moved on toward the trees, so it was likely that Tammy was still on the front porch.

"...thought I heard someone out here moving around, so maybe they're a little way over."

A familiar yowl filled my ears, followed by Tammy's scream.

And then two shots rang out.

At first, I didn't breathe. Every foul name in my lexicon ran through my head in that instant.

The crazy fool actually *shot at my cat*. Cronk could be lying on the lawn, bleeding or dead.

I had already known that Tammy had killed. I'd seen Nathan's body, and now Hanlon's, too. But it was that shot, the actual proof that she would fire on a defenseless animal, that hammered home the fact that Tammy Roscoe was a murderer. Up to that point, I'd thought that she might use Cassie as leverage against Joe, but I'd never emotionally grasped the reality of the situation. If she'd shoot Cronkite, she probably wouldn't hesitate to shoot Cassie if she didn't get what she wanted.

My hand closed around the gun. It was lighter than I'd expected, and the metal was cool against my palm. I slowly opened the door and for a split second I froze, fully convinced that the dome light would flick on even though I watched Ed push the override switch. But the inside of the cab remained mercifully dark as I slipped out into the night. I pushed the door shut as quietly as possible and scurried in a low crouch toward the woods.

"Ruth? Are you okay?" It was Ed. His voice sounded unnaturally loud, even though it was barely above a whisper and I had the speaker on low.

"I'm okay," I answered, hoping I was speaking loud enough for him to hear. "I'm in the woods. I think she shot Cronkite. She's heading this way, so I'm cutting the sound."

"Where are you?" Tammy yelled, mere seconds after I stepped into the brush and crouched down. Had she spotted me?

"Come at me again and I'll blow your stupid head off! Try me and see, you little demon."

Cronkite. She must have missed him. Or maybe she only thought she missed?

I pushed that thought firmly out of my mind.

Tammy's voice was closer now and the beam of her

flashlight grew brighter as she moved toward the truck. Had she heard me close the door? Or was her curiosity simply piqued by the truck now blocking the driveway? I slipped behind one of the trees as quietly as possible, gripping the gun.

"Is that you, Joe?" She continued moving toward me as she spoke. "It didn't have to be like this."

I risked a glance to my right. This angle provided a better view of the back yard than I'd had inside the truck, and I could now see that the door to the shed was open and someone had turned on the light inside. If that had been the case earlier, Ed would have seen it when he stepped out of the woods to find out if Joe was on the deck.

"We had a good thing going," Tammy said. "But then you and Nathan had to go and ruin it. And if you think ten thousand bucks is going to buy me off, you're crazy. Do you know how many hours I sat in those stupid realtor classes so that I could be your partner? I *trusted* you."

Joe and Cassie were now in the doorway of the shed, two dark silhouettes against the light. Cassie had a key to the shed on her keyring. Maybe she'd taken pity on Joe out in the rain and moved him inside.

Tammy was at the truck now. I heard the door open, and everything was quiet for a moment. Then she slammed the door and yelled, "Did you spend the money you stole out of the safe at Riverfront on this truck? Or maybe you borrowed it from the *friend* you told me you were staying with up in Clarksville. I should have known you'd go running back to wifey, you dirty *liar*." She slammed her fist against the side of the truck.

Risking a glance back at the shed, I saw Joe step out and close the door behind him. I couldn't see Cassie, and I prayed that she was inside the shed and not out of sight because she was already halfway across the lawn heading in this direction.

"Tammy!" Joe yelled as he ran toward us. "Is that you? What the hell? You just scared the freakin' daylights out of Cassie's cat."

Cronk was okay. I leaned into the tree as relief flooded through me.

"What are you doing here?" he said. "I thought we were going to meet in Clarksville. I've got the money, babe, like I promised—"

"You *promised?*" Her head was already turned toward him, but now she whirled her entire body around to face him. The cab of the truck was partially blocking my view, so I couldn't tell for certain until she raised the pistol to shoulder height. A deep red scratch marked her right hand from the index finger to the wrist. There was a second smaller wound on the side of her face. "What makes you think your promises mean anything to me, Joey Tate?"

Joey? Since when was he *Joey*? Ick.

Cassie was now on the side deck with Cronkite. Her curiosity was clearly too strong to keep her inside the shed. As much as I hated that the cat had been scared, it was probably a blessing in disguise because that forced my daughter to remain at a distance. Cronk was still pretty wound up, wriggling in her arms. Cassie gave me a little wave and disappeared into the house so she could put him down. I just hoped she'd stay there.

"Come on, Tammy," Joe said. "Be reasonable, hon. No need to get all emotional about this. We'll work it out." His tone was one that I remembered all too well from pretty much any time we'd had a disagreement. It was condescending and it set my teeth on edge. I doubted it was going to win him any brownie points from the crazy woman with the gun.

"You're right," she said. Her voice, which had been straining higher and higher with each comment, almost to the point of squeaking, was now a lot closer to her normal tone and for a moment I thought maybe he'd found the one woman on earth who was actually susceptible to that tactic. But then she went on, in a voice that was almost perfectly flat. "No point in being emotional about it. I haven't found the cash you mailed to your daughter yet, but *you're* here, which means the other half is around here somewhere. Assuming you didn't spend it on this stupid truck."

"No, that's not..." Joe stopped, and I could almost hear the wheels turning as he tried to figure out whether to admit the truck wasn't his. "It's a rental. The cash is in the house. We can split it. Or, um...you know, you can just take it all. Whatever you want."

I heard a rustling sound off in the distance behind me. Ed was making decent time, but I wasn't sure how much we had left.

"Where in the house?" Tammy asked.

"In an envelope on the kitchen table, sweetie. And it's all yours. You're right. I haven't been fair. Come on, put down the gun."

Even if I hadn't known Tammy had already been inside my house, I could have told from her tone that Joe had strolled into a trap. I wasn't sure how much time she'd had to search the place. Probably not long from what Jesse had said, but even the most cursory of searches would have included an envelope on the kitchen table. He'd just lied to her face, and I really didn't think she was going to let that slide.

"Or..." She cocked her head slightly to the side and raised the gun a bit higher. "Maybe I'll just shoot you instead."

I stepped out of the trees and aimed the Glock at her head.

"Drop it, Tammy." My voice was shaking, but to my surprise, my hands were not.

Joe raised his eyebrows. "Ruth. Come on. I've got this. Tammy's just upset. And scared. It's been a rough couple of days for her. I know her. She's not a killer, okay?"

"The other three people she murdered probably thought the same thing."

"Four," said a voice behind me.

I jumped at the sound, startling so badly that it's a miracle I didn't pull the trigger. I'd been expecting Ed, but it wasn't his voice.

Mark Webb stepped out of the woods and now his gun was also pointed at Tammy. He moved around to the other side of the truck. "Put the weapon down, Ms. Roscoe."

Apparently, hearing it come from a male voice finally made the threat real for Joe. The second Tammy's eyes twitched toward Detective Webb, he dove for cover into the trees.

Tammy's lip began to tremble as she crouched down and put the gun on the grass. "You're wrong. I didn't kill anyone. I want a lawyer."

"You'll have one," Webb said. "Now back away from the weapon."

She hesitated and looked for a moment like she was going to make a lunge for the gun she'd just relinquished. But then she took a few steps back. Webb grabbed the gun and then proceeded to read Tammy her Miranda rights.

Ed stepped up behind me and touched my arm, "You can lower your weapon now."

I looked down, a little surprised to see that my arms were still outstretched, the muzzle of the gun still tracking Tammy. I lowered them slowly and that's when my hands decided to start shaking. Ed took the gun from me and wrapped an arm around my shoulders, pulling me back toward him.

"Cassie's fine," he said softly. "She stayed back with Cronkite, who's hissing mad."

"Yeah. She just moved him into the house. Hopefully, that will calm him down."

Ed looked over at Webb, who was attempting to cuff his prisoner. She wasn't making it easy. "Personally, I'd like to lock that woman in a room with Cronk now that she doesn't have a weapon. He seems *really* eager to have another go at her."

"I'll bet. I'm glad Webb got my message. But where's his car?"

"He was heading this way already. Cassie called him. You'll have to get the details from her. But *your* message is the reason he parked over at the Faircloths' farm and came through the wood. If he was walking into a hostage situation, he didn't want to announce his arrival. Webb is who I heard behind me right before Tammy started taking potshots at poor Cronk. Luckily, Webb was able to move a bit faster that I was. Although I really do think you'd have done what you had to do if he hadn't made it."

I thought I would have, too. But I was also profoundly grateful that I hadn't been forced to find out for certain.

Flashing lights through the trees announced Billy's arrival a few seconds before he turned into the driveway, which was good, because Tammy wasn't exactly cooperating, and I could tell Ed was on the verge of stepping in to help him. Billy was thirty years younger, and if someone had to wrestle the woman to the ground, he was much less likely to feel the after effects the next morning.

"I'm going to go check on Cassie and Cronkite," I told Ed. He squeezed my arm and then headed over to talk to Billy.

As I walked to the cabin, I turned back to look at the scene behind me. Joe was apparently still cowering in the brush. That was quite a rapid turnaround from the guy who'd seemed convinced just a few minutes ago that Tammy wouldn't shoot him.

Cassie and Cronk were on the couch, peeking out through the windows. When I stepped into the living room, she jumped up and flung her arms around me.

"Thank God. I heard the shots, and I didn't know what was happening. Did she do this?" Cassie gestured at the room around us. Pillows and cushions were everywhere. Books had been yanked off the shelves. In the kitchen, pantry items were strewn all over the floor. The drawer was yanked out of the side table and junk was scattered about. My leaf lamp was on the floor, with the shade crushed, as if someone had stomped it. God only knew what the upstairs looked like.

"Yeah, this was Tammy's doing. She was in here when we pulled up." I knelt down to inspect my lampshade, which was beyond repair. "It's almost like karma came after me giving the crystal lamp away."

"You could always buy it back," Cassie said. "Tammy managed to do a lot of damage in not much time. She wasn't here when I pulled in a little after eight thirty. I

hiked out to talk to Dad, but it was raining so we packed
up his gear and went to the shed. A few minutes later, we
heard gunfire and Cronkite came running to the shed
like a bat out of hell. I thought you were going to meet
with Hanlon?"

"We did. He didn't show, but we found him dead in
his hotel room. Same method as Nathan. I called and
couldn't get you. Finally got up with Dean and he said
you came out to bring your dad some dinner."

She patted her pocket and then sank back down onto
the couch. "Pretty sure my phone is in the car. And yeah,
I came out to bring him some food and the stupid envelope. I don't want his money. But I also needed to let him
know what I'd figured out about Tammy, and to tell him
that Webb was on his way. I wasn't sure about Tammy
killing her husband until I found their wedding photo
online, but I had Dean call in a tip to the police while we
were in Nashville, telling them that there might be a
body buried in the strip of woods that runs behind the
houses on that side of the street."

"On the *bad side of the street*," I sighed and sat down
next to her. "Oh, Cassie. Why didn't you tell me you'd
seen something like that?"

She was quiet for a long moment, and then she gave a
helpless little shrug. "I wanted to so many times. But I
could never get the words out. Do you remember Dana
Biggles?"

I nodded, even though the question seemed like a
complete non sequitur. Dana Biggles was the main figure

in a story I'd investigated about six months before I was promoted to the editorial position. She was a nursery school teacher who had a mental breakdown and locked one of her charges in a closet. The child was frightened but unharmed. Dana said she'd done it to protect the kid, because she was scared that she might hurt him. That she heard a voice sometimes that told her the kids were whiny little brats who needed real discipline, but she was seeing a therapist and she would never actually hurt them. Several of the families and the daycare company promptly sued the therapist, claiming that he'd had a duty to warn that Dana was a potential threat to their children.

"What does this have to do with that story?" I asked.

"I just remember you talking to Wren about it on the phone a few days before the first time I saw Charlie Roscoe's ghost. You said the teacher was institutionalized, and that the parents had been right to sue, but you still felt sorry for her. That she'd probably have a hard time getting a job after that. And all I could think was that seeing and hearing dead people was probably a step up from just hearing voices on the likely-to-be-institutionalized scale."

She was probably right, but I shook my head. "I wouldn't have let that happen to you, sweetie. We'd have gotten you to a doctor..." I stopped. "Who would have thought it was mental illness. I get it. It just makes my heart hurt to think of you being that scared and not saying anything."

"It wasn't that bad, really. At least, after a while. I thought maybe it was a fluke at first, so I screwed up my courage and went back across the street. Just once. And... I saw him again. Thought I saw someone else that time, too, but I couldn't be sure. I decided to just stay away. Until yesterday, anyway. You made a comment about Tammy's husband running off with his secretary when we were at the Cheesecake Factory with Wren and I started wondering. I'd kind of forgotten she even had a husband, and I didn't have clue what he looked like until I found their wedding photo in the archives."

"So when did you call Webb?"

"I didn't. We hadn't really thought about the fact that they could track Dean's phone number when he called in the tip. Webb showed up a few hours back, and started asking a lot of questions, mostly about Tammy, given that her husband disappeared, but also some about Dad. I told him Dad *had* contacted me, but I didn't know where he was. That if he called again, I'd try to get him to turn himself in. And then when I found Tammy's wedding picture, I was sure she'd killed her husband...and most likely Nathan. So I came out to try and get Dad to turn himself in to Webb."

"But...what did you tell Webb? I mean, how did you explain knowing where the bodies were?"

"I told him the truth," she said. "I didn't want to, but..."

"And he believed you?"

"Not completely, but he did say the department had

worked with a couple of psychics before, so he didn't entirely discount it. When I got here, it was raining...and I told Dad just to move his gear into the shed for the night. I'd just finished telling him that Webb was in town and that I was sure Tammy was the killer when we heard the shots. I didn't know Tammy was in Thistlewood."

"I think she drove here with Hanlon. They were staying in the same hotel, and both had a reason to be looking for your dad. And maybe she was seeing Hanlon on the side. Your dad was convinced she wouldn't shoot him, but—"

I stopped when I heard two sharp raps on the door. Ed stepped in, followed by Billy. If it had been just Ed, I doubt it would have spooked Cronkite, even in his current nervous state. But Billy was a stranger and that was a bridge too far. Cronk arched his back and then bolted up the stairs.

"Where's Joe?" Ed asked as he scanned the wrecked room.

"Outside," I said. "He dove behind your truck as soon as Tammy lowered the gun."

"We thought maybe he came in with you to check on Cassie," Billy said. "He's not out there."

"Maybe he went back out to the shed?" Cassie suggested. "I was talking to him out there when we heard the shots."

The rain had picked up again, so I grabbed a couple of umbrellas and the four of us trekked out to the back yard. The front door of the shed was still open. But now the back door was open, as well. My camping gear was piled into a wet mass in one corner.

The only things missing were Nathan's motorbike and Joe's belongings.

And, of course, Joe.

Chapter Twenty-Five

THE 1992 ELECTIONS occurred just a few months after I began my job with the *Nashville News-Journal.* I wasn't a crime reporter at that point. For the most part, I simply wrote up whatever was dropped on the desk I shared with two other reporters. The presidential race was called a little after ten that night, but other results trickled in and it had been nearly three in the morning when I finished up and headed home. That was the first time I'd worked right up until the presses began to roll, but it wasn't the last.

I'd had a couple of late nights since taking over the *Star*, but this night was a clear record. It was nearly daylight when the last copy was pulled from The Collector and bundled up for delivery.

Dean had shown up at my place right after we discovered Joe's little vanishing act. That's when I realized the ringer was still off on my phone from when I was hiding in the woods. Wren had left several increasingly worried messages asking why I hadn't called to let her know how the meeting with Hanlon had gone, so I called her back to give her a brief overview, along with the promise of more detailed coverage the next day. Ed, Cassie, and I had to give statements to Webb and to Billy, and we didn't even get started with that until we'd combed the woods looking for Joe.

The only clues we had were the missing bike and a single tire track running from the back door of the shed through the mud and into the woods. None of us had heard a motor start, so he must have pushed the bike until he was far enough away that it wouldn't have been noticeable.

Cassie and Dean said they'd stay at my place so that Cronkite didn't have to be alone after his traumatic experience. I finally made it to the office just past midnight. Tammy had shattered the window glass on the back door, and she'd dumped out all of the desk drawers, but otherwise, the office had taken less time to put back in order than the house had.

Ed offered to stay and help, but he still had a few hours of work he needed to do on his manuscript, so I shooed him out, telling him that we both had deadlines to make. He seemed worried that Joe might show back up, but I really wasn't. I suspected that he'd be caught within a matter of days, and any chance he might have of the courts going easy on him was now out the window. Running had been a truly stupid move. But I still didn't think he was *quite* stupid enough to show back up here right now. He knew me and Cassie well enough to gauge how angry we'd be.

When I'd left earlier, I'd thought that all I'd need to do was print the outside pages. I could have taken the easy route and done precisely that, but the news would be all over town one way or the other, and yours truly had the inside scoop. Odds were good that I'd sell out, so I decided to print a few dozen extra copies to leave for sale at the diner and the other local businesses. I completely rearranged the front page, pulling out the minutes of the town council meeting and several other stories that could wait until next week.

The headline was *Murder at Mountain View*, with a picture of the Lodge that I pulled from a recent ad. I gave an honest and fairly detailed overview of what we'd learned, including a thorough discussion of Joe's suspected involvement in the money laundering enterprise. At the last moment, I remembered that I needed to pull out his obituary. I started to plug back in the filler piece from earlier, but instead composed a quick version of the all-points bulletin that Billy issued for Joseph Adam Tate.

I decided to leave it in Comic Sans. Let the readers make what they would of that.

Normally, I do most of my deliveries on foot, but normally, I've had sleep. So at five fifteen, I began loading everything into the Jeep. I was about to go back in for another stack of papers when Wren pulled into the parking lot in her Buick.

"Girl, you look like death warmed over. Did you get *any* sleep?"

"I did *not*. But the show must go on."

"That's a theater motto. Shouldn't yours be something like *can't stop the presses* or *the news never sleeps?*"

I gave her a tired grin. "I'm too exhausted and too hopped up on coffee and Pop-Tarts to be witty."

"Well then, you *definitely* shouldn't be driving. Let's load those papers into the back seat. I'll play chauffeur while you toss them out the window and tell me absolutely everything that happened last night."

And so that's what we did, just like we'd done back in high school. Only there were three of us back then, and we'd been rocking out to Madonna and The Bangles as I tossed papers onto doorsteps. The only time I'd ever been reprimanded by Mr. Dealey was when a subscriber called to tell him that they'd prefer to have their news delivered without the crazy music disturbing their morning coffee. There was no risk of that this morning. I suspected there would be a few grumbles about my lousy aim, but I was too tired to worry about that.

Once the home deliveries were finished, Wren made several curb stops downtown so that I could drop off bundles at the grocery store and the diner. I left bundles outside Miller's Drugs and The Buzz for them to stock once they opened. If someone wanted to unwrap and swipe a paper or two, they were welcome to them.

When I came back to the Buick, Wren was reading her copy. She folded it neatly and said, "There are no typos. None at all. Perfect from start to finish."

"You're a liar and I love you for it," I told her. "Just wish I could have written up the mystery you helped solve yesterday."

"What you need to do next week is give front page coverage to Olivia's trip to Nashville, regardless of whether she wins a prize in the state competition. Bobbi and Lillian will be green with envy."

"You have an excellent point. Assuming we don't have another wild week with murder and mayhem, Olivia will be above the fold on page one." I yawned widely in the middle of the sentence.

Wren laughed. "Let's get you home."

"Nope," I told her. "I still have one copy left."

Wren raised an eyebrow and then said, "Ohhh. Got it."

She dropped me at Ed's house a couple of minutes later. I told her that we'd meet her later for dinner at Pat's and headed inside to make my promised last delivery. I half expected Owen to raise a ruckus when I unlocked the door, but he kept it down to a few whimpers and a lot of enthusiastic tail wagging.

Ed opened his eyes when I crawled in next to him. I lifted the hand that was resting on his pillow and tucked the paper beneath it.

"I made my deadline," I said. "Did you?"

"Mmhmm. You got everything delivered?"

"Yep. Wren helped." I snuggled close and put my head on his shoulder. "Sleep now. Talk later."

We would both have happily slept until dinner time, but Owen had other ideas. He began barking a little after noon and between his howls and yips we heard the door-bell ring. Ed sighed, tugged on a T-shirt and pajama pants, and headed to the door. I just pulled the covers over my head, glad that I didn't have to get out of bed.

I could hear Ed telling Owen to hush, and then he said, "Oh. Hi, Miss Olivia."

"Good afternoon, Sheriff Shelton. I can't come in. Verna Phillips will be here to pick me up any moment. I'm all packed and ready to go. See my new suitcase? It has wheels."

"I see that," Ed told her, with a touch of amusement in his voice. "Pretty darn spiffy."

"It is," she said. "I just wanted to drop off these two loaves of banana bread to thank you for finding my quilt. This one is for you. And give this one to Ruth Townsend...*when you see her.*"

There was a hint of mild disapproval in her voice. Olivia was an early riser and her tone left absolutely no doubt in my mind that she'd seen me enter a few hours ago and hadn't seen me leave. Even though I was fully clothed, and we'd both been far too tired to get up to anything more than my head on his shoulder, I felt a blush rise to my cheeks.

Ed promised that he'd get the loaf to me and told her to have fun in Nashville. She laughed and said she hadn't been this excited about anything in years and she'd take lots of pictures to show him when she got back.

A few minutes later, Ed came back into the room, still holding the banana bread, packaged in multiple layers of Saran Wrap. Owen followed and immediately jumped onto the bed, sprawling out on top of my feet.

Ed tsked, shaking his head. "Well, now you've done it, you scarlet woman. You've gotten me in trouble with my Sunday School teacher." He sat down on the bed next to me. "But you're kinda cute and a deal is a deal, so I guess I'll still let you have one of these loaves."

"Oh, no, no, no." I reached out and grabbed both loaves. "This loaf is for Wren. I'm quite certain I wouldn't have spotted the quilt if she hadn't had me out on the lawn trying to track down Derrick Blevins's footprint. And this loaf is mine. But you're kinda cute, so maybe I'll share."

Owen made an indignant noise.

I laughed. "With both of you, apparently. I helped solve your mystery and you helped solve mine. Teamwork."

Ed took the loaves back and placed them on the nightstand next to his copy of the *Star*, and then pulled me into his arms.

"Teamwork," he repeated. "And there's absolutely no one I'd rather have on my team."

About the Author

C. Rysa Walker is the pen name author Rysa Walker adopts when she's in the mood to tackle mysteries that are a little more grounded in reality than her various science fiction and fantasy series. Author Caleb Amsel is her partner in crime on the Thistlewood Star Mysteries adventures. Learn more about the Thistlewood Star series on Rysa's website.

www.rysa.com/mysteries

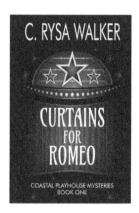

Tig isn't a detective. She just played one on TV. Will that be enough to help her find the killer?

Acting jobs are scarce now for former TV teen detective Antigone Alden. So when a teaching position opens up at Southern Coastal University, Tig packs up her teenage daughter and heads home to the Outer Banks of North Carolina.

But house she inherited from her mother isn't entirely empty. Her mom seems stuck between this life and the next, and now Tig is a local reporter's prime suspect in the murder of the former theater professor. Given his reputation as a ladies' man, however, there are plenty of people with a motive.

More from C. Rysa Walker

Thistlewood Star Mysteries

Baskerville for the Bear

A Murder in Helvetica Bold

Palatino for the Painter

A Seance in Franklin Gothic

Courier to the Stars

Comic Sans for the Ex

Coastal Playhouse Mysteries

Curtains for Romeo

Arsenic and Olé

Offed Off-Broadway

———

As Rysa Walker

The CHRONOS Files

Timebound

Time's Edge

Made in the USA
Coppell, TX
19 August 2021

60738738R00187